Carl Weber's Kingpins:

Miami

Carl Weber's Kingpins:

Miami

Nikki Turner

www.urbanbooks.net

2221   7846   0

Urban Books, LLC
97 N18th Street
Wyandanch, NY 11798

Carl Weber's Kingpins: Miami
Copyright © 2015 Nikki Turner

ISBN 13: 978-1-62286-935-0
ISBN 10: 1-62286-935-4

First Trade Paperback Printing October 2015
Printed in the United States of America

10 9 8 7 6 5 4 3 2 1

*This is a work of fiction. Any references or similarities
to actual events, real people, living or dead, or to real
locales are intended to give the novel a sense of reality.
Any similarity in other names, characters, places, and
incidents is entirely coincidental.*

Distributed by Kensington Publishing Corp.
Submit orders to:
Customer Service
400 Hahn Road
Westminster, MD 21157-4627
Phone: 1-800-733-3000
Fax: 1-800-659-2436

Carl Weber's Kingpins:

Miami

Nikki Turner

PROLOGUE

"This is Lisa Sanchez, reporting to you live from WYGH Action News, Miami, from the scene of Miami Memorial Cemetery where a young, vibrant, beautiful socialite is being laid to rest, as her promising life has been taken far too soon. Annalise Pierre-Louis, the sister of notorious, well-known drug kingpin Fitz Pierre-Louis, was tragically murdered five days ago."

Without appearing to, Fitz scanned the area and took in the debacle that surrounded this sad event. Inside, it all angered him, but he was a man who knew how to hide his emotions. He was pissed at the fact that not only was his sister gone, but these folks had turned her burial into a media spectacle.

Helicopters circled around, and the military tanks lined up, while countless camera crews, paparazzi, and reporters from all over the nation had been camped out since the wee hours of this chilly Miami morning. The cold had been record-breaking that winter, and this Tuesday was the coldest day that Miami had seen in its history. Fitz shivered yet kept his face muscles immobile, as he adjusted the Hermes scarf that matched his casket-sharp custom Hermès suit.

In spite of the "inclement weather," or the media feeding frenzy, not a soul had been deterred from showing up to pay their respects to Annalise Pierre-Louis. Even social media was screaming.

In a serious tone, the brunette anchorwoman continued her broadcast. "Annalise was a native and graduate from the University of Miami. She was a philanthropist who created so many programs and opportunities for the children in the Haitian community, so her premature, tragic death comes as a shock to many." Lisa paused, looking directly into the camera. She tossed her long, dark hair then continued. "But the gruesome details of her murder lead many to believe that she's an innocent casualty of an ongoing drug war between rival drug factions."

Lisa moved a little to the left as the camera focused on her backdrop, where the SWAT team was marching to their positions. "As you may notice, U.S. Army tanks and heightened security are present. This is an effort to prevent more outbreaks of violence. The mayor has devoted much of the city's resources, including the police's SWAT team, DEA officers, and even the Coast Guard on standby, to this effort, as this funeral service and the city of Miami are under siege at this very moment."

The newscaster delivered the news as empathetically as she knew how. "Anonymous tips have been pouring in with threats of acts of violence, which are expected today on this sad and tragic occasion. This is sending a widespread wave of fear that the retaliation will be coming swiftly. With a smorgasbord of mourners, ranging from some world-renowned singers, athletes, socialites, and political dignitaries leading all the way to the White House, security has been truly beefed up."

The camera began to focus on various celebrities as Lisa continued delivering her point of view. "Along with noted heads of the core organized crime families are, we are sure, some of the nations most notorious underworld representatives, who have flown in from as far south as Cuba, Peru, and Colombia . . . all with one motive—to pay their respects to the Pierre-Louis family."

She looked into the camera with compassion written all over her face as the camera turned to a massive fleet of black limousines and high-end foreign automobiles, which filled a two-mile procession as they cruised down the parkway and onto the cemetery grounds. Rolls Royces, Range Rovers, Escalades, Bentleys, BMWs, Jaguars, McLarens, Maserati, Lamborghini, and Ferrari kept the hired valets busy and vigilant.

Between the authorities and Annalise's family, security was tighter than a pair of size two, no-stretch jeans on a big booty.

As the crowd continued to gather, Señor Manuella of Peru sat graveside with aviator sunglasses covering his eyes and a blank expression on his face. Standing behind him, back ramrod straight, was Annalise's brother, Fitz.

Fitz stood six feet three inches tall, scanning the crowd while maintaining a poker face for his family. He was keeping himself together because he was fully aware that all eyes were on him—not only the paparazzi's and the alphabet boys'—FEDS, DEA, CIA, ATF, IRS—but enemies' and friends' alike.

The underworld had given Fitz the title Scarface of the Millennium. He, like Scarface, wasn't born with a silver spoon, but he had managed to win the admiration, love, and undying loyalty and respect of Señor Manuella, who was the cold, callous, infamous, sociopathic head of the Peruvian Cartel. The story went that Señor Manuella, who had no biological children of his own, met young Fitz one day when there was an attempt on his life. Having not a clue who Señor Manuella was, Fitz innocently told him about the hit. Not only was Señor Manuella eternally grateful, but he saw great potential in the little boy. From that moment, he took Fitz under his wing as his godson, and with Fitz's mother's blessing, he eventually adopted the Haitian-born boy. Señor Manuella embraced him as his own son, and when he was old enough, he passed the torch to his adopted son, making him the successor of his enormous heroin organization that supplied over seventy-five percent of the product to the United States.

So, the execution-style hit on Annalise had sent a message of direct disrespect to Señor Manuella and Fitz, and under no circumstances would it be taken lightly. That was the very reason why the heads of the core organized crime families came to Miami to mourn the loss, to pay their respects, and to assure Fitz that they were in no way connected to this heinous crime. As a sign of good faith, they would be putting a bounty on anyone they suspected had a hand in this hit. After all, at the end of the day, it was all business; none of the families wanted to be cut off from their direct supplier of the best uncut heroin on this side of the Equator.

Fitz tried to weigh the situation, to figure out which pain was the most intense—knowing his sister's remains were in the box, or seeing his mother Minnie's heart broken in a million pieces.

"Noooo! Noooo! Noooo! This is so unfair! It's not fair!" she screamed.

It hurt Fitz to his core to see his mother in shambles the way she had been ever since the news of Annalise's death was delivered to her five days before. He would have given anything for it to be him, not his sweet, energetic butterfly of a sister. He only wanted to get to the bottom of it. There was no doubt he needed answers so that someone would pay for this.

Annalise's boyfriend, Johnny "The Viper," tapped his feet continuously. He stared wide-eyed at the casket. His eyes never moved. She was his everything. The two had been together since the minute he laid eyes on her. At first he was a straight square, but once he found out about the family business, he had jumped through hoops to get

Fitz to give him a job. He had made a lot of money for Fitz and had gladly given most of his profits to Annalise, but now the poor guy was lost. Fitz surmised that he was also high as gas off the cocaine. After they'd left the funeral and headed to the burial grounds, Johnny had washed an eight ball down with a few shots of vodka in the back of the limo.

Annalise's twin, Caesar, couldn't stand to look at the casket, nor could he stop the tears from rolling uncontrollably down his face. It was something about that twin connection between the two that was always deeper than he could ever understand. Fitz, who was all about appearances, wished his brother would at least attempt to hold it together. In his eyes, the trembling of Caesar's lip was a sign of weakness—something that he always felt was his brother's flaw.

"Ashes to ashes and dust to dust," the pastor intoned to the standing-room-only crowd of impeccably dressed mourners, as they said their final good-byes and watched the casket being lowered into a freshly dug grave. Minnie, Annalise's mother, screamed to the heavens, crying for the loss of her youngest child. "Why her, God? Why?" she wailed. "Annalise was a good girl—a sweet girl. They could've killed anyone but her. They could've killed me. My Annalise was still just a baby, so full of life."

Several family members tried to console Minnie, but they couldn't contain her as she ran to the casket and tried to throw herself over it, not being able to bear the pain of seeing her only daughter being put into the dirt.

"I can't let her go! I just can't! Please, God! Please, just take me!" she begged. "Take me!"

Caesar went to his mother's side and embraced her with a hug as he fought to control his own tears, but her grief was too fresh to surrender its grip on her heart. The pain was too acute, and she still cried a river.

"Mommy, please," Fitz said to his mother. He was about to go to her side, but he felt helpless. His father saw it on his face. That's when Señor Manuella took his hand. Fitz leaned down to hear what his father had to say.

"Son." Señor Manuella spoke slowly, so his thick Spanish accent wouldn't be as hard to understand. "When pain is embedded this deep in one's soul, it can only be tempered by time, and even that's no guarantee. Everyone deals with grief in their own way."

The truth of the matter was, witnessing his mother's grief was killing Fitz on the inside, because there was nothing at this moment he could do to fix it. He nodded to his father.

"Yes, father, I understand." He turned to his mother's sister, Aunt Nadia, and some members of his security team, and said, "Please, please get her into the car and take her home. I will be there soon."

Meanwhile, the array of folks, along with the high-profile celebrities, socialites, and business affiliates, came to shake hands and give their condolences, and then they started to leave.

Fitz wanted to speak with his brother before he went ghost. He told one of his bodyguards, "Please, make sure my mother gets to the car safely." He wanted no one around when he spoke.

"Anything else?" Jacob was Fitz's most senior confidant.

"For now, just keep an eye on her." Fitz moved over to his brother, who had not left the grave yet. He was still standing there as the men began to fill the grave with the dirt. He continued to cry. Fitz pleaded, "Hey, Caesar, come on, man. Besides, I need to talk to you."

Caesar stopped, turned to walk away, and proceeded to finally make eye contact with his brother. Taking a deep breath, he gave his brother a sour, dry, "What up?"

Examining Caesar's eyes, Fitz said, "That emotion you're holding onto seems more like guilt than grief to me."

"Fuck you, Fitz!" he said with malice, hating that his brother would say that. "You so fucked up." He shook his head at his older brother.

Caesar tried to walk away, but Fitz wasn't having it. He put his hand on Caesar's arm. "Not so fast, playboy."

Sometimes it was hard for Fitz to even believe that he and Caesar shared the same blood, because they were polar opposites in every way. "Nigga, I ain't going to dance around it. Straight up, I blame you." He almost spit the words out.

"Nigga, you fucking crazy," Caesar shot back, wanting to swing on his brother right then and there, but he knew this wasn't the time or place for it.

"I leave the fuckin' city for three days—three fucking days—to take care of business, to make moves for this family, our livelihood, our business, and the only thing, the one fucking thing I ask of you while I'm gone, is for you to watch out for our sister, which should've been a given. And you fuck that up."

"What? So this is my fault?" Caesar still couldn't believe his ears.

"You's a fucking pussy!" he passionately accused of his brother. "And you just a disgrace to me."

Fitz tightened his grip on Caesar's arm. He stared at his brother, the twin of his sister, and all he could see was Annalise—minus the hair, makeup, and all the glamour girl stuff that his sister never left home without. The two, Annalise and Caesar, were the spitting image of each other. He sucked his teeth and shook his head in disgust. "I can't stand to look at you, because every time I look at you, I see and think of my sister, and it makes me want to kill you with my bare fucking hands."

Fitz's harsh words really put a hurting on Caesar, and before he could speak, Fitz did. He leaned in and spoke clearly and firmly. "If I didn't think it would kill our mother to lose another child, I would shoot your soft ass in the face right here. Right fucking now!" He pointed to the ground but never lost eye contact with his brother. "So that I don't hurt Mommy, please, do our loving mother a favor and yourself a solid, and get the *fuck* out of my sight . . . out of my fucking city."

"Fitz?" Caesar wanted to defend himself, but it was too late. Fitz had already spoken, turned, and walked away. Caesar had no choice. It was a done deal.

CHAPTER 1

Six Years Ago
in Virginia

"No freaking way!" Bianca tried to convince herself that her eyes were lying to her as she glanced into the foggy bathroom mirror and wiped it. Suddenly her heart dropped. "Oh, no!" She shook her head to see if that would help her shake away the image of her pudgy waistline.

Bianca was in true denial, even after missing two menstrual cycles. Even when she started getting morning and motion sickness, she still refused to accept the possibility that she could be pregnant. She prayed to God so hard to make the vomiting go away, but to no avail. For months, every time she went to the bathroom and wiped herself, she would be hopeful that blood would be on the toilet tissue, from either her period returning, or, if she were truly pregnant, as the symptoms of a miscarriage. Neither ever showed itself.

Before she knew it, she was four and a half months pregnant. Her mind was spinning with so much fear that she forgot to lock the door to the bathroom that she and her older sister, Bella, shared off their joint bedroom. She finally accepted it. There was no way she could deny it any longer. She was pregnant.

A butt naked Bianca had just stepped out of the shower and was reaching for her towel when Bella barged into the bathroom.

"Damn, girl. Can't you see I'm in here?"

Bianca's belly made her slow to the draw. By the time she covered herself with the towel, it was too late. Her big sister had already seen her growing baby bump.

"Oh my God!" Bella covered her mouth. She looked like she had seen a ghost. "What the hell?" a dumbfounded Bella said upon quickly shutting the bathroom door.

"Get out," Bianca aggressively said to her sister, not wanting to face the reality.

"Bitch, don't try to divert," Bella said, her eyes just as bucked as Bianca's. She kept her eyes glued toward her little sister's belly that was now covered with the towel, but not for long.

Bella ran over and tried to snatch the towel off of Bianca. "I know good and well my eyes are not deceiving me."

"Leave me alone. Please," Bianca said as begrudgingly as she could.

"No!" Bella firmly said.

"Get off of me," Bianca demanded, engaging Bella in a game of tug-of-war with the towel. She tried to plant her feet firmly and get a grip on the floor, but the tiles were wet and she kept sliding forward.

"Give me that towel," Bella ordered, using two hands to pull on it.

"Get the hell off of me," Bianca yelled, terrified of being found out. She didn't want her sister to know about her big, growing secret. She'd managed to ignore her own suspicions for months, hoping, praying to God, keeping her fingers crossed that someway, somehow God would make that baby go away before anyone ever found out.

So much for prayer, she thought.

"Naw, bitch. I know what I saw," Bella insisted. "And you better not be—"

"Get the hell off of me!" Bianca spat with all her strength as she continued to struggle with her sister. She was getting so angry and embarrassed that tears formed in her eyes.

Bianca and Bella were great sisters to one another. They were best friends. Unlike some siblings, they never argued, fussed, or fought. The term "bitch" was kind of like a term of endearment for them. They didn't mean it in a bad way. So, having this little fight truly was a first, and it was all love and love licks. There had never been as much as a small case of sibling rivalry or jealousy between the two of them either, even though people had always tried to ignite such a feud between the two.

Bella was the complexion of Wesley Snipes, clearly taking after her father, because Ella was a light caramel complexion. Bianca was a very light, even pale complexion, a trait that she was told came from her father, a different man than Bella's father, a man she had never known or met. In contrast, Bella's coarse, natural hair was longer than Bianca's, but Bianca had the whole "good hair" thing going on. Her nice, soft baby hair that edged her hairline was her trademark. People always assumed she was mixed with something, but as far as she knew, both of her parents were African Americans.

Upon telling people that they were sisters, no one ever believed them, and they always got the same reaction. They would always get the craziest looks from folks, eyes darting back from one sister to the other. Some people would be so brazen as to even outright say, "Y'all *must* have different daddies, huh?" There were the insensitive, rude ones that would say, "You're so pretty," to Bianca, as if Bella wasn't even standing right next to her.

Every now and then, someone would think they were giving Bella a compliment by adding, "But you're cute, too . . . to be dark-skinned."

It never went unnoticed by Bianca how Bella's spirit would take a nosedive then; sometimes her eyes would even water. Even after over eighteen plus years, to this very day, it still bothered her. It used to infuriate Bianca to see peoples' comments make her sister feel so bad about herself. So, Bianca, loving her sister the way she did, would start downplaying herself. She started hiding behind Bella, thinking if people only saw Bella, they wouldn't make comparisons or say hurtful things. Bianca never wanted others to hurt her sister, but at that moment, as the two struggled over the towel, she wanted to kill Bella her damn self; physically, mentally, any way she could.

"Let go, blacky," Bianca spat viciously.

Bella let that comment roll off her back like the water from the shower Bianca had just gotten out of. She just kept right on battling. She was not moved by her sister's words. She'd gotten over being called names such as black, tar baby, and darky. Besides, never once had Bianca ripped her for her complexion, so she knew she had only said it to upset her enough to let go of the towel and leave her be.

"I swear to God, if you don't let go of this towel," Bianca growled, holding onto it with a death grip. "I promise you, you going to be sorry." With anger-filled eyes, she threatened her sister. She was so filled with rage that she felt strong enough to rip Bella apart with her bare hands.

Bella was no more affected by her little sister's water-works than she had been by the insult she'd spewed. With all her might, she gave one hard tug, successfully yanking the towel from Bianca's grip, leaving her sister standing there in the middle of the bathroom floor, butt naked, with a very much visible baby bump.

Roaring like a lioness, Bianca's reflexes made her snatch the towel from Bella and hit her with it.

"Ouch, bitch! I'm going to kill you!"

Before either of the sisters had realized it, the door flew open, and Ella was standing there in shock.

All eyes went to the doorway, where Ella stood, arms akimbo. "What the hell is going on in here?" She poked her nose in the doorway. She craned her head back on her neck in the way she did when she couldn't believe something crazy was going on.

In all her years, she'd never heard her daughters have a fight, and she wasn't going to stand for it now. If she had not done anything else, she'd instilled in the girls that once she was long gone, they would be all each other had. So from the first time it sounded as if Bella and Bianca were going to almost have a disagreement that could escalate, she nipped it in the bud. She constantly reminded them, "Y'all sisters, no matter what. And friends come and go, but at the end of the day, when the dust settles, y'all all each other got." So, for the life of her, she couldn't imagine what on earth all the ruckus was about that she'd heard all the way from the kitchen downstairs.

Ella stood there, her eyes darting back and forth between her oldest and youngest daughters. Neither of them said a word.

"Did y'all hear me?" Ella said with her fists on her hips. "I said, what is all the screaming and cussing going on? And y'all know damn well I'm the only one allowed to yell and fuss up in this house, so somebody better get to talking, because neither of you want none of this."

Once again, Ella's eyes shifted from one daughter to the next as Bella tried her best to explain, but she wasn't fast enough. Bianca looked downward, while Bella looked down too—at her sister's stomach.

"Here," Bella said, handing Bianca back the towel.

Bianca snatched the towel to cover herself, but when she looked up into her mother's eyes, she knew she'd moved too late. Ella's eyes followed Bella's stare, which bee-lined down to Bianca's stomach just seconds before Bianca had a chance to cover it. Time stopped. The room fell silent.

For what felt like an eternity to Bianca, the mother-daughter pair stared into each other's eyes. With every second, Bianca could see her mother becoming more and more disappointed. It was as if Bianca could see through her mother's eyes, and she was watching all the dreams and hopes her mother had for her evaporate into thin air. Her mother's shoulders visibly slumped inward. She sucked her teeth and shook her head as if she was dumbfounded. Her mother seemed to be frozen in that space, in the doorway of the bathroom.

Bianca thought about all those times her mother had danced around with Bianca's report card in her hand, bragging about how smart she was. She would go on and on about how her youngest child was going to go off to any college of her choice and be chosen to study abroad and learn about other countries and cultures firsthand. On more occasions than one, Ella had bragged about how her daughters were going to be the ones to break the family curse and not have babies while they were still in high school. So far, she had broken the cycle with Bella, who had just graduated from high school. At that moment, though, Bianca had made a liar out of her mother in more ways than one.

Bianca really wanted to talk to her mother and tell her everything, but she couldn't. Instead, after she got the lump out of her throat, all Bianca could manage to say was, "Ma, I'm sor—"

But before Bianca could even get the words out, Ella had put her hand up to silence her. "I don't want to fucking hear it. You are a fucking disgrace to me. You silly little dumbass girl, fucking your life up!" she said with such disdain, as if Bianca were the hugest disappointment in the world. Ella took a look over her as if she were trash. She then shook her head and walked away.

Her mother's words cut her like a sharp knife. The pain of the cut hurt her feelings so badly that all she could do was tiptoe down the hall to her room, thinking about what she could've done differently so that she wouldn't be in this situation, which only brought tears to her eyes. She began to read her Bible, but that didn't stop them from coming, and she cried herself to sleep.

"Wake the fuck up!" She was startled awake by her mother's stern voice. "I said get the fuck up, girl."

Still half asleep, Bianca jackknifed up in the bed.

"It's shit everywhere down in that got-damn basement. I mean *everywhere*. Get your fast ass up and go down there and make yo' hot ass useful and clean that shit up, now! Right the fuck now!"

Bianca took a deep breath, pulled herself together, and headed to the basement to deal with the backed-up raw sewage that was due to the years of bad plumbing in the house. She tied a pair of tights around her face so that the smell wouldn't be so pungent as she began to clean it.

The night came and went, and she still felt like she hadn't put a dent into the swamp that filled the basement floors. It took two days to get the water up, and a whole other day just to shovel the shit up. Then it took another two more days of bleaching and sanitizing the entire basement, from top to bottom, walls and all. Bianca's poor body was so sore and her bones hurt so bad from all the hard labor that she was forced to do with no help that she secretly hoped that she would miscarry, but that didn't happen.

Finally, the hour came when everything was done, and it was clean and smelling like new money mixed with Fabuloso. She hoped that the Grade-A job she had done on getting the basement back intact would make her mother proud. With all her might, she raced up the stairs, hoping that when her mother saw how spic and span it was, it would take some of the tension off of the uncomfortable situation.

Before she could get to the top of the stairs, she heard laughter coming from the kitchen. By the time she walked through the basement door, she could hear her mother, her grandmother, and her Uncle Peanut's wife, Jackie.

"Welcome to McDonald's! May I take your order, please?" Grandma Williams mimicked Bianca's voice to the other ladies sitting around the kitchen table. "Yup, that's gon' be what Ms. High Yella Bianca gon' be saying." Holding her corpulent rolls round her middle, she fell into laughter, and the other ladies followed suit.

Though those were the words Bianca swore she'd never have to say a day in her life, at this moment, her fate wasn't looking good. Now that she had turned up pregnant at fourteen years old, the people she knew, including family, had already put the words in her mouth and had her marked for failure. They'd written her off as a typical teen mother who wouldn't amount to anything. They'd just given her a death sentence as far as making anything of her life.

"Fries with that?" another added to the cruel joke. It was Uncle Peanut's wife's voice, using a falsetto to imitate Bianca.

"Combo meal, or just the sandwich?" The ladies continued with their mean, sinister remarks. It was as though they were taking great pleasure in knowing that she was going to suffer and feel the full ball of scorn that they had gone through as young mothers.

Bianca shook her head in disbelief. She couldn't believe how they really had her dropping fries at McDonald's for the rest of her life. Even though she'd been an honor roll student and had even skipped third grade because she was so far advanced, with a baby in her belly now, no one saw her graduating high school, let alone going to college. Let them tell it, her life was over. Her life as she knew it was over—that much she knew—but something inside of her made a strong resolve. She wasn't going to let this baby's birth destroy her dreams.

It truly pained Bianca for the dreams of being the smartest and most successful one in the family to be ripped away. They hadn't necessarily been her dreams, though. They had been more like her mother's. Bianca's mother talked about the girl so much that people who didn't know any better would think Bianca was her only child, even though she had an older daughter, Bella. Her mother was living her own aborted dreams through her. Over the years, no matter how much Bianca's mother would praise her youngest daughter, there had always been that one person in the background with a big ole needle in hand, always ready to burst her bubble.

"I told you, Ella, outta both of yo' kids, Bianca was going to be the one that was going to give you the most trouble," Bianca's grandmother had said to her daughter, Ella. "Them yellow ones always think they better than everybody else and that the world should cater to them because they so damn light-bright, they almost white."

Growing up, Bianca swore Grandmother Williams hated her with a passion. She could not figure out for the life of her what she'd done wrong to make a churchgoing woman look at her like she was the devil. As respectful as Bianca had always been, it just seemed like it was never good enough for her grandmother. Even when Bianca got an A on a test, her grandmother wouldn't say a thing: no pat on her back, no compliment, and no "job well done, granddaughter." Just nothing!

Now Bella, on the other hand, would get a C-plus, and her grandmother would take her out for ice cream.

For many years, Bianca analyzed, wondered, and tried to figure why, but time and time again, she could never explain the favoritism, so eventually Bianca just chalked it up to her grandmother's own emotional scars. As a result of her being a dark skinned, bitter woman, she had taken out all the bad treatment she'd gotten because of her skin complexion on her own granddaughter.

"Ella, you should have had you another dark one like Bella," Grandmother Williams continued lecturing her daughter. "Now, that girl got some good sense. She got her li'l job at Goodwill, and she going to enroll in school next semester. That girl got her head on her shoulders. See, Bella know as black as she is, and the way these men folks run around sniffing behind women that look like Paula Abdul, Vanity, and Vanessa Williams, that she gotta be humble and take what she can get."

"Mm-hmm," Jackie, her uncle Peanut's wife, agreed.

"But that damn Bianca just stuck up and think she all that just 'cause she pretty." Grandmother Williams shook her head and continued, "Told you not to mess with that ole El DeBarge–lookin' Negro. He thought his dookie balls didn't stank, and now so does his offspring. You'd think the no-good gigolo would have raised Bianca every day of her life by the way she act just like him. And you better hope this bastard that she pops out with her hot tail is by a dark-skinned dude as black as charcoal, or you gon' have another high yellow heifer running around here thinking she cute." She rolled her eyes, leaned back into the kitchen table chair, and let out a *harrumph*.

"That is, if we ever even find out who the baby daddy is," Jackie added.

"Well, I do know this: Don't expect me to do nothing for that bastard baby. Not nothing. I'm not babysitting, making no bottles, or changing no shitty-ass diapers." Those were the words that, unbeknownst to Grandmother Williams, Bianca overheard her tell to her mother.

The old saying goes, "Stick and stones may break my bones, but words can never hurt me." *Whoever came up with that saying told a lie,* Bianca thought. They had never heard the words of Grandmother Williams.

Words couldn't explain the feeling that ripped through the fourteen-year-old ninth grader's body when she heard her own flesh and blood say those things about her. For a minute there, she thought she was having labor pains. And even though the words her grandmother spoke were killing her softly, she still decided to stand, hidden off behind the kitchen door entry, and continue to listen.

"Oh, Ma, please. Bianca just made a mistake," Ella said in her daughter's defense. "The same mistake both you and I made."

Bianca felt some sort of relief to hear that her mother was sticking up for her with the truth. Her mother was right; her grandmother was no saint. Grandmother Williams had her first child, Bianca's Uncle Billy, when she was sixteen. She would then turn around and have Anne at seventeen and Edward at eighteen. Ella, herself, had given birth for the first time at the age of fourteen. They were twins that were born premature, and both eventually died after a couple of weeks in the hospital.

"Your brother was no mistake," Grandmother Williams was quick to shoot back. "I ended up marrying his daddy as soon as I turned eighteen. I can't help it he got sent over to fight them Chinks in that useless war and was killed." Grandmother Williams used her tongue to push her upper false teeth around in her mouth. "I married your daddy, but that jive turkey ended up running off with that white woman he worked with. Light skin wasn't good enough for him." She let out a laugh that she hoped would cover the pain.

"Yeah, but with Angel and Angela's father," Ella, said, referencing her younger twin sisters, "you knew that man was married. You can't say that wasn't a mistake."

"And it wasn't. Got so much hush money out of that fool that I was able to maintain a nice house for all my children, and when they turned fifteen, that's when I had Peanut, to seal the deal all over again." This time when she laughed, it was the complete sound of victory.

"Umph, umph, umph." Ella shook her head, grinning at her mother. "Well, Bianca is going to be all right. I'm going to help her with the baby, and—"

"How you gonna do that? You work from sun up to sun down. Hell, you didn't even raise your own. I did," Grandmother Williams said, getting so turned up that her teeth almost flipped out of her mouth. "You do remember the girls stayed with me more than you," she reminded her daughter.

"I remember, Mama," Ella acknowledged. "That's why I'm going to pay it forward and help Bianca. I been saying for years Bianca is brilliant and smart." Her eyes lit up. "She's gonna graduate high school and get her a full ride to some Ivy League college. Graduate at the top of her class with job offers from companies everywhere."

"Chile, you fantasizing now," Grandmother Williams added.

Ella didn't pay her no mind as she continued to verbalize the dreams she had for her daughter. "No, maybe she's going to start her own business. End up young and rich." She looked at her mother with excitement in her eyes. The eyes staring back at her hadn't been moved by a word she'd spoken.

"Yeah, we'll see about that," Grandmother Williams said, full of doubt. "Them straight A's she was making in school before she got knocked up, you might as well forget about it. That baby is going to take up so much of her time that she won't even be able to think about studying. She'll be lucky to even make C's. Can't get no full ride to college making C's, and you ain't got no money to send her. The welfare she gon' end up living off of ain't gon' be enough to even get her through community college." She laughed.

"So a college scholarship to an Ivy League school is going to be out of the question." Jackie added her two cents.

Ella shot a look at Jackie and said, "We will see."

"You are right. We will see. I hope she'll be able to bring me some free chicken nuggets from McDonald's, because that's exactly where her destiny would be. Now that's it, that's all. It is what it is, and I don't want to hear no more." Grandmother Williams spoke like she had the power to speak all things concerning Bianca's life into existence. "You know how you used to brag about how Bianca was going to go off to college and become a doctor or lawyer or something, and take care of you for the rest of your life?"

Ella stared off, nodding. It was almost as if she were watching that dream she'd once had about her daughter float farther and farther away.

"Well, you might as well prepare your mind to settle for nothing more than free French fries for the rest of your life, because all she gon' be able to do now with a baby on her hip is drop out of school and work at a fast food restaurant, talking about, 'May I take your order, please?'" She let out a loud, wicked bellow that caused her to have to hold her stomach.

Ella watched her mother cackle away all the dreams she'd once had for her child. Before she knew it, she was giggling too. It was sad, but she had to laugh in order to keep from crying.

In her spirit, Ella knew her mother was right. The curse of becoming a teenage mother hadn't skipped a generation yet. Unfortunately, it had landed right in her baby girl's lap. That was that moment she decided that if she couldn't beat 'em, then she should join 'em, so she teamed up with all the other naysayers who thought Bianca wouldn't amount to anything. After all, she didn't want to keep holding onto a hopeless dream and be the laughingstock when Bianca proved her wrong. She'd rather be on the winning team, even if it was against her own daughter.

Listening to them get jokes off of her misfortune hurt Bianca's heart. Tears raced down Bianca's face, while the baby inside her womb began kicking. Bianca looked down at her belly and cupped her arms around it. She shook her head, questioning how this could have happened to her. What was worse was that she did not have a clue who the baby daddy was.

It was definitely true that even at her young age, she had experienced sex and things that she had no business experiencing, while looking for love in all the wrong places. But in spite of what people thought and said about Bianca, she wasn't a whore who just gave it up to any and every guy that hollered at her.

Grandmother Williams let off of her roaring laughter when she had what she could have sworn was a lightbulb moment. "What you should do is take that grown-ass little red heifer down to that abortion clinic and make her have an abortion."

"Mother, she has to be like four or five months pregnant. That's murder."

"Well, she should have thought about that before she went spreading her legs to every Tom, Dick, and Harry."

"You make the bed; you must lay in it," Jackie added.

Bianca couldn't take any more. She ran to her bedroom and slammed the door closed behind her. For a split second she thought that maybe her mother would come and console her, since the slamming of the door made it apparent that she had overheard them talking about her, but an hour went by and no one came in.

Bianca lay there, rubbing her belly and staring out the window in pain, trying not to let her thoughts run wild. No matter how much she tried, her mind just kept going to the same place. If only she could turn back the hands of time. She would have been smarter.

Before crying herself to sleep, Bianca's last profound thought came to her that would change her life forever. She might not have the power to control what had already happened in the past, but she vowed that she would damn sure control her future. In order for that to happen, there was one thing that she must take care of, something that if she'd handled properly in the first place, she wouldn't even be in the predicament that she was in now. It may take months or years, but one way or the other, it would get handled.

Before finally closing her eyes and drowning in her tears, her last words were, "God have mercy on my soul."

CHAPTER 2

Nine Years Later

"Ummmm, please, ma'am. Please take this order. I really need my shit like ASAP!" Frank, the owner of a franchise beauty and barber salon that focused on natural hair, said as he looked up from his desk with a friendly smile. His eyes were loving the fine specimen in front of him. With his bedroom eyes, he undressed the beautiful, exotic-looking twenty-three-year old woman standing in his office doorway. As always, he took his time in giving the young diva the once over, starting with her bad-ass patent leather red pumps, then to her turquoise khakis, her multi-colored silk short-sleeve blouse, accented by a gold belt, and her pearl necklace, earrings, and bracelet. The multi-colored Gucci oversized bag was the exclamation mark on the entire outfit. He took a peep at the cleavage she had poking out of the lacey push-up bra.

"Damn, girl, you know you be doing it with your fine ass." Frank licked his lips as he stood up from his desk. "You need to let me make you feel good. Real good."

The beauty sucked her teeth. "Sit your ass down, Frank! You know I don't play that," the pretty young thing said, strutting over to Frank's desk like a runway model. "You been trying to get this pussy for years now. Shouldn't you give up by now? At what point are you going to accept that I'm happily taken, and nothing you can do will be able to change that?"

Frank shooed her with a flick of his wrist and sat back down. "Girl, please. That doesn't mean shit to me. You know how many broads done sung that same song to me? And the next thing you know, the notes change."

"Oh, okay. I see. It's just a game to you."

"Oh, puh-leeze. You think it's not a game to all them niggas too? Especially that Latin lover you be fucking with?"

That right there—that last comment that Frank had just made—was when the needle was pulled off the record. The entire playful mood changed to a stone cold serious one. Bianca could joke all day long, but when it came to her man, women and men alike knew better than to put his name in their mouth.

"Oops, I touched that nerve. Forgive me. I surrender, baby," he said with a devilish grin. Frank put his hands up, trying to smooth things over. "My bad, Bee. I know you don't play when it comes to your King Caesar," he said with a raised eyebrow.

Bianca rolled her eyes and sat down in the chair at Frank's desk. She remained silent and counted to ten to pull herself together in order to allow her anger to subside. When anybody talked about Caesar, they were talking about Bianca, as far as she was concerned. It was like they were touching her eyeball with their fingernail. She felt that it was downright disrespectful. To her, she and Caesar were one in the same. Even though they weren't legally married, she was Caesar's rib. He'd been there for her in ways no other man had ever been, or any other person would or could be. Certainly not her disloyal, two-faced mother, who still to this day allowed Grandmother Williams to get in her ear, turning her against her once favorite daughter. And she wouldn't even mention her sister, who was her best friend, but yet and still, Caesar filled so many voids and was her everything.

There was no denying that there was something special about the love of her life. Caesar just knew how to handle Bianca. Even though he was known on the streets of Virginia as a cool dude that was about his business and only got rough when it was absolutely necessary, he was gentle with Bianca at all times. To her, there were no two sides to Caesar. He was always the same when it came to her, which was what she loved about him so much. He never once tried to front like he was this hardcore cat who could snap off at any minute. As a matter of fact, he was just the opposite. He was never confrontational or combative with her, and even if she got a little hotheaded, he knew how to calm her down. He knew just what Bianca liked, and that was to be loved and comforted.

Bianca loved the fact that they could lie in bed for hours and do nothing but talk, eat popcorn, and watch their favorite shows. They loved to watch the old school movies like *Car Wash, Shaft*, and *Foxy Brown*. Before Caesar, all the other dudes Bianca had messed with couldn't spend more than five minutes lying in the bed next to her before they were trying to jump her bones. And God Knows Bianca had dealt with guys who knew how to handle and take care of her physical needs, but they had left her feeling empty. Until she met Caesar, she had never known someone who was able to satisfy her mental and emotional desires. In her mind, Caesar was like her own living, breathing sanctuary. Best believe she wasn't going to allow anyone to make a joke out of that special something that they had, not even Frank, one of her loyal customers.

"Madame, ummmm, is it too much to ask to get down to business?" Frank finally said, knowing that money always made things better, especially for Bianca, because she was definitely about hers.

For a moment, remnants of her anger still lingering, Bianca just looked Frank over and frowned in dismissal. "Chill, boo. Go 'head with your order," she said with a sassy attitude.

"First off, those pants you rocking, I want three pairs of the red, black, and yellow, for all three of my main chicks."

"No problem."

"You know the sizes, right?"

"You know I do." She looked at him like he was crazy. How dare he ask such a stupid question? Everybody who was anybody in Virginia came to her, because Bianca was good at what she did. She could look at a woman and know her size. She even knew how to make a large woman look good in her clothes. She was a natural fashionista and stylist.

"Next, Michael Kors got this new bag out that is fire. It's—"

"Why not get them a little more elaborate bags?"

"Because that's what they like, and these still new hoes."

"Oh, okay. Well, you know I do more than Michael Kors, right?"

"I know. You can do anything my heart desires," he affirmed then continued with his order. "I want Robin jeans, whichever ones you can get for me."

She nodded as Frank went on to describe about ten other clothing items that consisted of purses, shoes, hats, and belts. Regular ticket price, the items would have totaled over twenty thousand dollars, but when all was said and done, Frank walked over to his shop safe, opened it, and counted out twelve thousand dollars. He then walked over to Bianca with the money in hand. "You know my sizes by now," he said as he molested her body with his eyes and then winked at Bianca while licking his lips.

"Ugh," Bianca said, taking the money and stuffing it into her bag. "I know your sizes all right." She looked Frank dead in the eyes. "I sized your ass up a long time ago."

Frank chuckled. "You know you love me, Bee. I know I'm your best customer."

Bianca tried to fight the smirk on her face, but she couldn't hide it. It was true. When she didn't count the dope boys, who blew money by the racks, Frank was her best honest-working customer. And he was consistent; she could count on him like clockwork. Some of her drug-dealing customers might end up locked up or dead, so she couldn't always count on their money to be consistent.

Nevertheless, it didn't hurt that Bianca secretly loved the attention and compliments he constantly gave her. She couldn't lie; it did do a little something to her ego to be hit on by a boss of his status. In an unspoken manner, she knew he admired and respected her as a business-woman, so that made her lighten up too.

Frank dipped his head, pointed at Bianca's face, and grinned. "Mm-hmm, there's that smile again," he teased.

Bianca turned her head, blushing. "Will you stop fuck-ing with me all the time?" Bianca said, playfully rolling her eyes up in her head. "Geesh."

"Then admit it. I am your favorite customer, and you love coming over here getting my money."

Finally Bianca admitted out loud, "You are my best customer, and of course I love coming to get my money. Duh, you know that." Bianca then turned serious to try to justify it from a business point. "Which is why you the only motherfucker who I do sixty-forty with. These other cheap niggas don't get enough shit in a single order. I mean, you already getting the merchandise for half off. Live a little. Splurge, goddamn it!" she said in regards to her other clients.

"And they don't pay up front like Big Daddy do," Frank reminded her.

"Yeah, yeah, yeah! If I give you the money now, what if you get caught and go to jail or something? Im'a be out of my money," Bianca said, mocking some of the other people she'd dealt with.

Frank burst into roaring laughter, as if he had heard the craziest thing ever. "If they knew better, then they'd know that Bianca Williams don't ever get caught boosting—and if she do, somehow that bitch know how to wiggle her ass up out of it."

"They better know it," Bianca said, raising her hand to high-five Frank.

"You should be like an act in Vegas or some shit." Frank continued to stroke her ego. "You the great escape artist, 'cause, baby, you know how to maneuver your ass out of any situation." Frank flashed a big smile, lusting after her still.

"You better let them bitches know," Bianca agreed as she stood. "Let me get my butt on out of here. I have to go to work." She winked at Frank this time.

Frank headed to the door, "Come on. I'll walk you out." He then added a joked in a conspiratorial manner. "Before I have you down on that couch, back here in this office."

Frank led Bianca out of his office and into the main salon area. She gave him a friendly hug before she said, "I'll call you when I have your order filled."

As she was walking from the back of the shop, all eyes were on her.

"You know you killing those shoes, right?" Marvin, the nail tech, asked Bianca as she sashayed by his nail station. He pointed his nail file at the stylist that was doing hair at the station about five feet from him. "Cynthia was just saying she needs that whole outfit you have on to wear to her cousin's baby shower tomorrow."

"For real, I really do," Cynthia said as she did a flat two-strand twist on the client who was sitting in her chair. "It's a perfect outfit for something like that."

Bianca stopped in her tracks and looked herself over. "That's very doable. You can have it for a hundred twenty-five."

Cynthia's eyes lit up like a Christmas tree. She said, almost in a whisper, "That's a real hookup for days. Less than fifty-fifty. I've seen how much the pants alone cost."

"That is a hot outfit," Marvin cosigned, because he knew that Bianca always gave him a little something-something in the form of a kickback whenever he helped her make a sale. So he hyped it up even more. "And you already know, Cynthia, you will outshine everybody at the shower. Girrrrl," he said, flapping his hands and lifting his eyebrows in a dramatic fashion. "You gon' kill it."

Pretty much everyone in the salon knew who Bianca was and how she got down. She could get them damn near anything they wanted from almost any store for half of what the ticket price was—and depending on her mood, maybe even lower.

"So, you want the outfit or not, diva?" Bianca asked.

Cynthia was a new stylist to the shop and was still a little confused as to how things worked. "So, you mean you can go cop that now and have it back to me in time?" She looked perplexed.

Before Bianca could say anything, Marvin answered, "If you want it and got the money, no doubt about it."

Cynthia was getting excited about the possibility that she could be the best dressed at her cousin's baby shower. She loved looking like big money even though she had small budget.

"No," Bianca said, sauntering over to Cynthia while she checked her out. "What are you, about a size six? I can't tell with your smock on."

Cynthia looked down at herself and rubbed her hand down the front of the black plastic apron she was wearing. "Yeah, I'm wearing a six now."

"And so am I," Bianca said. "Which brings me to the deep discount of a hundred twenty-five for the pants and blouse, based on the fact that the outfit has been gently worn once. I've only had it on for about an hour. This is my first stop of the day since leaving my house."

Cynthia looked over Bianca again, contemplating whether she wanted the outfit, but if Bianca was literally going to give her the clothes off her back . . .

"So, what you wanna do?" Marvin jumped in and asked. "You were damn near salivating over that outfit. For that little bit of change, bitch, you betta snatch that up quick, fast, and in a hurry. Before I do." Marvin rolled his eyes and began organizing his polishes as he waited for his next client to arrive.

Cynthia dug into her pants pocket. "Shit, if you serious, I'm all for it."

"I know one thing," Frank interrupted. "Y'all gon' stop all that damn cussing in this shop. Y'all need to be acting like ladies." He pointed to one of the signs that hung on the shop walls. It requested that neither the stylists nor customers used foul language.

Both Marvin and Cynthia looked at Frank like he was crazy.

"What?" Frank shrugged. "I can cuss all I want. I own this muthafucka."

There were chuckles throughout the beauty salon side of the shop. The barber side with the men couldn't really hear what was going on, as they were all engaged in their own conversations and dick-measuring contests.

"Anyway, I need to get back to my office and finish taking caring of some things," Frank said. "Y'all go ahead and handle y'all's business. And call me, Bee."

"All right, honey. You know I got you," Bianca said as she gave Frank a hug. "I'll connect with you in a few days."

"Take care, sweetie. Be careful out there in those streets." Frank kissed Bianca on the cheek and then went back into his office.

Bianca turned her attention back to Cynthia. "So, what's up? You gon' do this or not?"

With the money in hand that she'd pulled out of her pocket, Cynthia extended it to Bianca. "Here you go, girl, and I appreciate you."

Bianca took the money, counted it, and dropped it down into her oversized tote bag that she'd also gotten at a five-finger discount. She knew the street code that one should never be her own client, but in her case, it paid off. Modeling the merchandise and using the merchandise were two different things, and modeling had definitely paid off in this instance.

In the middle of the floor where she stood, Bianca slipped off her shoes. She then unbuttoned her pants and slid out of them, revealing the lace full bottoms that matched her lacey bra.

"Oh, shit. This girl is crazy," one of the patrons said in disbelief.

Bianca couldn't care less what anybody had to say. She handed the pants to Cynthia. Next, Bianca took off the belt. "This is on the house. I didn't even figure the cost of this in." She handed it to Cynthia and then slipped out of the shirt, handing that to Cynthia as well.

"Well, thank you!" Cynthia managed to somehow get the words out.

"It was a pleasure doing business with you." Bianca slipped back into her high-heeled patent leather pumps and strutted off, displaying her flat stomach and long legs, looking like a Victoria's Secret angel. Every eye and mouth on the barber side was open wide.

"Damn, did you see that shit, man?" a couple of the men said to one another, while others high-fived, feeling like the luckiest men in the world.

"Did anybody record that shit?" was the final afterthought, followed by sighs of regret.

On the salon side, all eyes had been glued on Bianca as well, as one stylist said, "Damn, I wish I was her."

And that was the story of Bianca's life: Men wanted her, women wanted to be her, and she was none the wiser. She was just stuck in her own little world that consisted of her and Caesar.

As the door shut behind her, Marvin spoke up. "Now that's a real hustler for you. When they sell the shit off the back, with no shame in it, you know she on her grind. Bad bitch all day long!"

CHAPTER 3

"Baby, where you at?" Bianca said into her cell phone.

After dropping Nique off at home, Bianca stopped off at the store to pick up a few things before heading home: a thank-you card, some votive candles, incense, and Caesar's favorite candy, grape Mike and Ikes. After that, she zipped by the grocery store for a couple bottles of wine, roses, a meat and cheese tray, and a fruit tray.

"Hello to you, too," Caesar replied. Caesar was a stickler for greetings and pleasantries before just diving straight into business. He said it showed a person that you cared somewhat about them and not just what you wanted from them at that moment.

"Oh, my bad." Bianca blushed. She'd been with Caesar almost a year and a half, but he still gave her butterflies. "How are you, my love? How has your day been?"

"That's more like it," Caesar said.

It was still mind-boggling to her how just the sound of his voice had her squirming in her seat. The mental connection and sexual attraction between the two from the day they met could not be denied.

Bianca had met him one day as she was leaving Frank's shop. Caesar had been in the city for about three years, and had settled in and made a life for himself, but he still had not found the right woman for himself.

He had his Friday routine down pat. He'd just gotten a fresh haircut and was walking through the parking lot, heading to his black Range Rover, while Bianca was just getting out of her black Land Rover.

As he was approaching her, she was hit by the smell of his Bond No. 9 cologne. Bianca was an aficionado when it came to scents—particularly good men's cologne. Spellbound, she looked up to see where the intoxicating smell was coming from. She felt as though she had been hit by a bolt of lightning. Suddenly, she was mesmerized by the specimen in front of her; she almost couldn't contain herself. Hands down, he was the finest thing she'd ever laid eyes on. He was so gorgeous that he was almost pretty.

He had become used to women staring at him. He smiled.

Bianca couldn't help it. Before she knew it, "Hey, handsome," had slipped out.

"Hi, beautiful," he responded.

"There is no way you are from here." Bianca had started the conversation. This was a first. She'd never been the one to strike up a convo with a guy. Men always came at her before she had the time to even notice them.

"Actually, I'm not," Caesar replied with what Bianca described as a sexy-ass Latino accent.

"Where you from, papi?" Bianca asked, deciding to give him a little Latin flavor of her own.

"Florida. The sunshine state."

"What are you?" she asked. Though he looked black, with a smooth caramel skin, his accent let her know he was from somewhere else. The second the words came out of her mouth, she could have kicked herself for it. It was funny how she despised when people asked her that question, and now here she'd done the same thing. She prayed in her head that she hadn't offended him like people did to her all the time. They always assumed that her high yellow self was mixed, or even sometimes an albino.

"Dominican," he replied then shot it right back at her. "What about you?"

Bianca shrugged. "I don't know. I guess I'd have to find my biological father one day to find out, but right now, I just say black."

"Well, black is beautiful, indeed!" He gave her a quick once over. "And I hear once you go black . . ."

"You never go back!" Her cheeks were probably as red as a jar of maraschino cherries.

"Aww, home girl blushing?" Caesar teased. He smoothed his finger over his thin moustache and eyed her with a bemused grin on his face.

"Stop it." Bianca laughed and shooed her hand. After a couple seconds, she turned her head back to face him. "So, when do you go back to Florida?"

"Who says I'm going back?" Caesar said.

Bianca shrugged. "I don't know. I just figured who in their right mind would want to leave the beautiful, sunny beaches and palm trees to come here, where we have the ugliest winters?"

He chuckled. "All that glitters isn't gold, baby. You like Florida?"

"Never been. Only seen pictures or Disney World commercials."

"Well, that's Orlando. I'm from Miami. The heat, baby!" Caesar said proudly.

"Well, I guess if LeBron doesn't want to go back, why would you?" she said.

"Oh, home girl got jokes too," Caesar said, playing with the few hairs on his chin. "Well, if you're a good girl, maybe I'll take you to visit someday. Roll out with me and hit the beaches. Do a little salsa." He did this sexy little salsa step that made Bianca want to cream her panties right then and there.

"Oh, wow. I don't even know your name and already you trying to take me home to meet the fam," Bianca said.

"Oh, my bad." He chuckled and laughed into his fist. "I'm Caesar." He extended his hand. "And I ain't say nothing about meeting the fam." He quickly corrected her. "I was thinking more like you and me, a little one on one time."

"Well, I'm Bianca." She extended her hand. "Nice to meet you, Caesar. And ya girl ain't mad about a little one on one time." She looked him up and down.

"Not at all."

The two just stood there shaking hands, staring each other in the eyes.

"Well," Bianca said, barely able to keep her composure, slowly sliding her hand out of Caesar's. "I better, you know, ummm, like, head inside." She nodded toward the shop.

"Not without giving me your number first. I mean, we need to connect so we can plan this trip to Florida and all." He smiled and winked.

Bianca had to be imagining things, because she could have sworn she saw a twinkle in his eye when he winked. Or perhaps it was the twinkle in hers that was blinding her. Some might have said that she was blinded by love, but she swore it was love at first sight.

After giving him her number, they went out that very same night. Within a week, they were claiming each other as boyfriend and girlfriend. Bianca was the first to put herself out there, telling Caesar all about her life and her reputation on the streets, the good and the bad. She even told him how she earned her money.

Not holding back, Caesar didn't play games with Bianca about who he was and what he did either. The instant trust they had for one another was priceless. Caesar claimed to have never let a woman in that quickly. Both had thrown caution to the wind and had an instant love and trust for one another. Even more so, they had a respect and gratitude for one another.

The two had decided that since they both had issues with their families, which they never discussed, they would become each other's family. Each one would be all the other ever needed. That meant the world to her, and it was something Bianca never wanted to take for granted. She felt an unconditional love with Caesar. She always felt like she was in the nonjudgmental zone when they were together. In fact, when she was with him, for the first time in a long time, she felt like she was home.

It wouldn't be long before Bianca showed Caesar her gratitude, all right.

CHAPTER 4

"Hey, babes, where you at?" Bianca tilted her head to the side as she took her ear plugs out and put her iPhone on speaker.

"Just leaving my last stop, heading home. Do you need anything?"

"No, babe, just you," she said as she walked through the front door and kicked off her heels.

"You always know what to say to make me speed home to you."

"Well, hurry. I will be waiting," she reminded him while putting the wine on chill.

The second she hung up the phone, she rushed through the house to get candles and everything in place for his arrival.

Home sweet home. Their one-bedroom apartment was nice and cozy. It was small, but it was luxurious. The newly built domicile had only been up and running for about a year. The couple was the first to have ever lived in that unit. The apartment included a guest bathroom, located to the left, as soon as you walked through the door. Boasting marble counters, it looked like the bathroom of a five-star hotel. Unlike most guests bathrooms that only had a sink and a toilet, this one had a shower as well. It had a smoked glass door, so that you couldn't see the person taking a shower, but their silhouette could be seen.

The thick, cream-colored carpet put to shame that standard beige carpet most apartments came with.

Bianca had always been funny about walking around the house barefoot, but here, she had no qualms. The soft fibers connecting with her feet were like getting a foot massage. The one bedroom was huge—a master bedroom indeed, with its own private bathroom equipped with a walk-up shower, no doors, curtain, or anything. It had dual shower heads, which could each be set to one of five options. This bathroom was all marble everything, from the walls to the floor.

Bianca loved to cook, and she felt like a gourmet chef every time she prepared a meal in their all–stainless steel kitchen.

Before meeting her, Caesar was a true bachelor. He had never cooked a thing, and was a restaurant consumer. On days she didn't feel like cooking, he was always happy to take her to some lovely place for fine dining.

The two loved backgammon, board games, and dominos, and it was always done in their sitting room, which wasn't that huge, but it had two glass French doors that opened up to a patio with the view of the huge water fountain in the pond.

The huge, sunken bedroom was Bianca's favorite place in the house to hang out anyway. After a day's hustle, for both her and Caesar, retiring to their California king-sized bed was the life. Caesar had stayed at a hotel once that had the most amazing bedding. While there, he went right to their Web site and ordered the set to be overnighted to the apartment so that when he got home, Bianca could have it all set up. Bianca, too, had fallen in love with the bedding that made her feel like she was sleeping on a cloud. So most evenings, after eating dinner and showering, this was where the two retreated. In the winter months, it was even cozier due to the gas fireplace. The flickering flames lit the room to make it even more romantic for the lovebirds. This was where they replenished their souls from their day's work and nurtured their burgeoning love for one another.

However, tonight their lighting would come not only from the candles Bianca had set up all around the bedroom, but the sparks of intense lovemaking that were guaranteed to fly off between the two. After lighting all the candles, Bianca pulled all the petals off the roses and randomly placed them throughout the room. She placed the fruit tray on Caesar's side of the bed and the meat tray on hers. The Mike and Ikes she placed right on his pillow. She lit the huge candles that rested on the stand of the flat screen television. Bianca gave the room another once over. Now she was sure everything was in its proper place.

Bianca smiled. She let out a sigh of contentment. She was satisfied that everything was in place and fit for her king. Everything was set up for a romantic, enchanted evening. She took a quick shower, dried off, and headed to the closet to see what she could entice her man with tonight. She found a sheer negligee with a sheer robe over it. She dabbed her favorite perfume, Bond No 9 Chinatown, behind her ears, behind her knees, and on her wrists. Out of habit, she did her Kegel exercises to tighten up her vaginal muscles, and gave herself a throwaway douche. She couldn't wait to see her man so she could jump on his waist as soon as he strolled through the door.

As she waited for him, she thought about a conversation they'd once had.

"You know, you should use your gift of fashion for good," Caesar had told Bianca. "You have great style and an amazing business sense. I could actually see you running a legitimate boutique, being a personal stylist or something like that."

"I do use my gift for good," Bianca had replied. "For the good of the hood. Please . . . these designers know hood chicks can't afford all this high-priced shit. What we supposed to wear? Target and Wal-Mart stuff? Forget that. My people pay what the stuff should be priced at in the stores anyway."

"So you the fashion Robin Hood, huh?" Caesar laughed.

"If that's what you want to call me, there it is."

And there it was. Bianca loved the fact that Caesar believed in her, but he had some nerve. He sold every kind of drug a dope head could fiend for.

He was well respected in the streets, took care of his workers, and never brought work home. There was something about his method. Bianca had never once heard him say anything about a worker stealing from him, or any of his connects trying to set him up, mainly because he used middlemen to handle his business. This dude was like the Wiz behind the curtain, controlling everybody with the super powers everyone thought he had. Meanwhile, he was just a man. But he was Bianca's man, a man whom she loved and believed in too.

"You could run Wall Street if you would use your gift for good," Bianca had said to Caesar.

He looked down while he laughed.

"What's so funny?"

"I used to tell my brother that all the time." His laughter drained out. "He's the one that taught me everything I know."

Caesar stared off like he was contemplating his words regarding his brother. Caesar had spoken very little about his family to Bianca. However, she did know that he had one brother, who was almost three years older than him, and a twin sister, who had tragically passed away.

"Then why'd you leave it all to come here?" Bianca had asked Caesar.

His reply was, "People may love you when you're coming up, but sometimes a king just doesn't get praised in his own throne."

Caesar had shared with Bianca how he was that young, trusted kid on the streets in Miami that everyone knew and had grown up with. It was just unspoken that nobody messed with him and he messed with nobody. But he was getting too high up there in the ranks. Cats started dropping his name when they'd get busted, so he said he knew that was his sign to relocate, which was how he ended up Virginia. He had been there for three years.

From the day they met, they stayed joined at the hip. And even though they loved being up under one another, they knew that when it was time to take care of business, they had to dip out and handle that.

"At least if we lived together, we'd be able to come home to one another," was what Bianca had said to Caesar when she brought up the idea of them moving in together.

It didn't take much convincing, because after five months of seeing each other, they became roomies. To Bianca, even though Caesar was all man, she often felt like she was living with her best girlfriend. She really could share everything with Caesar, and he understood her. He could relate to her feelings. He listened, and when he had something to say, he talked. He told her how he hadn't spoken to his brother since leaving Miami. His brother was disappointed and ashamed of him for leaving the so-called family business.

When Bianca questioned him about his and his mother's relationship, he told her that he hadn't spoken to his mother either. His mother saw him as being a coward, running away and abandoning his family. "She just didn't understand what my brother and I were involved in," Caesar had said. "She just didn't understand me."

His mother had disowned him. Even though his brother had disowned him as well, Caesar was still family, so his brother wasn't going to have him in another town scraping to survive. He broke him off a piece of the business, making sure Caesar still had work, but he didn't deal with Caesar directly. He left that to his right-hand man, Jacques. Caesar's younger sister was the only one who still loved him openly. He communicated with her directly through her cell phone.

That was the one and only conversation Bianca had had with Caesar about his family. After that, seeing how talking about his family filled Caesar's eyes with pain, she never brought them up again. Every now and then, she'd mention them taking a trip back to Florida. She had hopes of reconciliation for them more so than she did her own relationship with her mother. The difference between her and Caesar was that he cared; Bianca didn't. Caesar longed for that family bond and unit. It was important to him and his culture. So, she vowed that she would be his family. She would give him all of her, so much of herself that he wouldn't need anyone else.

She smiled while in the closet, thinking about how they had made the pact, "Since we both have family problems that we don't discuss, let's be each other's family."

They shook on it, and it had been nothing less than the best ever since. Life, for the first time in years, was good for Bianca. She was in love, and from all indications, her man was in love with her. With that being said, she wanted this night to be a night to remember for them both . . . and boy, was it destined to be.

CHAPTER 5

"Looky here, looky here," Caesar said as he entered the candlelit bedroom. His voice woke Bianca from her little catnap.

"Hey, babe." She gave him a big smile. "I don't know how I dozed off." She was too groggy to jump up and wrap her thighs around his waist, so there went that plan out the window.

"You were tired." Caesar ruffled her hair. "Had a long day, huh?"

"Not too long. What about you?"

"Uneventful. Nothing too heavy, baby." He came and sat down on the edge of the bed beside her.

"I know nothing you can't handle," she reminded him. She thought so much of her man. Lying on top of the heavenly white comforter, Bianca stretched out of her slumber, extending her long, fair legs. "Hey, Cee," she said, her eyes closed, with a soft smile on her face.

"You doing that shit on purpose," Caesar said. "Making my dick all hard and shit." He grabbed his manhood.

"What?" Bianca said playfully as she continued to wake from her slumber, purposely in a slow, sexy motion. She did a feline stretch and yawned.

"Don't *what* me. You know what the fuck you doing." Caesar grinned. "Look at all this." He looked around the room. "Baby, this is so nice." He took off the jean jacket he was wearing and climbed on top of Bianca's stretched-out body, his combat boots hanging off the edge of the bed. He pecked Bianca softly on her lips. "I love that you love me, but I love you more." He gave her another long kiss. She kissed him back, but when he tried to use some tongue, she turned her head away.

"I been sleeping. My breath is probably tart," Bianca said. She'd brushed her teeth earlier, but the toothpaste and mouthwash had worn off. Her mouth tasted funny.

"I don't care. I'll take you how you are, stank breath and all." He used his hand to turn Bianca's head to face him. He then parted her lips with his tongue.

"Mmmm," Bianca moaned, giving in and participating in the French kiss. Bianca grabbed Caesar by the back of his head and began running her hands up and down his head while kissing him with increasing passion.

After a few seconds, Caesar pulled away, staring Bianca in her eyes. "I don't know what I did to deserve this special setup." He looked around the room. "Thank you." He kissed her again.

"You're welcome," Bianca said when Caesar pulled his lips from her.

He gave her a quick peck before standing up. "Let me go jump in the shower, then we can pick up where we left off." He nodded toward the bowl holding a wine that he had brought in the room.

"Why don't you go grab us a couple glasses, unless you planned on us taking it from the bottle?"

Bianca got out of the bed. "No, sir. I got other plans for that bottle." She spanked him on the butt as she walked away.

Caesar watched Bianca walk out of the bedroom to the kitchen, shaking his head the entire time. He had the sexiest female in the city, if not the whole state.

Fifteen minutes later, he was in the bed, still slightly damp from his shower, indulging in all of Bianca's sexiness.

"You know what I love?" Bianca asked as she lay between Caesar's legs, holding the glass of wine the two took turns sipping from.

"What's that, baby?" Caesar moved Bianca's hair to the side and kissed her on the neck.

"The taste of wine on your tongue." Bianca crawled around to face her man. She fed him a sip of wine and then sucked it off of his tongue. The two engaged in a kiss.

"Mmmm," Caesar said, running his tongue across Bianca's lips. "And you know where I love tasting wine from?"

A smirk took over Bianca's lips. "That I do." Bianca handed Caesar the wine. He sipped it while he watched Bianca get up on her knees, displaying her perfect physique. She let it slide down her arms and land on the bed. She went to turn around on all fours.

"Not on the bed," Caesar said. "Bathroom."

Bianca got up and walked into the bathroom. Caesar swallowed the last of the wine in the glass and then refilled it before heading into the bathroom himself. When he got in there, Bianca was sitting on the floor, waiting for him.

"One more second. Let me get my magic potion." He set the glass of wine down on the counter.

Bianca sucked her teeth. "Come on, baby, I'm so ready for you. You don't need that."

"You know I like to drive all night," Caesar told her. "I need to make sure my gas tank is on full. And stop whining. You know you like to ride all night too."

Bianca stopped pouting. "Well, you do have a point there."

"Thought so. I'll be right back." Caesar made a trip to their closet.

Bianca wasn't the only one who stored her merchandise in their closet. Caesar had a nice little pharmaceutical

section tucked away. And once again, Bianca wasn't the
only one who sometimes used, or in her case, wore, her
own merchandise. Caesar dipped into his product every
now and then. It was nothing heavy like crack or the heroin that he sold. Just Ecstasy pills, and he only popped
them when he wanted an all-nighter with his woman.

At first, Bianca found it strange that Caesar couldn't
seem to get into sex unless he popped an X, but then
she chalked it up to him having had so much sex in his
younger days that it affected him now. She'd once heard
a commercial saying something about lots of men having
problems getting it up and keeping it up, but that was men
over forty. Caesar wasn't even thirty. But once she saw
the effects of him popping an X, and how she benefitted,
she had no complaints. She stopped questioning why and
just kicked back and enjoyed the effects it took on him.

Caesar bent down and pulled out the four-tier shoe
rack that housed the tennis shoes he only wore on special
occasions. Taped behind it were two very large manila
envelopes. One held nothing but hundred-dollar bills.
Caesar had a few places he stored cash, but most of it he
kept in a safe deposit box where he did his banking. Yes,
he actually did have a bank account. The most he kept in
it was twenty grand. He used the account the same way
any everyday, hardworking man would. He paid bills
from it and deposited his paychecks into it. His paycheck
came from Lawson's Entertainment, LLC. That was the
company his brother had hired a lawyer to incorporate
for him back in Florida. On paper, it looked as if the
company managed artists and booked them for gigs in
nightclubs, private parties, etc. In his legal business,
Caesar was a booking agent.

A few months ago, Bianca became an artist at Lawson's
Entertainment as well. On paper, she was a model, so
she kept a legit bank account as well, in addition to her

own stash she kept in the house. Caesar's big money was in the corporate account back in Florida, but the same way Bianca kept some just-in-case money in her middle console, there was enough just-in-case money in their apartment to take care of any legal fees Bianca or Caesar might encounter if ever busted out on the streets.

But cash wasn't what Caesar was looking for at the moment. It was the second manila envelope, which held some of his product. Caesar retrieved what he needed, put everything back in place, and then went back into the bathroom.

"You ready for this?" Bianca sat on the floor, balanced up on her elbows, her knees bent, with feet flat on the floor and her legs wide open.

Caesar popped his pill with some of the wine, then stood over Bianca and said, "Assume the position."

Bianca turned and got on all fours. Caesar picked up the glass of wine and walked over to Bianca. He got on his knees behind her. He held the glass at the small of her back and slowly poured, the red liquid sliding down Bianca's crack. Caesar filled his mouth with the last swallow of wine then set the glass down. He spread Bianca's cheeks wide and then proceeded to clean her of all the liquid with his tongue.

"Mmmm. Yeah." Bianca moaned at the feeling of Caesar's tongue stroking her up and down, every now and then plunging into her.

"Ooooh, baby, you taste so good." Caesar smacked her on her right butt cheek. "Literally." He laughed and then began eating her backside out while fingering her vagina.

"Oh, Caesar, baby. You make me feel so good. It's fucking out of this world." Bianca continued to tell Caesar how good he was making her feel while his tongue and fingers sent her into ecstasy without the use of an actual Ecstasy pill.

Caesar pushed Bianca's back toward the floor so that she was arched like a true feline. Her ass was tooted high in the air, and her pussy was open wide for him. His tongue went from one hole to the next, as did his fingers. It was like he was in a race to put a Rubik's Cube together with both his tongue and his fingers. As far as Bianca was concerned, with his skills, he was definitely going to make it into the *Guinness Book of World Records*, and he would probably hold the title for the rest of his life.

"Oh, baby. Oh my God." The juices coming from Bianca's body turned into a waterfall. She felt that she would drown in all of her wetness. She didn't know which way was up. Her body was tingling and trembling. Her natural wetness was mixing with Caesar's saliva and creating an ocean of bliss. She didn't want anybody throwing her a life jacket.

She began arching her back, trying to find a rhythm to Caesar's beat, but he was drumming all over the place—from the front to the back. Even though Bianca was arched like a cat, she began panting like a dog.

Caesar knew Bianca well, just like a book. If God was the author of all lives, then he was the co-author of Bianca's. Sensing she was about to cum, he plunged his finger into all the natural wetness of her womanhood, while he hunched over her, plunging his manhood into the river he'd created with his saliva in the back. He bucked in and out, quickly and wildly, while his fingers danced inside of Bianca's ballroom.

"Oh, uh, oh, yes," Bianca cried out, her muscles tightening around Caesar's fingers.

"That's right, baby. Make yo' man nut all up in this ass," Caesar said as his eyes rolled to the back of his head, on the verge of cumming himself. "Shit. Fuck. I love you, baby! I swear I love this ass. I love you! I do, baby! I really do," he confessed.

A string of expletives released from both their mouths as their bodies simultaneously released. Caesar rested his body over Bianca's as the two breathed heavily. Finally, Bianca collapsed to the floor on her stomach, Caesar's vessel no longer inside of her.

"Oh, baby. I can't even explain the way you make me feel," Caesar told her as he ran his finger down the middle of her sweaty, glistening back.

"Ditto," Bianca moaned, still trying to catch her breath and bask in the moment. "Start the shower water," she ordered.

After a couple seconds of trying to catch his own breath, Caesar finally stood to his feet. He padded over to the shower and turned on the water. Once he got it to just the right temperature, he stepped under the showerhead. Bianca stepped in behind him, wrapping her body around his from behind. They both just stood there, allowing the water to beat down on their skin as they rested against one another.

Caesar turned around and looked Bianca in the eyes as water streamed down her face, causing her to blink rapidly, trying to look at him and keep the water from getting into her eyes at the same time.

"I love you, Bianca. I really do." He had such a serious and heavy look on his face.

Bianca smiled, like she always did, to try to break up the intensity of his words and the look on his face. Quite often, after the two would make love, Caesar would always look at her and tell her he loved her. To Bianca, it felt more like an apology. She would often wonder if she was going to wake up the next day and find him gone. "I love you too, babe. You know that." Bianca smiled with her eyes only. "Now, finish what you started." Bianca placed her hand on top of Caesar's head and pushed him downward.

Caesar lifted Bianca's leg over his shoulder, while she held onto his head, and he began sucking on her clit.

"Mmmm," Bianca moaned, closing her eyes and lifting her face, allowing the water to pour right down on her. "Yeah. Suck it," she ordered. The more demands she gave Caesar, the harder he sucked.

Right when Bianca's clit began to swell and throb, he threw her up against the shower wall and stuck himself inside of her. "Come on, do it. Do it," he yelled, pumping in and out of Bianca.

With his forehead against the wall, he pounded deep inside of Bianca, while she parted his buttocks with her hands and played with his anus. She allowed her fingers to plunge in and out of him as he plunged in and out of her.

"Damn it. Fuck! Oh, shit!" Caesar stood trembling inside of Bianca as his cum shot up inside of her like a bullet.

"I love you," Bianca panted. "I fucking love you." Bianca closed her eyes and rested her head on Caesar's shoulder. She ran her hands down his back. This was where she wanted to stay forever, in the most comfortable place on Earth, in his arms.

Caesar kissed Bianca on the forehead and then pulled out of her. For the next few minutes, the two took turns washing each other up. Afterward, they dried one another off, and they made their way back into the bedroom.

They enjoyed the fruit tray, finishing off the bottle of wine. They talked about their day, while Caesar popped Mike and Ikes into his mouth. Eventually, they began doing a repeat of their earlier sexual acts, and Bianca almost wished she'd popped an X this time, in order to keep up with Caesar.

"I see you on your *Fifty Shades* shit tonight."

"Yes, baby! This is what you bring out of me," he said as he had Bianca press a pillow over his face while she rode him, then had her give him head right before he was about to cum, so that he could flow in her mouth.

Bianca had been with her share of men in her young age, but nobody made her want to do the things she'd experienced with Caesar. Some of the things they'd done might have been a little hyper-erotic and over the top.

"For real, baby?"

"I swear, you the only one I ever did this kind of kinky-ass shit with. Only you hold the title to that."

Caesar knew that those words alone reminded her how special she was to him. But what really made her feel the ultimate high was when he said that she held the key to his heart.

"And you hold the key to mine, baby. I love you so much." She smiled, and there was nothing else in the world that could top the high that she was feeling at that moment.

The sound of Caesar's heartbeat in her ear was like a lullaby to Bianca. It was a heart that only she could unlock. She could honestly say that Caesar was the man who was going to be in her life forever. Only death could part them. She just had no idea that death would come knocking so soon, and that she, too, would have the key to unlock that door as well.

With Bianca's head resting so peacefully on his chest, Caesar looked down at his lifesaver. He admired how naturally beautiful she looked without makeup. He slowly reached for his phone over on the nightstand, trying not to wake Bianca. Once he had the phone in hand, he took a selfie of him kissing Bianca on the head. He then pressed a few buttons and laid the phone back on the nightstand.

What would my brother say now? he wondered.

Smiling and feeling serene, he had wonderful thoughts about the life he'd made for himself in Virginia with Bianca, a woman who truly loved him for him. Peace and much contentment dominated his brainwaves until he, too, fell off to sleep.

CHAPTER 6

The vibrating of Bianca's cell phone startled her, waking her up from her sleep. She hit the ACCEPT button and listened.

"Bianca? Bianca? Girl, where are you?"

Bianca held the phone to her ear, still half sleep. Her body ached from all the positions Caesar had her in just a couple of hours before. "Where are you? What time is it? Is everything okay?"

Her sister ignored the questions. "Oh my God! What have you done?"

Bianca was oblivious to what her sister was talking about. She pulled her phone away from her ear and looked at the time. It was almost one in the morning. "Girl, what's up? What you talking about?"

"Oh my God, what have you done?" There was terror in her tone.

Bianca was clueless as to what was going on, and she was tired of asking for details in the middle of the night, "Chile, what is your dramatic ass talking about?" Bianca held the phone to her ear, still half sleep, giving her sister one more chance to see if she was going to hang up on her or what.

"I'm at Mama's, and . . ." Bella said in this whisper-shout sort of tone.

The first thing Bianca thought was that maybe Bella had gotten into it with her husband again and escaped to their mother's with her three children in the middle of the night. It wouldn't be the first time. But what did that have to do with her? She had seen Tony out with a chick and cussed him out recently. It was a known fact that Tony cheated, and if Bianca saw him, she didn't bite her tongue.

Then Bella said, "The plumber came, you know, to fix the backup. This time it's the worst it's ever been."

"Now we getting somewhere," Bianca said as she slowly sat up in the bed. That still didn't explain why Bella would be waking her up in the middle of the night to tell her about the sewer backup.

"This is the worst it's ever been. Pipes broke, the backup is all through the basement and backyard."

Bianca peeped over at Caesar, who was peacefully sleeping like a baby. She got up and tiptoed into the bathroom to talk to her sister. As soon as she got into that bathroom, she let off on her sister. "What are you calling me for? Like, really? I've had my share of cleaning that fucking basement. You know this. And I'd even offered several times to get that plumbing fixed."

Prior to turning eighteen, Bianca stayed with her mother. With their estranged relationship, when Bianca was at home, she pretty much just stayed in her room and kept to herself. She wouldn't even go down to the kitchen and eat if she heard her mother in there. Their relationship was just too volatile. Just looking at one another wrong could strike up an argument. So, to keep the peace, Bianca was like a hermit when she was home.

On her eighteenth birthday, she moved into an efficiency, which was still tight quarters, but it gave her peace. She stayed there for a couple of years, until she finally moved in with Caesar.

Moving in with Caesar had been her saving grace. She was now free to move about the cabin.

Not that Bianca missed anything about living with her mother, but the one thing she knew she wouldn't miss for sure were those ridiculous plumbing issues they had, which resulted in a major backup every couple years. The entire basement would flood, and most likely she'd be the one to have to clean it up. Not anymore! And boy, was she glad that those days were gone for her. Yet even now, it was still such a headache to Bianca, because she'd have to listen to Bella go on and on about how much of an inconvenience it was to help Ella get that basement right, and how nobody ever did that basement right but her.

The last time it happened, even though Bianca wasn't living there, she'd offered to help chip in and pay for whatever it would cost. Hell, she'd much rather be dropping fries for the rest of her life than cleaning up a basement backed up with piss and feces everywhere. When she proposed to pay, Ella just laughed and said, "Yeah, right. Where you going to get thousands of dollars from?"

The truth of the matter was that Bianca had been boosting for the last few years and had been saving damn near every penny. She was boosting on a much larger scale now, versus when she was staying with her mother. That was her beginning stages, when she was learning the life, so even though she hadn't been making as much money a couple years ago as she was now, she still had a nice little amount of money put away. That was after she gave her mom a little something-something every month back then.

With Caesar now taking care of all the household bills: rent, food, utilities, and whatever they needed, Bianca had really been able to form a nice nest egg. But even when she lived with her mother, besides the change she threw at Ella, Bianca didn't spend much money. Hell, she basically stole everything she needed! And if she couldn't steal what she needed, she knew somebody who could, and they bartered.

Bianca had first started boosting one day when she was at the mall and wanted this designer pair of jeans. She'd been saving up birthday money, Christmas money, and money she'd gotten from graduating high school. That was her life savings, literally, and the pair of jeans would suck it all up, but Bianca was so tired of always being labeled the bummy-dressed hood rat, so she went for it and doled out everything in her change purse for those jeans. She barely had enough money for her bus ride back home after the purchase. So when Bianca sat at the bus stop with these two girls who were pulling out items and bragging about what they'd stolen and how much they were going to sell it for, Bianca was sick.

"Only a fool pays full ticket price for shit on these racks," one girl said to the other, the two high-fiving one another.

All of a sudden, Bianca wasn't feeling too proud about her first major purchase of a name brand clothing item. That entire bus ride home, Bianca began planning in her head how she was never going to be the fool those girls were referring to again. That very next day, Bianca tried her hand at boosting. She stole stuff that she really didn't need or could even fit. She just had to take advantage of certain opportunities. Besides, she had to practice, didn't she?

Not wanting her efforts and successful boosting gigs to be in vain, Bianca learned of this website that mostly teenagers and young adults frequented. They would post pictures of clothing items they wanted to sell, and others would bid on it. Bianca made $200 her first week. She'd started her own online business with zero startup money. Now, between her online store that she still had on the website, her closet, and her trunk, she was handling hers for real. She could have paid the entire plumbing invoice if she wanted to—but she didn't. Now that she thought about it, that was probably why Bella was calling. Their mother was probably too cowardly to eat her words, saying that Bianca couldn't afford to help out, and now she needed her help after all.

"You don't understand. This shit over here is real," Bella firmly informed her sister.

"Yeah, I know!" she agreed. "You keep forgetting I've been there and seen it firsthand. Look, I'm about to go back to sleep. Find out how much the plumbing bill is and let me know in the morning. I will take care of it," Bianca directed her sister.

"No, no, no! You don't understand. The plumbers aren't the issue. It's the police I'm more worried about."

"What? Huh? Police? Damn, the shit is that bad, huh?"

"The police."

"Why are the police there?" Bianca was the one who was now whispering. "Did that nigga put his hands on you? Fuck that!" Bianca instantly got upset at just the thought of Bella's husband, Tony, putting his hands on her. Bianca had once suspected it one night she called Bella up to talk and Bella answered the phone, huffing and puffing, all out of breath, with him yelling in the background.

"No, he didn't hit me. It's not that."

"You sure?"

"Yes, I'm sure." Bella swore on her firstborn's life that he'd never put his hands on her.

He must have hit one of the kids then, was the next thing that popped into Bianca's head. "I know he didn't touch my niece or nephew, because I will—"

"Bianca, stop it. Just stop it and quit playing with me," Bella snapped. "What have you done? Bianca, what did you do?" Bella broke out crying.

Bianca was completely confused. "Bella, what are you talking about? I'm home. I haven't done anything."

"They found it, Bianca." Bella was crying her heart out. Bianca could barely understand her.

"They found what? Who found what?" Bianca tried to get Bella to just spit it out as sweat beads began to form on Bianca's head. Some things were starting to register. The hairs on the back of her neck stood up, and a sheer thrill of sadness and fear went through her entire body. Pieces of the puzzle were starting to come together.

It was making her go back to a very dark place that she had blocked out a long time ago and vowed to herself to not think about again . . . but now here she was, having to relive the second most painful thing she'd ever experienced in her life.

CHAPTER 7

The horrific thoughts went back to when she was fourteen years old. It was a snowy day in Virginia, and all the schools were basically out for the day. The streets weren't bad, but the officials were worried about the back roads. She had to stay at her grandmother's house while her mother was at work. She remembered it just like it was yesterday.

Grandma Williams pulled on her long, red wool coat and red hat. She was on her way out to play bingo. "Your fast ass need to have this house spic an' span by the time I get back," she said.

At times, Bianca couldn't stand her grandmother. The woman treated Bianca like a black Cinderella. The only difference was that she wasn't a stepchild; she was this lady's blood. The woman wasn't anything like any of the sweet grandmothers that she had ever seen portrayed on television. In Bianca's eyes, she was nothing but a mean old witch. All she needed was a flying broom between her legs, some pointed toe boots, and a big black hat.

"How come I gotta be here? Why can't I stay at my own house?"

Grandma Williams tossed a crooked smile her way. She had a gold tooth on the top left side of her mouth that always stuck its head out when she was about to get fly out the mouth, which seemed like all the damn time. "First of all, Ms. Thang, you ain't got no damn house, your mother does," Grandma Williams was quick to point out. "You don't have a teacup to piss in. And secondly, if your mother hadn't come home early and caught you with that white boy in your bed, maybe she would let you stay at home by yourself while she was at work. But that ship done sailed, much like your virginity."

"We weren't doing anything but studying. And he wasn't in my bed. He was helping me study for the advanced geometry class that I'm taking." Bianca was a virgin and always made above average grades, but math wasn't one of her favorite subjects. She'd always preferred English and history. She asked, "When did studying become so wicked?"

Grandma Williams rolled her eyes. "Two things the Lord can't stand," she said, ignoring Bianca's question, "liars and fast-ass girls." Then, with two fingers of her right hand, Grandma Williams touched her forehead, the left side of her chest, then the right side, as if she were warding off evil spirits.

As Grandma Williams stepped out the door and got into her red Cadillac, Bianca thought, *The only thing evil up in here is you.* But she would never say it to Grandma Williams's face. Not for a few more years, anyway.

At that moment, Bianca had no other choices, so as always, she did as she was told. She cleaned the house from top to bottom. She started in the kitchen, washing dishes, then she vacuumed the living-room carpet, dusted the tables, and wiped down the plastic on the sofa and chairs. After knocking out the bathroom, the only rooms left were the bedrooms and the den. Since no one was allowed in Grandma Williams's bedroom, Bianca made her way to the den.

Uncle Peanut and two of his friends were in the den watching a football game. A team dressed in yellow pants with a thick black stripe down the side had the ball. Their quarterback threw the ball to a guy wearing white pants with red and blue trim. Peanut cursed at the TV. "That muthafuckin' kick cost me fifty muthafuckin' beans!" He was hot as fish grease. "Fuckin' bums!"

One of Peanut's friends, slim built with a bald head, ragged him. "You know got-damn well the Steelers wasn't gonna beat no mu'fuckin' Tom Brady," he said. "You ain't lose no fifty beans, nigga. You gave that bread away."

"Pay it so you don't owe it," the other one said, with an open hand. "Let me get that—"

It was obvious, Bianca thought, that the team in yellow wasn't supposed to just up and give the ball away. Even she knew that, and she knew diddly squat about football or any other sports.

Peanut looked up in her direction. "What the fuck you doin' in here with grown folks? Don't you see we busy?" He was only four years older than she, and nowhere near as mature, if you asked her.

"Boy, please!" Bianca put her hands on her shapely, fourteen-year-old hips. "You aren't hardly grown," she said. "I'ma need for you and your friends to bounce so I can straighten up in here before Grandma get back from bingo."

Peanut checked his phone then smacked his lips. "Momma gonna be at bingo for at least another four hours. Holla back," he said.

"Let her chill," said Peanut's friend, the one who'd won the bet. They called him Cockroach. "Baby girl reminds me of my baby's momma." He licked his lips as if he were thirsty.

If Bianca could've read Cockroach's mind, or had been a little more streetwise, she would've beat the pavement and got as far away from those fools as her feet would carry her. But she couldn't read his mind, and she wasn't streetwise.

Cockroach, with a slippery smile, said to Peanut, "Aren't you going to introduce us? Shit, we may be able to work something out on that bread that you lost, plus let you make a li'l sum-sum on the side. Ya feel me?"

Bianca saw Peanut nod to Cockroach. Cockroach grinned that same slippery smile, like the guy in the movies that no one likes, or the villain who eventually gets killed by the time the ending credits roll.

Cockroach said to Bianca, "Come sit beside me, ma. We can clean up later. Don't worry. I'll help you."

"No, thank you." She didn't need to be street smart to know that Cockroach wasn't anyone she wanted to sit next to. She told Peanut, "I'll just come back later."

When she turned to leave, she felt a hand take hold of her wrist. It was Cockroach.

"Why you in a hurry?" he said. His breath smelled like onions. "We 'bout to have some fun." He forced her hand onto his crotch. It was hard.

She frowned her face up and tried to pull away, but he was too strong, his grip too tight. He palmed her ass real hard. She cocked back and slammed her fist into his face with her free hand. The blow surprised Cockroach, but it didn't hurt him. It only seemed to make him more eager to finish what he'd started.

Bianca screamed, "Help me!" to Peanut.

Peanut laughed. "Don't act like you ain't already fucking, girl. Go 'head and give ol' boy some of that, so I can squash my bill."

Bianca didn't want to believe what she'd heard. She knew Peanut was a follower, but she never would've imagined that he would stand by and watch her get raped in their grandmother's house.

Cockroach spun her around, yanked down her jeans, and bent her over the couch. He had both her hands pinned behind her back. The other friend said, "My next! That li'l bitch thicka than a bowl of oatmeal."

Peanut said, "You gotta pay if you wanna play, playa."

"You ain't said nuttin' but a word, my nigga."

While Peanut was negotiating payments for Bianca's body, Cockroach was digging his fingers inside of her. Bianca tried to jerk away, but Cockroach kept pulling her back. When she screamed, the one who said he wanted to rape her next put his palm over her mouth, silencing her protests and pleas to stop.

Bianca couldn't have imagined, not in a million years, that anything worse than this could ever happen to her. Why hadn't she seen this coming? How was she to know she was not safe in her grandmother's house? To paraphrase what Sophia said in Alice Walker's novel, *The Color Purple*, a girl child ain't safe in a houseful of men.

But Bianca had always been safe in her mother's home. Say what negative things she could about her mother, Ella never brought men in the house near her daughters. Unlike a lot of her friends' mothers, who naively brought men home to live with them and their children, often getting their daughters molested, Ella had never exposed her girls to that trauma. After Bianca's father abandoned her, she gave up on men. She was also careful about whom she brought around her developing daughters.

The other reason Bianca hadn't seen danger brewing was she had grown up in a houseful of women. She had never been around horny boys growing up in a house. Therefore, she had thought she was going to be safe going to her grandmother's house. How wrong she was, though.

A pain so sharp and intense reverberated throughout her entire body that it felt as if she would split in two. Her last thoughts, she remembered before passing out, were: *How could something like this be happening to me? I wanna kill these motherfuckers. I swear I never in a million years thought that I'd be losing my virginity like this.*

CHAPTER 8

"Bianca! Bianca! Bianca!"

Hearing Bella's voice snapped her out of the daze she was in. She had not thought about that night in a very long time.

"Look, sis, you know I love you. God knows you know I do. I will do anything for you. But I can't back you on this one."

"Huh? What?"

"I just can't," Bella informed Bianca.

"What do you mean?"

"I can't have your back after you killed my nephew."

"Killed the baby?" Those words snapped Bianca out of her trance. "Bitch, are you fucking crazy? I mean, fucking out of your got-damn mind? Do you really think that low and little of me, like I would do some sick shit like that to the one thing that did look to me for real love?" At this point, she had flipped out and was screaming at the top of her lungs.

"Look, I don't want to believe it," Bella whispered into the phone as if hoping no one would hear, "but I see them bagging up the remains of a little baby."

"That has nothing to do with me."

"It's almost impossible to believe, but I hear you and want to believe you."

"I will explain everything."

"Okay, cool, so just come over here and talk to the police. You just needs to get over here quick, because they are really asking me a lot of questions."

"Look, I don't have shit to do with that, and I'm not coming over there for them to haul me off to jail."

Bella heard nothing she said. "Look, just tell them you were young and scared. I will be here the entire time, and everything will be okay."

"I'm not going to jail for no bullshit that I didn't do." Bianca had lowered her voice by now.

Bella, with her one-track mind, had no type of understanding of the matter. "Again, sis, I love you, but what you did was wrong. And if you don't hurry up and get over here and face the music, I will have to tell them where you at."

Bianca took a breath. She couldn't believe her ears. *How dare she*? she thought. She was going to hang up the phone, but caught herself before she did. Instead, she robotically replied, "Okay."

Hell, no. That wasn't her final decision, but she knew that was what she had to say to at least appease her sister for the moment, to kill time, to think. She had to play this thing out right, until she figured out what to do, and there was only one person's advice that she truly trusted.

"Someone's coming." Bella's voice got lower. "I gotta go. I love you. I'm here for you. Please, just do the right thing."

The phone clicked in Bianca's ear. She looked down at the phone and hit the END button. She turned her head, facing the mirror. She hadn't felt the tear running down her cheek, but now she saw it. For a moment, the reflection staring back at her in the mirror was her fourteen-year-old self. The same fourteen-year-old who was scared to death and had no one in the world to lean on or to protect her.

At that moment, she could vividly hear her grandmother's voice in her head, the day she brought the baby home from the hospital. *That bastard was born as a punishment to your hot red ass. You shame your mother! And I promise you, it's going to make your life a living hell.* She spit those words like balls of fire, and they burned like hell.

"Babe?"

"Oh God!" Bianca turned to see Caesar standing in the bathroom doorway. There had to have been a hole in her chest from where her heart jumped out and landed on the floor. She looked up into Caesar's concerned eyes, and without saying a word, he took her in his arms.

A wailing sound escaped her throat as she balled into his chest. She didn't feel like the independent young woman he had fallen in love with anymore. She felt like a scared fourteen-year-old who needed her daddy, a father she never even knew.

In that second, she imagined that she was a girl in her daddy's arms and that he was her father, the superman who would make everything all right.

Caesar tightened his arms around her. "What's the matter, baby?"

Bianca couldn't even speak. She trembled in his arms.

"What's wrong? Talk to me."

Bianca's phone slid out of her hand and onto the floor, cracking the screen. Next, Bianca began to slide to the bathroom floor.

Caesar was able to scoop her up into his arms before she hit the tile. "Come on, baby, you gotta talk to me." Caesar carried Bianca into their bedroom and laid her on the bed.

Bianca's limp body didn't even have the strength to sit up. Caesar had to sit down and lean her against him. "You're scaring me, sweetie. Please talk to me." He kissed her on the forehead. "Who was that on the phone? Did something bad happen?"

Bianca was unresponsive to anything Caesar said.

"I want to help you, but I can't if you don't talk to me," Caesar told her desperately.

Bianca wanted to talk to him. She really did. She just couldn't get her brain to react. She felt like a mute, and that she'd have to end up communicating by blinking her eyes, once for no and twice for yes. She opened her mouth and tried to talk, but only another wailing sound came out. It sounded like she was in physical pain, and she was. It had nothing to do with the way Caesar had worked her body out either. This had to do with all the pain that she had been concealing for her entire life. Finally it was coming crashing down on her like a skyscraper falling. All the secrets she'd harbored had been like a low-grade infection that had grown into a full-blown case of AIDS.

Caesar decided that all he could do was hold her until she was ready to talk, so that's what he did for the next five minutes. Finally, Bianca was able to muster up the strength to at least lift her head.

"The police are at my mother's house. They want to question me. They think I killed my baby."

"I thought you took the baby to the firehouse," he said, recalling the story that she had told him and everyone else.

Bianca felt awful. She looked into his eyes. "That's the only thing that I lied to you about."

Caesar rubbed her back the entire time, coaxing her, at the same time letting her know he was there for her. It was almost the same feeling that a child would get from its mother. That thought alone made Bianca's shoulders begin to heave up and down. Her mother would never be there for her like this, no more than she'd been there for her own child she'd given birth to.

The thoughts that Bianca had been able to sweep under the rug and cover with her and Caesar's blissful relationship were now exposed. The cover had been pulled off of the messy bed she'd made, and now she'd have to lie in it. If she was ever going to share what was going on in her mind with anybody, it would be Caesar. She was afraid, but she still had to come clean. He was the only one who could help her.

"Tell me what's wrong, baby." Caesar made another attempt to get his girl to talk to him. Caesar grabbed Bianca by the shoulders and turned her to face him. Her eyes were puffy and red from all the crying she'd been doing. She looked like a totally different person. Her eyes were just blank. Whatever was going on was clearly detrimental and life-changing, but no matter what it was, Caesar knew one thing: Nothing and no one could ever make him stop loving her.

"I will always love you." Whitney Houston might have said it best, but Caesar was saying it again. "I refuse to believe that you don't know that about me by now. Nothing you can ever say, nothing you could ever do, will change that. Now, please, tell me what's going on."

"They think I killed my baby."

"What happened to the baby?"

She took a deep breath and began to reflect on everything that happened.

CHAPTER 9

After the guys finished passing her around—while Bianca lay on the floor, warm semen dripping down her legs like a vile gumbo soup—Peanut threatened, "I'll make you regret that you were ever born if you utter a word to anyone about what you've done."

Peanut's words—*What you've done, what you've done, what you've done*—careened around her head, over and over and over.

Scared and unsure of what to do, Bianca kept quiet. After all, who was she going to tell anyway? Her mother? It would break her heart to know that Bianca had been passed around like a church collection plate, having all the men put something in her. Her grandmother? Hell, no. She would believe Peanut over her any day. Besides, after all, she was sure that Bianca was already fucking one hundred miles in running anyway. And the lady loved the ground her dear Peanut walked on. In her eyes, he could do no wrong, so for Bianca to accuse him of rape, her grandmother would find that inconceivable. She was sure that no one was going to do anything but make her life more miserable.

She felt she had no choice but to keep quiet. But Bianca's body . . . that was a different story. Her body never got the text, nor had it promised to keep any secrets. While getting dressed for school, four months to the day after being gang raped, Bianca noticed that her jeans no longer fit over her hips. If this was a joke, she thought, God had a strange and warped sense of humor.

A hundred and four days later, she gave birth to a five pound, eight ounce little boy. Bianca named the baby Babylon. Beside the fact that she'd been reading the Bible incessantly since the entire ordeal, she had no idea why Babylon was the name that came to her when, for the very first time, she looked into her baby's liquid-brown eyes.

While her mother was at work, Bianca was sent to her grandmother's with the newborn. As Bianca was gazing down at little Babylon, she couldn't help but wonder, *How can something so innocent have been created from something so evil?*

Suddenly, Peanut walked into the room. It was the same room in which Babylon was conceived.

"What's crackin', B?"

Bianca wanted to throw up. She could barely stand to look at Peanut, much less occupy the same space, breathing the same air.

"If I didn't know better," he said, "I'd think you didn't fuck wit' me." He smiled. "Don't you fucks wit' me?" He already knew.

"No, Peanut. I don't fucks wit' you. So, what do you want?" She hated him with a passion.

Peanut cut his eyes at her then looked toward the baby. "So, this here's yo' li'l nig, huh?"

Bianca watched Peanut watch the baby. She trusted him about as far as she could spit in his face—which she would've done if the fear of what he might do in retaliation hadn't dried up all the saliva in her mouth. She refused to let Peanut know that he had that type of power over her. He was wicked enough as it was.

Suddenly, Peanut's casual observation of Babylon mutated into an intense scrutiny. His brow furrowed like dry trenches on the side of barren a road, eyes narrowing into laser-like slits. Bianca thought something must be wrong with Babylon. For the first time since Peanut had walked into the den, Bianca switched her focus from him to the baby, hoping Babylon wasn't choking, or something worse. God, she thought, if something was wrong with the baby, what would she do? She was clueless. And besides her and Peanut, no one else was there. Her mother was at work, and her grandmother was . . . shit, she had no idea where Grandmother Williams had gone. In the split-second it took Bianca to divert her attention to Babylon, she'd nearly worked herself into a full-blown panic attack.

"Thank God," she whispered. *Nothing is wrong*, so she thought.

Then what was Peanut looking at?

The answer would hit her like a punch in the gut, knocking the wind from her lungs and leaving her stunned

The ears, she thought. How could she have missed it?

Babylon's ears were pointed. The only person she'd ever seen with ears like that was the guy from *Star Trek*, and . . . Peanut.

Peanut noticed it too. That's what he was staring at. And it wasn't just the ears that were similar. They were the same complexion of milk chocolate and had the same pug nose.

To conceal the rape, she'd told her mother and grandmother that she had no idea who the baby's daddy was—and she didn't, but she had lied when she said it was "one of maybe ten to fifteen different boys at school." She told the bald-faced lie, but she had just assumed the baby belonged to Cockroach or Dog.

This can't be possible, she thought.

But it was possible, because Peanut had not only sat back and watched his friends violate Bianca. He'd also joined in on the perverted fun.

At that second, he put two and two together, and shit got real. Peanut knew that things could go badly for him if anyone else noticed the similarities. Most likely a long stint in prison, plus he'd lose Jackie, and that wasn't going to happen. He had to do something, but what?

"Yo, give me that fucking baby," he said nervously. He was breathing hard and sweating.

"You crazy." Bianca wasn't having it. "You're not taking him anywhere." She reached for Babylon to protect him, but Peanut swooped him up from the bassinet first.

`"Give 'im back!" she shouted. "Give 'im back!" She tried to pry her baby away from Peanut's left arm, but he used his right arm to fend her off.

"I swear I won't utter a word to anyone. Just leave him alone."

"I know you won't."

"I haven't said nothing this far, and if you just leave him alone, I promise I won't say nothing."

"You ain't going to have the chance to say shit, bitch." He shoved her. Hard. Bianca stumbled backward. She was about to charge forward when Peanut pulled out a six-inch pocketknife and put it to the baby's neck. He barked, "Don't make me hurt the li'l nigga."

The threat of the knife biting into her son stopped Bianca cold in her tracks. She gave him a look that only a lioness could possess over her cub, and that's when he pushed her down, completely knocking the wind out of her.

"Bitch, I swear, I will kill you if you say a word." His eyes had fire in them. With his Timberland boots, he stomped her down as if she had stolen something, causing her to go black. She never saw her baby again.

When her family asked her about the baby, she said she had dropped him off on the steps of the fire station.

To this day, the words of her grandmother still rang in her head: *It was probably the best thing for it. The best thing you could've done for that retarded baby anyway.*

CHAPTER 10

"Damn." Caesar sat in disbelief. "That's really fucked up. They are fucked up. Your uncle, he's a sorry mother-fucker."

"Don't I know it," she agreed, secretly wanting him to say he was going to kill him for hurting her. But he didn't. It was okay, because at that second, Bianca was reminded that nobody but her was ever going to be her saving grace.

He rubbed his hands up and down her back. "It's going to be okay. Everything is going to be all right." Caesar stared off in thought while holding Bianca. "All you have to do is go and talk to them, and I know you don't want to live through that again, but you gotta tell these people what happened. I assure you, there is nothing that your pussy-ass uncle can or will do to hurt you."

"My uncle? I'm not worried about him. I'm worried about me—about facing the police."

"I don't condone telling on nobody, but this is different. You are the victim."

"Listen, baby, this is already becoming a witch hunt. Nobody is going to believe me. Not my momma, my sister, and damn sure not my grandma. The police already got me convicted and under the jail."

"No, no. I'm going to help you get through this," he said, still thinking, putting together a plan in his head.

Bianca pulled away, wiping her nose with the back of her hand.

"One of my boys has a sister who is an attorney," Caesar started. "She helped him get off after shooting this house up that resulted in a dude being paralyzed. He did that shit, too, so I know she can work something out for you." Caesar headed over to the nightstand where his phone was. "I'll call him and—"

"Whoa, wait!" Bianca said. "No, don't tell anyone." She had horror in her eyes.

Caesar stopped and looked at Bianca. "We can at least ask her some questions. We have to be prepared for what to tell the police, and of course, we will have her there with you while you are being questioned."

"I'm not telling the police shit," Bianca snapped.

"Don't be stupid. We're gonna have to tell them something."

"We? So, are you saying you're going to talk to the police?" Bianca started pacing again.

Puzzled, Caesar looked at Bianca. "This ain't no Maxwell song. Girl, the cops gon' come knocking in real life, so we need to be—"

"Gone," Bianca finished the sentence.

"Gone where?"

"Baby, we can pack up and just go. No, we don't even have to pack. We can just go. We've got the money to start over somewhere." Her eyes lit up. "Miami! We can go back to Miami. We can set up camp there. Your brother can—"

"My brother can't do shit!" Caesar cut her off. "I told you, he don't fuck with me and I don't fuck with him. He'd turn you in just to spite me. That's how ruthless the life he lives has made him. Trust me, my brother is no safe haven, and neither are those thugs he keeps close to him." He paused, wanting to say more, but he caught himself. "Just believe that."

"Well, the police haven't touched him, which means even in all his wrongdoings, he's doing something right."

Caesar shook his head. "No, no. I'm not involving my brother."

As far as Bianca was concerned, this was the best solution. Why wouldn't Caesar just hop on board? A part of her was starting to do something she hadn't done since meeting Caesar, which was doubt his love and loyalty to her. Did he want her to go to jail? Did he have another chick on the side that he was going to replace her with the moment they threw her in jail? She didn't know what to think, but she hoped she was wrong about the things she was thinking. Her next line of questioning, though, would let her know where his head was at for real.

"Then where are we gonna go?" Bianca asked.

Caesar took a deep breath and looked at Bianca regretfully. "Like I said earlier, I think Bella is right. I think you have a better chance of fighting this if you go to the police instead of them coming after you. You even have a way better chance if you turn yourself in, versus you running and them hunting you down and finding you. If you run, it makes you look guilty, and we both know you are not. I hate to say it, Bianca, but this all will catch up with you. It's catching up with you now. Can't you see?"

Bianca shook her head adamantly. For her, turning herself in to the police wasn't an option. "Caesar, even if I do get an attorney and get off, I'll still have to sit in jail while I await trial." Bianca's eyes filled with fear. "Do you know what they do to baby killers in jail? They have a special place underneath the jail for baby killers. God, they're going to destroy me. When I come out, I'm going to be all fucked up. No, I can't do it. I won't."

"But you are not a baby killer."

"I know, but in this world, you are guilty until proven innocent, and do you know what the media alone will do to me?"

"You were a young girl victimized, and this animal took advantage of you too many times. He's the one who committed the crimes, and he's the one that should be under the jail."

"Nobody is going to believe me."

"I disagree. I believe you, and many others will too."

"I don't want to risk it." She was adamant.

Caesar continued trying to reason with Bianca. "Okay. So, hypothetically speaking, let's say we did run."

She listened closely, because he was now starting to see things from her point of view.

"No matter where we went, we'd always be looking over our shoulders. That's not the life I want to live. Why do you think I left Miami in the first place? I'm not ashamed to say it, Bianca, but I'm truly not 'bout that life. I tried it. I put many years of work in. It's not me. I want to live with a clear conscience, not aiding and abetting a fugitive."

His last comment right there let Bianca know not only where Caesar's head was, but where his heart was, and he saw it written all over her face.

"I love you, Bianca." He walked over to her, detecting the doubt she was having for him on her face. "I'd rather lose you for a couple years than forever. I'll be here for you. I promise. I'll do whatever you need me to do. Just don't ask me to get caught up in murders and killings and shit like that. I love you so much, baby, but I wouldn't do it for my brother, and I'm not doing it for you."

His words hurt Bianca to the core. "But you told me there was nothing you wouldn't do for me. You told me you couldn't live without me," Bianca reminded him.

"I know, and I meant it, but—"

"Then no take-backs," Bianca said, sounding like a five-year-old. "You have to really mean what you say."

"And I do." Caesar held Bianca tightly. "But every person has their limits."

Bianca pulled back and stared Caesar in his eyes. "But love doesn't. Love doesn't have any limits, Caesar. At least I know my love for you doesn't."

"I hear what you are saying, and I can understand how you might feel I'm limiting my love for you by putting boundaries on what I'm willing to do for you, but this is the right thing to do. You can't keep running."

"Like you? Like how you ran away from Miami?" Now Bianca was being condescending and nasty. She couldn't believe her man wanted her to turn herself in. She thought he would have her back in this situation.

"It's not the same thing. You can't even compare the two," he said, a little frustrated that he really couldn't get deeper into his own situation.

"Well, from my vantage point, you don't want to go back to Miami any more than I want to go to jail. So what's the big deal? We can both live life on the run in our own certain way." Bianca smiled, hoping her facial expression and words would give Caesar a change of heart. She watched him contemplate for a moment. She was once again becoming hopeful.

"I want to run away with you."

Bianca's eyes lit up.

"But that's just not realistic."

Her eyes dimmed once again.

"Okay, so you pulling my strings, playing with my heart and emotions," she said, wondering whether he had been doing this all along, and she'd just been too blinded by her feelings for him to see it.

"We are not in some rap video or gangster movie, and I'm not going to pretend to be. I've always been real with you. That doesn't stop now. You have to listen to reason, Bianca. Five years from now, you'll look back and all of this will be done and over with. The consequences will have been faced, and you can live life free, or you will be totally exonerated from any charges. And I think being free is something you truly haven't experienced since . . . you know."

Bianca paused. She'd always thought it was her and Caesar against the world, but now she wasn't so sure. "But I have been free. You made me feel free." Bianca shook her head and walked over to the dresser. She looked at herself in the mirror. "You made me forget who I was. I wasn't that chicken-head hood rat everyone else thought I was. You made me feel like a queen." Bianca's head fell.

"And you still are my queen." Caesar walked up behind her. "A king takes care of his queen. If there's one thing we've always had in our relationship, it's been trust. I've always taken care of you, and I always will." He kissed the back of her head. "You do still trust me to do that, don't you?"

Bianca slowly lifted her head and stared at Caesar through the mirror. She nodded.

He turned her around. "Then let me get in touch with my boy, so he can reach out to his sister. We'll figure out the best way for you to do this."

Like a deer in headlights, Bianca simply nodded. "Okay," she said. She was saying okay to Caesar for the same reasons she'd said okay to Bella before hanging up the phone with her.

Caesar exhaled like he'd just saved his own life.

Bianca watched in the mirror while he walked over to his phone and picked it up.

"Wait a minute." Bianca spun around. She hurried over to Caesar. "If I do this, it's going to be a long time before you're even able to touch me again. I just know it. I'm going to have to just sit in there until I beat the charges."

Caesar stood there, looking at her with questioning eyes.

Bianca looked around the room. "Tonight was supposed to be so special. It was my thanks and appreciation to you for just loving me and always giving me great advice and steering me in the right direction."

"Ironic, huh?" Caesar said.

"Yes. And just think, now this night might be more special than you and I ever imagined." Bianca leaned in so close to Caesar that her lips were grazing his. "Make love to me, Caesar, like never before. Like it's the last time. And this time, I want to experience the same high as you."

Caesar raised an eyebrow. "Are you saying what I think you're saying?"

"Yes, I want a Molly too. Please. For these next hours, I don't want to think about anything but how good you are to me. How good you make me feel. Please, Caesar." Bianca began kissing Caesar all over his neck. "Take me higher," she whispered, "than ever before."

Caesar's neck rolled back as Bianca sucked on his Adam's apple. "Hold on." Caesar headed over to the closet. After a few seconds, he came back out of the closet.

Bianca met him halfway as he walked toward her. He opened his hand, where two pills rested. Bianca took one out of his hand.

"I'll be back. Let me get us something to drink. We do still have another bottle of wine." Bianca walked away as if she were walking to the electric chair. She returned a few minutes later with two glasses filled with wine. Caesar was waiting for her in the bed. She went and sat beside him. "Here you go."

Caesar took the glass of wine from Bianca, placed the Ecstasy pill on his tongue, and then chased it down with wine.

Bianca stared at her balled-up fist where she held her pill. Ecstasy had always been Caesar's thing. Bianca had never been into any type of drugs, not even smoking weed. She knew she was pushing the envelope tonight. It was as if she had an out of body experience. She was walking on the wild side, releasing all of her inhibitions.

"Go ahead. You'll love the way it makes you feel."

Bianca contemplated for a few more seconds and then gave in. "If it will take me higher with you, then I'll take it, because I want to be wherever you are." Bianca threw hers down her throat and then sipped some wine. "Keep drinking," she told Caesar. "I want to taste it on your tongue. I want to get so full off of you."

Bianca climbed on Caesar while he drank, causing him to spill some wine. As it flowed down his chest, Bianca licked it up. The two were still in all of their nakedness from their earlier sexual escapades.

While Caesar drank, Bianca licked and sucked. Once all of Caesar's wine was gone, she grabbed her glass and fed it to him. "Fuck these sheets," she said when some spilled on them. "Fuck me."

For the next couple hours, the rewind button was in full effect, as Caesar and Bianca repeated all of their earlier sexual acts and then some. She felt like they were in a magical microcosm. Perhaps Caesar hadn't really needed to take a second pill, because he was all the way turned up. Bianca had been jaded and not able to keep up with him any longer a half hour ago, but knowing it would be the last time she had Caesar between her legs and in her mouth, she continued to engage.

She laid there with her eyes closed, taking in every touch, stroke, lick, and kiss. Caesar's hand slid from her hipbone up to her neck. The harder he pumped, the tighter his hand squeezed her neck. The adrenaline was pumping between the two of them as she began bucking back. For the first time ever, Bianca could not keep up with him as he moved at the speed of lightning. She knew when to bow out gracefully. Besides, he was about to cum, and hopefully he would be full, or at least want to catch his breath, giving her time for a breather.

"I'm 'bout to fucking cum," Caesar moaned. "Shit!" he cried out as he ejected his fluids inside of Bianca.

Bianca couldn't breathe because he had such a tight grip around her, but she knew it would only be momentary, and she could hold her breath for a pretty long time. A few seconds later, Caesar's body collapsed on top of her. His heartbeat was like a drum, beating faster and faster.

With her eyes now open, she looked up at the ceiling. Slowly, she began to rub Caesar's back. "I love you, baby," she said as a tear escaped her eye. This time, it was Bianca who seemed to be apologetic after their hours of lovemaking. Little did Caesar know that there was so much she had to be sorry for . . . so very much more. She knew she was coming into another chapter in her life, but she wondered what lay ahead for her future.

CHAPTER 11

And just like a light, Bianca was out.

She stared out of the Greyhound bus window as the scenes of farmland and cattle went by in a blur. In her head, her life was going by in a blur as well.

How the hell had she gotten here?

She was many hours and hundreds of miles away from the home, the place that she had made for herself and the love of her life. Her journey had started off in her car with two oversized suitcases, a backpack, her tablet, and her purse. She'd ditched her car last night, though, knowing it was a smart move to make. With that GPS technology, it would have only been a matter of time before the cops tracked her down. That OnStar was a double-edged sword. She hadn't brought her phone with her. It still lay on the bathroom floor, shattered. Her backpack was filled with cash. The envelope that held some of Caesar's Molly pills was in her oversized tote. She'd taken the cash he had in the house and on his person with her as well. One of her suitcases was full of her clothing, and the other was full of merchandise. If she had to make a fresh start, then she would need some things to start up with. She carried with her the most valuable and fastest moving items she had. She left behind everything else . . . and everyone else.

God knew that she loved Bella and Caesar with all her heart. Over the years, they'd each given her their share of advice, never steering her wrong, but this time she just didn't see eye to eye with them. There was no way she could turn herself in to the police. Maybe at first the police would buy her story. After all, it was true. When she confessed to Caesar what had really happened to her baby, that she hadn't really taken him to the fire station like she'd led both him and her family to believe, she'd told the whole truth. If she got on the stand, raised her right hand, and swore on the Holy Bible to that same story, a jury of her peers might be sympathetic to her. Though she had only been a teen mother and hadn't known any better, she still should have said something and not covered it up, which made it easy for her uncle to basically get away with murder.

It was believable because it was the truth, but sometimes the truth is stranger than fiction.

She sat on the bus, trying to convince herself that leaving was the best thing to do. After all, Virginia was a Commonwealth state, and when it came to the laws there, they could definitely be unpredictable. She could have been thrown in prison for the rest of her life, and she wasn't willing to take that chance. The fact that Bella and Caesar would even want her to take that chance struck a nerve deep within her. The fact that they'd be okay with only being able to see her through bars for the rest of her life left a bad taste in her mouth when it came to them. But none of that mattered anymore. She'd left all of that behind. The same way she'd managed to sweep her crime under the proverbial rug before and move ahead with life, she'd do it again. She was a survivor. God had given her the strength to survive a gang rape and the birth of a baby out of her fourteen-year-old body, and now God would give her the strength to overcome her grief and rebuild her life in a new place.

Until now, she hadn't known what Peanut did with her baby boy. She had always assumed her baby was alive somewhere. Now she knew her baby was dead, and she felt a strong sense of sorrow sweep over her. She began to cry again. Her heart went out to her little baby, who, from all appearances, had had Down syndrome. Small wonder, with his uncle being his father. One day, she knew, Peanut was going to pay for killing her baby. His baby.

She cried some more as she thought of her sister, Bella, who had been the only person in her family who seemed to love her since her pregnancy. She hated leaving town and not being able to say good-bye to Bella. She cried for hours straight as she exited the city limits, knowing that it was more than likely she'd never see her sister again. There was no statute of limitations on murder, so the police would always be on the hunt for Bianca. Bella had a good heart and a conscience. Besides Caesar, she was one of the most truthful people Bianca knew. If the police asked her where Bianca was, if she knew, she'd tell them. Bianca didn't want to put her sister in that position. It would be too much to bear for her.

Bianca was used to being able to let things go and slide off her back. She'd learned that growing up. So, once she'd made up her mind to let go of the entire incident concerning the baby, that was just what she did. Carrying around those thoughts would have hindered her life, even more than if the baby had still been alive for her to have to take care of.

No questions asked: That was the promise that the law allowing children to be dropped off at fire stations or hospitals made to the mothers who dropped them off. Even when Bella and her mom asked Bianca where the baby was the day they came home to find the bassinet empty, once she told them what she'd done, they didn't even ask questions.

"I knew she couldn't take care of no baby. She can hardly take care of herself," were the words Ella had said to Bella before rolling her eyes and walking off.

It was just like déjà vu for Bianca. The same way her mother had walked off when she found out that Bianca was pregnant was the same way she walked off when she learned that Bianca had dropped her baby off for someone else to take care of. She expressed no type of sadness. Bianca wasn't surprised. She could count on one hand the times her mother had even held her son in the few short days of his life with Bianca.

Bella, even though she didn't ask questions, seemed to be the most emotional out of the three. "I'm sorry, Bianca. I can't imagine what it feels like to feel alone, like you have no help and can't take care of your baby," Bella had told her. "I wasn't there when you needed me, but if you want to get your baby back, I promise, even if it means I don't ever get to sleep again, I'll help you. I just don't want you to live with the regret that I—"

Even though Bella stopped talking, Bianca knew what she was going to say. She was going to remind Bianca of the regret she would have to live with as a result of her leaving her baby. A couple months prior to Bianca giving birth, Bella had turned up pregnant. After witnessing how Grandmother Williams and their mother had reacted to Bianca's pregnancy, there was no way Bella was going to put herself in the line of fire. She got an abortion without their mother ever knowing.

"He's better off," was all Bianca had said to her sister before packing up all of the baby's things and setting them out on the curb. The same way they never talked about Bella's abortion again, they never talked about Bianca's baby. When anyone asked, they were told the baby had been given up for adoption.

Within the last twenty-four hours, all had learned that that hadn't been the case. For years, no one even talked about it, nor had she let anyone know of Peanut's actions. Now she planned on moving far away, where she wouldn't be found out in her new spot. One slip up and she'd be back in Virginia, being charged for the murder of her very own infant son. That was not going to happen. She was sure she'd long for conversations with her sister, but memories alone would have to suffice.

Getting over Caesar would prove to be more difficult, as even now, tears escaped her eyes, knowing that the person she truly felt was her soul mate would no longer be a part of her existence. Every now and then she had to catch her breath. It was hard to breathe without him, indeed, but she had to choose herself. She knew she had to look out for her. At the end of the day, if nobody had her, she had her.

I got me! I have to have me! It's got to be a given! A must! I got to have me! she kept telling herself.

All Bianca could picture was him lying in that bed. The sex. The Ecstasy. The wine. The fire from the candles. It created an emotional tornado in her mind. "Caesar." The word fell off of her lips with such regret, but something gave her reason for pause. Caesar wanted her to turn herself in. What happened to his "I got you" declaration? No, he didn't mind if she did five years, locked up in a cage like an animal. Maybe he didn't love her after all, she thought. Maybe he didn't put her first. Suddenly, a small voice said to her, *You've got to have your own back. You are your own best friend.*

It was like a well opened up inside of her, a deep shaft of light. *I got me! I have to have me! It's got to be a given! A must! I got to have me!* she reminded herself again.

She closed her eyes, praying sleep would come and take over. Hopefully, when she woke, she would be at her final destination, ready to start a brand new life.

CHAPTER 12

When Bianca stepped off the bus, the Miami heat nearly melted the poor child. No breeze, just humidity and heat. She felt like she was blundering through an oven. The palm trees looked wavy, as if she were seeing them in a mirage.

"Got-damn, it's hot as hell," a girl, wearing some short shorts that barely covered the cheeks of her behind, swore. She sported a baseball hat and aviator shades, holding a Louis carrier and a Victoria's Secret Pink sequined bag. Bianca noticed that she had a different Southern accent than the one she was used to in Virginia.

"Hell, yeah!" Bianca agreed, about to buy a water from a guy peddling refreshments.

"Your first time in Miami, huh?"

"Yeah," she said, "and this right here is a different kind of heat."

The scantily-clad girl chuckled. "You got that right." She turned to the guy slanging the water. "Two, please." She took the waters from the guy in exchange for two dollars and handed one of the no-name-brand waters to Bianca. "Welcome to Miami."

Bianca smiled. "Thank you."

"I'm Yogi, by the way, and you are going to need a good friend here."

"I'm Bianca, and I bet."

"No, for real. It's a real beast here . . . a whole different animal. Trust me."

"I believe it." Bianca agreed, still in awe of the palm trees and the weather.

"You dance?"

Bianca was confused. "Huh?"

"Dance. You know, strip?" Before Bianca could answer, Yogi straightened it out real fast. "Hold on to your drawers before you get offended. Understand now, and you will soon see for yourself that pretty much everyyyyyybody here dances and is bi. It's nothing for chicks to strip. And you know I'm not lying, because it's a strip club on every corner."

"Oh, okay," Bianca said, taking it all in, while taking off her shirt and thanking God that she had her camisole under her top. Right away, she wondered if Yogi was checking her out, since she had said everybody was bi. She quickly returned the same question. "So, you dance?"

"Yup. Been doing it for five years now. Get money, travel to dance, but this is home based."

"I hear ya."

"You got somebody picking you up?" she asked.

"No. About to head to this taxi line over there."

"My boy coming to get me. We could drop you somewhere."

"Nah, I'm good, but I appreciate that though."

"Look, take my number in case you need anything," Yogi said. "Plus, I'ma take you out for a drink later."

"Okay," Bianca said slowly, wondering what Yogi was really into.

Yogi caught her hesitation. "Look, let me get yo' number so I can call and check on you later."

"I gotta go get me a phone. I left mine by mistake at the rest stop bathroom and didn't realize it until we was gone," Bianca lied. "Had me real fucked up."

"I know how that can be. Shit's the worst." She turned to a lady walking by. "You got an ink pen?"

The lady gave her a pen. As Yogi went to write the number down, Bianca stood there wondering if Yogi was bi, too, and trying to come on to her, or if she was just being nice.

"Here, girl, call me. No strings attached. Trust me. I know what you thinking."

"Really?" Bianca said sarcastically.

"Yeah, I don't want to try to get at you. You a bad bitch and all, but it ain't that kind of party. I'm from Memphis, and I've been the new girl, too, and wish I had a 'me' in my corner when I got here, 'cause I went through so much shit." She paused for a second. "I don't wish that shit on my worst fucking enemy, man."

"For real?"

"For real." She nodded. "I'll tell you 'bout it some other time."

"Damn," was all Bianca could say as she took the number out of Yogi's hand, folded it, and put it in her purse.

"There go my boy right there." Yogi pointed over to the Maserati that pulled up. She waved to him, then put a finger up to motion to him that she was coming, as the two girls stood at the end of the taxi line.

"Well, it was good meeting you," Bianca said with a deep breath.

"I know we gon' hang for sure," Yogi said as she gave Bianca a hug and told her, "I work at The Den. If you wanna come out tonight or tomorrow or the next day, let me know. I got you."

"Okay. Thanks again."

Damn, what is the temperature? Bianca thought, as she watched Yogi walk away. She wished she had checked the weather before she left so she would have worn something other than black skinny jeans, but her mind hadn't been on what Mother Nature was doing. It had been on one thing: getting the hell out of dodge.

"Damn," Bianca said, wiping the back of her hand across her forehead. She couldn't believe that sweat had formed within seconds. She waited for the next cab and looked around for a moment, taking in the sights of what she would now call home. She'd definitely have to get familiar with her surroundings, but not today; not in this heat, for which she was dressed so inappropriately.

The next cab rolled up, and a guy hopped out to assist with her luggage.

"Where you going to?" the cabbie asked Bianca.

His question stumped her. Her only plan had been to make it to Miami, and she was there. Exactly where she would lay her head in Miami, for now, was still up in the air. "A hotel," Bianca said. "One with a pool. Maybe near life, fun, beach, malls . . . where I can easily get around."

The cabbie began rambling off the names of several hotels as he loaded Bianca's two suitcases into his trunk. Her other items she kept on her persons. By the time they'd pulled off from the bus station curb, Bianca had decided on the Marriott. Who could lose with the Marriott? She just hoped the location was right. Having no transportation, she couldn't stay anywhere where things weren't accessible and transportation was limited. She would utilize the services of the hotel staff to learn as much about her new city as she could.

She was glad she'd taken all of her savings and some of Caesar's stash from his private safe. In all, she had a little over half a million in cash on her.

As she rode in the backseat of the taxi, she made sure to pay special attention to her surroundings and the direction in which the cabbie was taking her. She made a mental note of all the landmarks and street names.

The driver noticed her looking around. "The ocean and the beach are as far east as you can go, so everything away from the beach is west. That will help you in getting around. Most things are east and west or north and south. Miami is south, and going toward Fort Lauderdale and West Palm is north."

"Thank you," she said. "That was a nice little jewel. I definitely appreciate that."

Once she began to put her plans in place for the city, she had to at least act like she knew, even if she didn't. The last thing she wanted people to think was that she was a little lost Dorothy looking for a group of sidekicks to help her find her way. Thin and petite in stature, she had to make it appear as though she was larger than life, and she was more than ready to do it.

Although Bianca had cried all the way to Miami, she knew there was no more time for tears. It was time to get down to business and make a new life for herself.

Caesar had come from Miami to Virginia, ignorant of what the streets had branded her as: a hood rat, a ho, a chicken head, a bum bitch. He'd fallen in love with her for the woman he'd met that day in the beauty shop parking lot. He didn't care what other people thought of her. But now, from Virginia to Miami, there was no reputation waiting for Bianca that she had to offer up an explanation for or defend. She had the prime opportunity to create her own, and she knew exactly what reputation she was seeking: that of a boss bitch. She didn't know what type of business she was going into, but whatever it was going to be, she would continue to be her own boss.

In years past, what people thought of and said about Bianca had affected her decisions in life. She vowed to never let that happen again. The world was not going to run her; she was going to run the world. At least a little slice of it in Miami, anyway.

"The beach is not too far from here," the cab driver said as he approached the hotel. "Folks like to get up early in the morning and run through the sunrise." He looked over his shoulder back at Bianca as he threw the cab in park in front of the hotel doors. "But you don't look like you need to work out." He looked her up and down, removing one article of her clothing at a time with his eyes.

Bianca looked at the cabbie, and for the first time realized what an overweight, lowlife he looked to be. He probably had a wife and a slew of kids at home, yet he was checking for her.

Men. She was about to give him a dirty look, but then decided that a lowlife like him may be just the friend she needed to get what she wanted. It might have been nice to have friends in high places, but sometimes it was more valuable to have friends in low places.

A mischievous grin suddenly spread across Bianca's mouth. "Well, you know I try to keep it tight." She ran her hands down her body.

The cabbie licked his lips. "Mmm, I bet it's tight all right."

Bianca leaned in, placing her hand on the front seat and then resting her chin on it. She was almost nose-to-nose with the cabbie. "Uh . . ." she looked at his ID that was clipped to the rearview mirror. "Samuel, I'm new in town, and I might need a little help getting around, getting to know the right people, if you know what I mean. I was just wondering if you had a card or anything, so perhaps I can call you if I need you." She looked him up and down. "Or need anything." She gave him a coy schoolgirl look.

Without taking his eyes off Bianca, and with a bulge forming in his pants, he reached into his front shirt pocket and dug out a business card. "That's my cell phone number on there." He handed Bianca the card.

She slipped it out of his hand and tucked it into her bra while he watched, practically salivating at the mouth. "Thank you, Sammy." Bianca quickly covered her mouth with her hand, as if she'd said something she hadn't meant to. "Is it okay if I call you Sammy? I'm really into nicknames." Her voice was flirty.

"Mami," he said, glancing at his passenger, who looked about twenty years his junior, "you can call me whatever the hell you want."

She winked at him. "Thank you, Sammy," Bianca said, as a bellman from the hotel opened the cab door for her. They had gone to a Marriot near the ocean. Bianca looked out at the placid, azure ocean and felt a sense of peace come over her. Today there were no waves and the ocean looked still. Bianca took a deep breath. Yes, everything was going to work out fine.

"Welcome to the Marriott," the man said. "Are you checking in, ma'am?"

"I am," Bianca said as he helped her exit the car with her things.

Sammy got out of the car and went to the trunk. He took Bianca's things out and set them down. The bellman immediately took possession of them.

"Thank you, Sammy." Bianca handed the cabbie a hundred-dollar bill that she'd pulled from her purse. She had no idea what the fare was, but she knew it was nowhere near a hundred books for a fifteen-minute ride.

"Anytime." He took the bill, stared at it with excitement, and then flicked the bill. "I gave you my card, but do you have a number, Miss . . ." He searched for the letters of her name, but she hadn't told him yet.

"It's Bianca," she said. "No, I don't have a phone, but you know where to find me." She gave him one last wink before turning and following the bellman into the hotel lobby.

CHAPTER 13

Bianca checked into the Marriott, paying for a week's stay. She used her real ID. What reason would the Virginia authorities have to come looking for her in Florida? And even if they did manage to connect any dots, it would take them much longer than a week to do so. She'd be gone by then, depending on how quickly she got things done.

Bianca knew better than to use her real debit card to book the hotel. Besides, she'd drained her bank account dry of every dime before departing Virginia. It took a sob story and the shedding of a few tears to get the reservations clerk to allow her to use the cash for security and incidentals. The clerk bought the act hook, line, and sinker, but made Bianca pay for the entire week's stay up front in cash and another thousand-dollar cash deposit

The bellboy rode up the elevator to the fifth floor with Bianca with her luggage in tow. Once they arrived at her room, he pulled the curtains back for her, revealing the beautiful Atlantic Ocean. She gave him a ten-dollar tip and watched as the door closed behind him.

Wow. She took a deep breath and took everything in. *This is it,* she thought as she gazed out of the window. *Beautiful Miami, the place I will call home for now!*

Bianca smiled, thinking of all the things that Caesar had told her and all the beautiful things she had imagined it to be. Then she turned around and looked at the new place that she would call home, at least for a week anyway. Hot and sticky, Bianca removed her clothing where she stood. When she unsnapped her bra, Sammy's business card fell to the floor. She scooped it up and placed it on the little kitchenette table. She cut on the radio; it was already on the hip-hop station. She headed straight for the shower.

In the shower, she let her mind race to past, present, and future, trying to put everything together in her head. Once out of the shower, she dried off, and the second her head hit the king-sized pillow, she drifted into a deep, much-needed sleep.

Waking up an entire day later, almost forgetting where she was, Bianca turned her head toward the curtains. The drapes were still open, and the sunset was breathtakingly beautiful. It painted the sky a vermillion color with streaks of purple. The sun was on the verge of going down, and the streetlights and business signs were starting to light up the Miami skyline.

Bianca couldn't believe she'd slept the entire night and day away. No tossing and turning. No nightmares, and no regrets. Bianca was up, feeling refreshed, brand new, and ready to get down to business. She got out of bed, walked over to the window, and peeked out. Everything was so foreign to her, yet she felt right at home. She couldn't help but stare out and wonder what awaited her. Curiosity poked a smile on her face.

Bianca had gotten a burst of energy. She lotioned up with the complimentary toiletries the hotel had supplied. Packing her Bath and Body Works products had not been a priority when she'd packed to leave. Thank God the complimentary toiletries included a small, travel-sized toothpaste. Unfortunately, she'd forgotten to pack her toothbrush. She called downstairs, but the toothbrush they brought her couldn't do anything. As a matter of fact, she decided to run to the corner store and get everything she needed.

Hitting the Miami streets gave her life. The valet guy suggested that she hit Lincoln Avenue, and her first stop was the Apple store. It was a must that she got her electronics. She bought herself a computer, an iPhone, and an iPad. From there, she managed to pick up everything that she needed most on her five-finger discount.

She dropped her things off at the hotel and went back out. There were a few things she had seen in the window of a store she had passed on her way back to the hotel. She decided that she would go back and get them.

When she was almost at the store, she heard a voice calling out, "Hey, baby." She turned around and saw one of a group of guys wearing a pair of duck boots.

"Hi," she said but kept it moving.

Another said, "Yo, baby." She turned her nose up. "Bitch, you too cute?"

"Nigga, go get you some fucking respect," she shot back at him.

He shot her a look that was more powerful than an AK-47, and before he could say anything, his boy in the duck boots grabbed him and pulled him away. "My apologies. My boy's an asshole. No home training."

"You got that right," she said, never stopping, leaving them way behind and entering into the store.

Once she was inside, no one greeted her or said a word to her. Even better. Especially after they spoke to the group of white girls who entered behind her. She continued to browse, but the saleslady was following her around the store.

"So you have this in a size four?" Bianca asked.

"No," the woman said, not even looking.

"What about this in a size eight?"

"No." The clerk's eyes were still averted.

"This is an eight?"

"No, ma'am. No and no."

"Oh, okay," Bianca said. "I get it." She put down the dress she had in her hand. "You don't want my money. It's not good enough for you, huh?" She rolled her eyes and headed for the door. The clerk had already pegged her as a thief anyway.

"Ma'am," a man called out to her then started coming toward her.

Bianca kept it moving and was out the door, but the man, who must have been the owner or the boutique's security dressed in plain clothes, was relentless. "Ma'am, you need to stop, please."

She kept going, but the man was running her way, and just when he was about to put his hands on her, Duck Boots appeared out of nowhere. "Nigga, what the fuck you doing?" he asked. "This is my girl," he firmly said. "Get your fucking paws off of her." He cut his eyes and lifted his shirt, flashing his chrome 9 mm.

The steel stopped the guy from the store dead in his tracks. He raised his hands and backed up. "I don't want no problems, man. I don't," he said then turned around and made his way back to the store.

Bianca was half a block ahead. She moved into the cut as she saw Duck Boots head down the street to look for her. She had fallen out of his sight, but she could see him heading her way. When he thought it was no hope in finding her, she stopped, and that's when she popped out of her stash spot and said, "Thank you. Lifesaver!"

"No problem. Just wanted to make sure you good. You need a cab or anything?" Though she was walking fast, he kept her same stride as they made their way down the crowded, tourist-filled street.

"I'm good. Just wanted to tell you thank you for that."

"You new to these parts, so in case you need a friend, call me."

"Ummm, I just got a new phone," she said with a coy smile to the big, tall black guy with the smoothest skin standing in front of her. She had been so anxious to get back to that store that she left the phone back at the hotel, still in the box.

"Yo, papi, let me get that pen," he said to a guy working as a host at a restaurant on the strip, trying to sell a lobster dinner special. He grabbed a napkin and wrote his number down on it and passed the pen back.

As he handed her the napkin, he told her, "Look, Northern girl, don't let these palms trees and crystal blue water fool you. These Miami streets ain't no joke. Trust no one and watch your back at all times. Nothing—I repeat, nothing and no one are what they seem."

"A'ight, thanks . . . lifesaver."

"It's actually Black."

"A'ight now, Black. Thanks again," she said with a smile and a raised eyebrow.

"Why the look?"

"Just seems so cliché that your nickname would be Black." His chocolate skin said everything.

"Yeah, that's what they been calling me my whole life," he said, and for the first time, she noticed his deep Southern drawl.

"Okay." she nodded and thanked him again.

"Take that shit for face value, ya heard?" he said, strolling away.

She heard him loud and clear, but she was wondering how in the world she could take anybody seriously wearing some damn hot-ass duck boots in ninety-five degree weather.

CHAPTER 14

Back in her room, she dropped the things that she had used her discount to get on the bed and smiled. In spite of everything, Miami had been good to her today. She had gotten some really great pieces.

Bianca decided to go unpack her suitcases. Her own, previously worn personal items were placed in a shopping bag in the corner. Sooner or later, she'd find a dry cleaners to take them to. She didn't usually wear her clothes over again, but at home she had had a deep closet of clothes waiting to be worn. That was no longer the case. The things she would keep for herself were folded neatly into the drawers and closet. Unworn, tagged items she kept in their lone suitcase. She had plans of what to do with the items, but first she had to get her essentials together and get back connected with the real world.

Bianca cracked her new laptop open and set up an entire new eBay account using the prepaid Visa card that she had gotten from the drug store under the name of Alexis Williams. Once everything was set up, she took pictures of the things she had brought with her in her suitcase, and the other things she didn't keep for herself that she had gotten earlier. She posted them for sale, and within minutes, Bianca starting getting offers for the items.

"Ching, ching! I still got it," Bianca raved. She was back in business.

Now, did Bianca really need the money right about now? No, but for what she intended to set off in Miami, she needed this site to make her legitimate on paper. That was something that Caesar had always stressed.

By midnight, Bianca had taken a picture of and uploaded all of her merchandise to the site, as well as sold over a thousand dollars in products. Now all she had to do was use the hotel business center to print off the shipping labels and find the nearest post office to package and mail the items.

Fearless didn't even begin to describe the attitude Bianca had at that very moment. Knowing that the police would be looking for her for the rest of her life, she was still hell bent on living life to the fullest. She was not going to look over her shoulders twenty-four seven, but instead she was going to stay headstrong and keep it moving. If ever she did go down, she wanted to go down while on top. She wanted to prove to herself that she was something great and could do great things, in spite of her past and in spite of the choices she had made. She'd really hoped that Caesar would be the one by her side to see her rise above the hood life, but that was never going to happen.

Caesar's good heart was what Bianca had loved about him so much, but his good heart wanted her to turn herself in to the police and face the music. That was just not something Bianca could ever bring herself to do. The police could take her kicking and screaming, but she would never go willingly. It was her word against her uncle's. Knowing the fate of all the others before her who hadn't gone willingly, still, Bianca was determined to put up a fight. She'd been fighting this long. Why not go out with a fight as well?

***

For the next three days, Bianca spent her time sightseeing, trying to get a feel for the city, and of course, casing stores. She even managed to swipe a few more pieces of merchandise and upload them to sell through her online account. Thanks to that online store, she'd been in Miami all of three days, and other than the money she spent on her electronics, she hadn't had to spend one dime of the stash she'd brought. If she had things jumping off like this in just a few days, there was no telling what things would look like a year from now when she was good and settled.

She was determined that she would stay focused and keep her eye on the prize, but first, she had to find the prize in the first place. Her goal was to go completely legitimate. She didn't want to continue boosting the rest of her life. She wanted to stay beneath the police's radar, and she could do that if she wasn't leading a life of thieving. Yes, she was going to have to find a way to make her money through a team doing the work, if the work was not legitimate.

Nightfall had come again, and she needed to get out of the hotel and see some of the nightlife. So, she finally called Yogi. It was almost ten o'clock.

"Hey, doll face," Bianca said.

"Hey, beautiful," Yogi shot back.

"It's Bianca from the bus station."

"I know. You ready for that drink? I owe you."

"Sure," she said.

"What are you doing tonight?"

"Girl, I have no plans as of yet. I truly need to get out."

"Well, good. Come up to my job."

"The strip club?" Bianca asked.

"Don't say it like that. Trust me, it's not what you think. The strip clubs down here are like clubs. It's like a meeting spot. Trust me when I tell you it's more than ass-shaking and pussy-popping going on in there. You're going to be cool. I got you," Yogi said.

"Umm, okay . . . I guess."

"What else you doing? Hanging on the strip? That gets old after a while. Come by, have that drink, mix in with the locals, and get you some laughs and probably some numbers."

"Numbers at the strip club, girl? No, I think not. I can't compete with pussy just everywhere."

"You'd be surprised," Yogi said with a friendly laugh. "So, get cute and get a cab to The Den. I'm going to leave your name at the door. If you have any problems, just ask for Roscoe, and he got you too. Heading there now, and I'll be there until at least seven."

"In the morning?"

"Yup. The trap don't ever close."

"For real?" Bianca questioned.

"Girl, you got a lot to learn, but don't worry. I will teach you the ropes."

CHAPTER 15

Bianca stared at her reflection in the bathroom mirror as she smoothed the red lipstick across her lips. She puckered her lips to even out the lip paint. Next, she turned her head left to right, admiring the way that her hair fell down from the doobie that she'd had it in. She hoped and prayed that she could find a good Dominican shop that could wrap the heck out of her hair, but for the time being, if she kept it wrapped up in pins and in a doobie, it would fall pretty for the next couple of weeks, until she could find a good hair spot. She hoped soon, because she knew for sure that the Miami heat would not be nice to her hair.

"Time to have a little fun in this hot-ass Miami heat," Bianca said to herself. She'd been doing a lot of talking to herself lately. It was moments like this that really made her miss Caesar. No matter what, she'd always had him to talk to. Those days were gone. She'd never hear the sound of his voice again. She shook her head, ridding herself of those sad thoughts. She was about to hit the streets. She couldn't go out looking all gloomy, so she plastered a fake smile on her face.

"Yeah, that'll do it. Time to go play. All work and no play makes Bianca a . . ." She thought for a minute. "Hell, who am I kidding? Even when I'm playing, I'm working." She picked up the bottle of body spray from the set she'd picked up yesterday at Bath and Body Works.

Hopefully, once she got her feet wet, she'd be able to put a crew together out here.

"You really need more than one go-to person in business," Caesár had once told her. "Never put all your eggs in one basket. If that one person knows they are all you have, they'll end up taking advantage of that . . . and you."

Bianca shook her head. "Still following your advice, Cee." She smiled, sprayed the body spray on her, set the bottle back down, and then exited the bathroom.

It was after one a.m., but by Miami's standards, still kind of early. From what she was told, things really didn't start happening until two, so she would be a little ahead of schedule, but better to be early than late any day. Bianca looked around the room and grabbed her gold Fendi cross-body purse. She made sure she had her hotel room key, and then she did one more sweep of the room before leaving.

Bianca made her way to the elevator and took it down to the lobby. The elevator doors opened like the Red Sea parting. Bianca strutted across the hotel lobby like she owned it, and she commanded everyone's attention. Folks nearly stumbled on top of each other, staring at the beautiful young girl in the tight, form-fitting, knee-length red tube dress with gold, strappy heels. The only accessory Bianca carried was her purse. She wasn't all iced-out with jewelry. She had learned through it all that less was more to her.

The one thing Bianca knew about men was that they needed to be needed. If she looked like the strong, independent type who could do everything for herself and buy everything for herself, that could definitely be a turn-off. By the same token, with a powerful man, a woman sometimes had to show just a hint of how powerful she was as well. She didn't want to look like no bum bitch, but at the same time, she had to let a guy think there was a void in her life that he could fill, be it with material things or whatever else.

"Can I help you, miss?" one of the bellboys asked. "Do you need a ride?"

Bianca shook her head. "No, thank you. I'm waiting on one."

"No problem. Have a good evening," he said, doing a slight bow, only as an opportunity to let his eyes glide down Bianca's body.

"Thank you," Bianca replied. For the next couple of minutes, Bianca stood there, looking from left to right, ignoring all the glares from the women whose men were doing all the staring. Finally, Bianca's ride arrived.

"Sammy, you're late," she said as soon as he got out of the cab.

"I'm sorry to keep you waiting. I got stuck in traffic." Sammy hurried to open Bianca's door for her.

"Traffic? At one o'clock in the morning?" Bianca asked, not believing her cabbie's excuse.

"There was an accident. We had to wait for the vehicles to be moved out of the way. Then the bridge was up. You know," he said, struggling to plead his case, "just the Miami bullshit."

Bianca stood face-to-face with Sammy. "Next time, go another way." She then slipped into the backseat.

"Yes, ma'am." Sammy closed the door and did a light jog back into the driver's seat. "Where to?" He looked over his shoulder as he closed the door.

"There's this place my girlfriend was telling me about," Bianca said. "The Den, the Dungeon, I don't know, something like that."

Sammy's eyes widened. "I know what you're talking about. The Den. And trust me, a nice girl like you don't want to go anywhere near that spot." He turned around and put the car in drive. "I know a better spot that you'll love. It's over on—"

"Sammy," Bianca said in a singsong voice, "I'm the customer, and you have to take the customer where she wants to go."

Sammy sighed. "I do not recommend you to go there. Especially since you are not a dancer and into that kind of thing. You seem like a nice lady. I'm telling you—"

Bianca cut Sammy off again, but this time with just the wagging of her index finger.

"Okay, ma'am, whatever you say."

As they made the twenty-five minute drive, Sammy did what a cabbie does and told Bianca some of the history of Miami. He told her where to shop, where to eat, where to relax and enjoy the beaches, and where to go out for a good time. One thing for certain, The Den was not on that list.

"You know, very bad people hang out at this spot," Sammy said as they approached a red light. He nodded forward, so Bianca figured her final destination must have been just up the block. "Bad men."

Bianca leaned up. "What makes you think a girl like me don't like a bad man?" Bianca was being silly, using a fake Jamaican accent.

"I'm serious," Sammy warned, not in a playful mood at all as the light turned green and he proceeded to drive.

"Oh, relax, Sammy." Bianca laughed and leaned back in her seat. "You're acting like a worried father. I'm a big girl. I'll be okay."

Sammy paused for a minute. "It's just that I do have a daughter your age. I'd never drop her off at a place like this, or want anybody else to, for that matter, so I don't feel comfortable dropping you off here either." Sammy seemed sincere as he tried to hide his emotions.

"Awww," Bianca said as she texted Yogi to let her know that she was almost there. She then told Sammy, "I appreciate that. I've never had a daddy to care. Feels good, but I know how to handle myself. I'll be fine."

Sammy pulled up in front of a club that didn't look nearly as bad as Sammy had made it out to be. "Here we are." Sammy sighed. He shook his head, still not too thrilled about dropping Bianca off there. "You're going to need me to come to get you. You're not going to find another cabbie to come pick you up here."

"Yeah, I've got your number, Sammy," Bianca said as she pulled another hundred-dollar bill out of her purse to give to him.

He took the money, gave out one last sigh, and then walked around to let Bianca out of the car.

"Thank you," Bianca said, stepping out of the car with the assistance of Sammy.

"I'm going to hang out here for a couple of minutes just in case you walk into the place and change your mind."

Bianca put her hand on her hip. "Sammy, you can go. I'll call you later. I'm good. Geesh." She smiled, shaking her head.

That really must be what it feels like to have a father figure worry about you, she thought. Initially, Bianca had thought she was going to have a different kind of relationship with Sammy. She thought it was going to be the barely legal, young girl–dirty old man kind of relationship, but here ol' Sammy was turning out to be a thoughtful old man. Bianca preferred that type of relationship anyway.

As far as the line of people outside the club shooting the breeze, they didn't look like any type of weirdos or any different than the patrons at any other club she might have gone to. This club had the usual bouncer standing outside, not only to check ID, but staged to intimidate anyone who might be there to cause trouble. However, no matter how big a bouncer was, they never seemed to deter trouble. If trouble was meant to happen, it was going to happen. Tonight, Bianca was looking for trouble with a capital T. She hadn't been doing the club scene while she dated Caesar, and now she felt like a single woman on the prowl.

Once Bianca got up to the bouncer, without him even having to ask, Bianca stepped to him with her purse wide open. "Take a look."

The only thing inside her little clutch was cash, lipgloss, Sammy's business card, and her hotel room key. Tucked in the zipper compartment were several Ecstasy and Molly pills. But he was still looking.

"I don't have anything to hide," she said, immediately wishing she hadn't. People who said they had nothing to hide usually had everything to hide.

The bouncer looked her up and down. "I bet you don't, ma." He looked her over again. "You good," he said and pointed her to the window.

"Fifty dollars," the dry, expressionless lady told her when she got to the window.

"Okay, but Yogi said that she left my name here with you."

"What's your name?"

"Bianca Williams."

The woman looked at another piece of paper with some chicken scratch written on it. Meanwhile, two gentlemen just walked past without paying or stopping to say anything to her.

"ID, please," she said to Bianca.

Bianca passed the woman her ID, and she examined it. "G'on 'head."

Bianca was surprised by just how large the inside of the club was. From the outside, it looked like a storefront, but now that she stood inside the club, she saw that it was more like a huge warehouse. Once Bianca realized she was standing there, looking around like Alice in Wonderland, she quickly put a pep in her step.

As Bianca made her way through the dimly lit, smoke-filled club, the loud music wasn't the only thing popping. So were the chicks, popping vagina everywhere. There were half dressed and naked women strutting their stuff in the club, looking for dances and dates.

When the DJ put on Juicy J's "Bandz a Make Her Dance," the club caught fire, igniting the vibe in the club, and even more girls appeared on the floor. There were so many now on the dollar chase, moving fast to try to find where they could drop it like it was hot. Now, finding Yogi was going to be even more difficult than she could have ever thought. The hunt was on, but by the end of the night, it might be a toss-up on just exactly who was the prey.

"Excuse me, are you working tonight?" a tall guy asked Bianca.

"Hell, naw, she ain't working." Yogi walked up and gave her a hug.

"Girl, I was looking for you." Bianca gave a deep sigh of relief. She smiled, looking Yogi up and down, admiring her neon green, high-waisted thong body suit that was covered in clear rhinestones that only covered her breasts and pubic area. She also wore tall, lace-up rhinestone boots.

"I was over there in VIP," she said and looked her over. "Girl, I almost didn't know who you were. You look so good, girl. You really clean up good." Yogi smacked her on the butt.

"Umm, I would've never found you." Bianca looked her over. "You look rather sexy, and you are all dolled up."

"Girl, don't get your panties in a bunch," Yogi said, noticing how uncomfortable Bianca was when Yogi hit her on the behind. "I smacked your ass as a way of endearment, not on no lesbo shit."

Bianca shot from the hip. "Are you gay?" She didn't know what to think.

Yogi answered, "Sometimes," and then switched the conversation. "What are you drinking?"

"They got rosé?"

"Yeah, we got it. I got ya," she said. A tall guy with a tailored suit came and whispered something in her ear. She nodded. As Yogi was talking to the guy, Bianca noticed a girl wearing a zebra print outfit with rhinestones on it, watching Yogi and the guy.

Yogi took Bianca's hand and led her to a bar in the back of the club. "Hey, Tee, this is my homegirl. Give her some rosé and whatever else she wants. Look out for me."

Tee, the bartender, nodded her head. "I got her."

"Look, girl, duty calls for me in VIP. You can respect that, right?"

"Go get yo' money, girl. I'm a hustler too, and ain't gon' never stand in the way of nobody getting their paper."

Yogi high-fived her. "I will be back and check on you, but for now, drink and have fun, babes." Yogi leaned in and gave her a friendly, sisterly hug.

Bianca watched her friend go off into the crowd. She surveyed the club to try to get an idea of what was what, as she eyed where other exits might be. She spotted the area where the restrooms were. Of course, she'd already peeped the VIP section, but there seemed to be another doorway, opposite of the VIP, that certain patrons would slip through every now and then.

"Hey, babes." Tee, the bartender, leaned in and said, "It's going to be about thirty minutes before the rosé comes. Can I get you something else?"

"Yes, make me something fruity. Just hook it up. Oh, yeah, and make it sweet."

"Could it get any sweeter than you?" asked a guy sitting next to her at the bar.

Hmmmm, she thought then said with a smile, "Ah, no, I don't think so."

She continued to watch everything going on around her. The man sitting beside her was very observant of the things happening as well.

"Here you go, sweetie." Tee placed the drink down in front of her.

"Thanks, doll." Bianca smiled and passed her a twenty-dollar bill.

"Oh, no." She shook her head. "Yogi got you."

"I know, but this is for you."

"Very nice of you, big spender," the guy next to her chimed in.

She smiled and took a sip of her drink. "You gotta look out for those who look out for you, right?"

He nodded. "Good philosophy to have."

She just kept drinking her drink, trying to allow the effects of the music and the alcohol to sink in. As she was almost done, the guy who was sitting next to her, the one who'd thought her little comment earlier was real, noticed her drink was getting low. "What did you have?"

She looked at the drink. It didn't have a name as far as she was concerned. Just some concoction the bartender had mixed up because she liked sweet-tasting drinks. "It's called a . . ." She thought for a moment before she came up with something. "Bianca on the Run."

"Bianca on the Run, huh?" He nodded. "Never heard of it. Looks good. New and refreshing." He looked Bianca up and down. "Kind of like you are to this spot." He took a sip from his own drink. "So, what brings a sweet lady like you to The Den?" he asked with a raised eyebrow.

"Here, baby." Tee set another drink down in front of her.

"Thanks so much," she said, sliding her another twenty.

The guy still sat there with a raised eyebrow, waiting for her to answer.

"What brings anybody to The Den? The girls." She looked around.

"So, you are a girl who likes girls."

"No, don't humor yourself," she joked. "No, the drinks, perhaps." She lifted her glass and threw him a smile. Then she said, "No, seriously, my girl invited me. She works here. In fact, I'm going to get her to give you dance, on me, when she comes back out of VIP."

"Really?"

"Why the hell not?" Bianca said.

"Why would you do that?"

Bianca looked at the man for a moment. He was in some casual slacks and a nice button-up shirt. Again, with the way folks talked about The Den, she was expecting to roll up to some kind of biker club joint where everybody was in cut-off leather jackets with no shirts underneath.

"Why not?" she said. "I mean, honestly?"

He stared at her, waiting for her to finish.

"I mean, look at you. You look uptight. Seems like you can really use a nice dance, and plus, I always support my friends no matter what their hustle is." She looked him over then took a swig of her drink.

He chuckled a bit. "It's really nice to support your friends and the hustle. I can respect that. But a dance I don't need, honey. Maybe I will get you one."

Bianca started moving to the song that the DJ was playing while she drank her drink. Once the liquid was gone, she began picking the edible fruit out and eating it one by one.

"Yo, Tee," he called out to the bartender. "Can't you see the lady's drink is empty?"

"No dances for me. I'm a lady, honey." Bianca picked up the napkin off the bar. "It's a gentlemen's club." She ran her fingers across the word *gentlemen* on the napkin. "So it's a playground for gentlemen, not ladies. This isn't the place for me to indulge in dances. Plus, I'm not a girl who likes girls," she said with a smile.

"Nice to know, Miss . . . lady."

She nodded and then stood up. "I have to go to the ladies' room. Will you save my chair please?"

He looked at her as if she had said something insulting, but then he nodded. "Yes, I will be your chair-sitter for you."

"Why, thank you, sir. By the way, my name is Bianca. Now you know me," she said, then walked away.

En route to Miami, while on the bus, she had contemplated for hours what her alias would be, but she decided on nothing. She made up her mind that she was not going to come to Miami and live under an alias. That's why she'd given the man her real name, as well as used her real name for everything else. Running from the truth and keeping up with a lie were two different things. The latter was much harder. Lies resulted in distrust. Bianca would need people to trust her.

Bianca's eyes couldn't help but notice the mystique behind the blue velvet door. Everything in Bianca wanted to "accidentally" walk to the back room that she saw a few patrons enter into every now and then, but the restrooms were clearly marked. Besides, she'd planned this all out in her mind. That was the problem, though. Sometimes things can be planned out to the T, and in the blink of an eye, it all goes straight to hell.

Bianca had to do a double take when she entered the restroom. It looked more like a restroom one would find in some high-class private clubhouse or something. It was plush! When Bianca first entered, there was a quaint little sitting room with a round couch to the left and a table in the center. To the right was a round table with four tall, high, upholstered chairs surrounding it. The room was carpeted. Not only did it look absolutely amazing to be a bathroom in a nightclub, but it smelled good. There were a mixture of perfumes and women's fragrances on top of the lavender scent that seemed to be permeating through the vents.

Once again, Bianca got crabby looks, like the whole freaking joint was a clique, and she was the ugly, pimple-faced new girl. It did not matter that Bianca was a beautiful dime piece. She was an intruder in the eyes of these ladies.

"Hey," Bianca said to a group of women who were clustered over on the couch, each with either a drink in hand or one sitting on the table in front of them.

Not a single one of the women replied.

Bianca looked to the couple girls on chill in two of the four chairs. Whatever they were doing prior to Bianca entering the bathroom, they ceased immediately upon seeing her. They looked like two high-school girls caught smoking in the girls' bathroom by the school principal. Bianca was about to speak to them, but she just flipped her hand and kept it moving instead.

After exiting the little lobby area, Bianca moved into the area where the sinks were. There were four sinks on each side. Nothing fancy here, but again, everything was nice and sparkling clean. Ahead, there was a row of bathroom stalls. There were six on each side, but the stalls were huge, like those ones meant to fit a wheelchair, only these weren't for the handicapped. Bianca walked by to find an empty one. She noticed multiple pairs of high heels in a single stall a couple times. There was giggling and chuckling coming from one stall, while moaning and groaning came from another. Bianca finally found an empty stall and went inside.

What the fuck? The stall was like a little gathering area. There was the toilet, of course, with a nice oblong lid that could kind of be used for a table if need be. There was a chair on each side that flipped out of the wall. There was also a shelf.

"Do people come in here to piss, or hold business meetings?" Bianca mumbled under her breath. That's when it hit her. She'd been so focused on the mysterious pathway out in the club, when this was probably where she really needed to be.

When Bianca came out of the stall, she began touching up her makeup and fixing her hair in the mirror. As she touched up her lipstick, she spent the entire time ear-hustling two girls standing nearby.

"Girl, I ain't make no money tonight. I swear shit kinda slow for me."

"Bitch, you seen Mikey? That nigga always spend."

The first woman sucked her teeth. "Yeah I see that motherfucker over there dancing with that bitch Treasure."

"But didn't you go home with him yesterday?"

"Bitch, don't throw shade."

"I seen you talking to ol' boy from Overtown. That nigga right there, you can get a grip out of him."

"I know! But I got be in the Mollyworld to fuck around with that weirdo."

Just then, Bianca went in her purse and into her secret compartment. "Here you go." She spoke up.

Both girls looked at each other and then looked at her.

Then one smiled and said, "How much you selling them for?" while the other girl looked on, waiting for an answer.

"That one you can have. Just let me know if you know anybody else looking for them."

"Oh, really?" the other said, chewing gum with her arms crossed.

"Yup." Bianca nodded. "You want one?" She offered it to her.

She took it out of Bianca's hand. "Thank you." She smiled. "I know somebody who would love to see you right about now. Stay right here and don't move. I'll be right back," she said and walked out of the bathroom.

Bianca kept playing in her hair in the mirror, and all she could think about was the money she was about to make. She knew the Mollies were going to move. After all, it was the perfect relationship. Sex and Mollies went hand in hand. She tried not to let her grin out as she thought about her good fortune. *A hustler is a hustler. It doesn't matter the city or product. If you a hustler, you gon' make it happen, and, baby girl, you making it happen!*

CHAPTER 16

"Hey, you're back," Bianca said when the bathroom door opened ten minutes later and the woman that she'd been discussing the pills with returned. Bianca smiled as the woman walked her way, but then her smile faded when she saw two men enter behind her a few seconds later.

"That's her." The woman pointed to Bianca.

"Oh, my new friend," a third man coming up the rear said.

Bianca followed the voice and noticed that it was the gentleman who had been sitting next to her at the bar.

"I've been waiting for you to come back and join me," he said.

"Rocco, you know her?" the woman asked, looking back and forth from him to Bianca.

Bianca decided to run with it. She went over and grabbed Rocco by his arm. "Yes, he knows me." Bianca looked at the woman the entire time, hoping and praying Rocco would back up her claim so that she could stick her tongue out at her like a five-year-old.

Rocco peeled Bianca off of him like she was trash and pushed her away. Bianca lost her balance and landed on the floor.

She looked up at Rocco. "Hey, that's no way to treat a lady." Bianca sat up on her bottom and began wiping her dress, not that anything was on it. The floor was spotless.

By now, every person that had been in a bathroom stall had exited. Any women who had been in the lounge area were now standing in the sink area. They were all watching, waiting to see what would go down next.

But when Rocco yelled, "Out!" they all scattered like roaches. It was only Bianca, Rocco, the woman, and the other two men left in the bathroom. "You too." Rocco looked at the woman in the zebra suit, still holding the folder. "I ain't stutter."

Her face begged for him to allow her to stay, but her lips knew better than to verbalize it. She hurried out. Before she was all the way out the door, Rocco called out to her. "Good work, Sasha. Go see Slim."

Sasha's eyes lit up. Now she couldn't get out of there fast enough. Rocco watched her leave and then looked down at Bianca, who was still on the floor.

"Rocco, that was very rude," Bianca said. "Not just you pushing me to the floor, but you never telling me your name. After all, I told you mine."

"That's because you hurried off before I could return the introduction," Rocco replied. "Too busy coming in here, disrespecting my place of business."

"Oh, this is your club? I'm sorry. I meant no harm." She looked around. "This is a nice, respectable business. I should have known better than to think that type of thing went down here. You know what I mean." Bianca cupped her hand around her mouth and whispered, "The use of drugs, narcotics, and stuff." She then let out a taunting chuckle. On the inside she could have pissed her panties from fear, but on the outside she had on her game face.

Out of nowhere, Rocco kicked Bianca in the stomach, pushing her back to the ground. He rested his foot right there on her stomach while Bianca looked up. He bent down, and with one strong pull of his hand, he ripped Bianca's dress completely off of her. It was a perfect rip, as the left seam totally came undone.

Bianca lay on the bathroom floor with nothing but panties and pumps on, feeling the throbbing pain as a result of his kick. "Damn, Rocco. You looked like the kind of guy who liked it rough, but this is not what I expected." She looked him dead in his eyes. "You definitely looked fuckable, and after a couple more drinks, I would have at least let you eat my pussy and hit it from the back, but rough sex on the bathroom floor . . . " Bianca looked around, letting the liquor talk for her. "Not what I had in mind, but if this is the way y'all do it in Miami, fuck it." Bianca kicked her shoes off and then took her panties off. She sat right there on the bathroom floor, holding herself up with her hands, her knees bent and full front throttle in the men's faces.

"Boss, she's not wearing a wire," one of the men whispered in Rocco's ear.

"Hell, she's not wearing nothing," the other man said.

The two men laughed. Rocco didn't find anything funny, so as soon as they detected the hard look on his face and the fact he didn't plan on joining in on the laugher, their own ceased.

"Get up," Rocco said to Bianca then threw her dress at her.

Bianca looked at him, puzzled. "All this pussy right in your face and you're not going to do shit with it? What will everyone out there think when I tell them you passed up all this?" Bianca nodded between her legs while giving Rocco a sensual look. "They'll probably think you're gay or something. Are you a homo, Rocco? I mean, it's okay if you are. Back home I have plenty of gay fr—"

Rocco snatched Bianca up off that floor with one hand, by her throat, with a quickness. He squeezed while he stared her in the eyes, wanting her to say some shit like that one more time, so that he could watch her take her last breath.

It hurt. Bianca couldn't breathe worth a damn, but she stared back at him without even blinking. She didn't even try to pry his hand from around her neck. She was just going to take it.

Rocco tightened his lips. Bianca held her own breath, not willing to accept the fact that someone else was responsible for her lack of oxygen. Things in Miami would be on her terms, even if it was her own death.

Back in Virginia, both Bella and Caesar wanted her to handle her situation on their terms. It's not to say that their way wasn't the right way. It just wasn't Bianca's way. When she said things would be different in Miami, she meant it.

Jesus, please let him stop. Bianca prayed to God, but she would never beg a man for anything in her life. The entire time, she talked to God, all the while staring Rocco down, keeping the tough girl persona up, not knowing how much longer she would be able to hold her breath.

Looking into Bianca's eyes, a very subtle smirk flirted with his lips. This girl was not going to bow out of this power struggle. She was not going to beg him and plead for her life, like so many people before her had done. There would be no groveling on her part. It was almost like the young girl in his grips was begging him to take her life. It was like she was begging him to end the story for which she couldn't care less about the ending. There would be no pleasure in such on his part. He wasn't used to giving people what they wanted, at least not without a fight. His smirk now turned into a full-fledged grin as he opened his hand, releasing Bianca.

Bianca fell back to the floor in a coughing fit. She managed to crawl over to the sink and pull herself up. She fiddled around for the faucet, before remembering that the pedal to turn it on was on the floor. She pressed the pedal, and as the water shot up, she cupped as much in her hand as she could. She guzzled until her throat was no longer scratchy and the coughing had stopped. Afterward, she looked at herself in the mirror, wiped her mouth with the back of her hand, and then walked back over and stood in front of Rocco.

Once again, the two were eyeballing each other, only this time he didn't have his hand around Bianca's throat.

After a few seconds passed, Rocco spoke. "I let you live. Aren't you going to thank me?"

Bianca paused for a moment before allowing a smile to grace her lips. She then took a step closer to Rocco, closing in the previous one-foot gap. Her vision fluttered between Rocco's left and right eyeballs then all of a sudden, she spit the mouthful of water she'd been holding in her mouth right into Rocco's eyes.

There was darkness, even before she hit the floor.

CHAPTER 17

Bianca woke up, grabbing her throbbing forehead. She was in so much pain that she couldn't even open her eyes. She was afraid that would make the pain worse. Why was she in so much pain? What the hell had just happened? She moaned, burying her face into her hands while using her fingers to massage her head. She put one hand down on the ground, prepared to force herself up off the bathroom floor. No matter how many times Rocco kicked her down, she was not going to stay down.

When Bianca put her hand down on the ground, she was thrown off by the softness beneath her hand. The last thing she remembered was spitting water in Rocco's face, his fist coming toward her, then after that, nothing. The blow must have instantly knocked her out. Since the last place she recalled being was in the bathroom, that's where she expected to still be, but unless Rocco had been so kind as to make her a nice, soft spot on a mound of toilet paper and paper towels, that's not where she was.

With her head down, Bianca opened her eyes. She could see that she was now wearing a grey T-shirt with the word "Security" on it. It was about four times her size. She was swimming in it. Noticing a huge red spot down the front, she immediately wiped her hand underneath her aching nose. She then looked at her fingers. It didn't appear as though there was any blood. Perhaps it had dried up. She massaged her head. She felt a huge lump on the side, but when she looked down at her hand, again, there was no blood.

She looked to see what she was resting on. It was a
double bed with bronze-colored bedding. She twisted her
body to look behind her and saw that she'd been lying on
four thick pillows. Grabbing her head again, she began
looking around the dimly lit room. The only lighting was
coming from a lamp on the table next to the bed.

The walls looked like they were painted a lighter
bronze than the bedding. There was nothing fancy about
the bedside table, or the headboard or footboard of the
bed. Just wood, from what Bianca could see. To the right,
there was a small, free-standing bar with three stools in
front of it. Straight ahead was a large, abstract painting.
Bianca was sure that if she didn't have a throbbing headache, she would have been able to stare at it long enough
to figure out just what all the different shapes, sizes, and
colors formed into. But not right now. Staring at that
thing any longer and forcing her brain to do more work
than necessary would only make her headache worse.

"So, she awakens."

"Ugh!" Bianca screamed and grabbed her chest. Her
eyes followed the sound to the corner of the room,
between the painting and the entry door on the left,
where the voice had just come from. There, she could
make out a male figure. She couldn't focus in on his
face, but she could tell that his legs were crossed. One
of his arms rested on the wooden arm of the oversized
upholstered chair, while another one looked to be up
near his mouth. There was a flickering red spark at his
mouth, letting Bianca know that he was taking a puff of
something. From the large size of the tip, she was willing
to bet it was a cigar.

Bianca exhaled, gathering her bearings. She'd come
too far to appear weak now. "Rocco, if all you wanted
to do was get me in bed, you should have said that from
the start." Bianca used her hand to wiggle her nose

bone. "You didn't have to punch me. Besides, didn't your mother ever teach you that boys shouldn't hit girls?" Bianca waited for an answer. She could hear him exhale.

"For one," he started, using a strained voice as he tried to speak and exhale the remaining smoke at the same time, "mi madre taught me very well." He stood, taking a step toward the bed. "For two—" He paused, taking another puff from his cigar. Once again, he spoke as he blew out a puff of smoke. "I'm not Rocco."

The mystery man now stood in the light of the lamp, and Bianca could see clearly that he was not Rocco. He reached down to the lamp, pushing a button that now gave the bulb a brighter glow. Bianca could now see the gentleman's facial features in detail. She observed his eyes, nose, mouth, and complexion. They were all so familiar to her. She had no doubts that the person her entire night revolved around was now standing only a couple of feet from her.

"Who . . . are you?" Bianca asked, trying to keep it together. "You're not Rocco."

He sat on the bed, his back to Bianca. Once again, he crossed his legs and puffed on his cigar, only now Bianca could tell by the scent of marijuana flowing up her nostrils that he wasn't smoking a cigar, but instead a blunt. He exhaled. He then held the blunt over his shoulder, offering Bianca a puff.

"No, thank you," Bianca said. "I don't do drugs."

He snickered and then took another puff. "You don't do drugs, huh?"

"You heard me," Bianca said. "And I usually don't share a bed with strangers, either."

He turned his head to the left, just barely able to see Bianca sitting behind him. "You come to my place of business, you try to sell drugs right here on my turf, in my fucking house—" He beat on his chest—"and you don't even know who I am?"

Bianca put up her hand. "Whoa. Is that what this is about? Me offering some skeezer bitch a couple of pills?"

"You didn't offer her shit. You tried to sell them to whoever she could find for you," he said. "That's a big difference. Either way it goes, you're fucking up my business." His voice rose with anger.

"Sorry," Bianca apologized, as diplomatically as she knew how.

"Sorry, huh?" he said in a disgruntled but calm tone. There was something about this guy's swagger and demeanor that let her know that he wasn't one for her to play with. All she could do was be as respectful as she knew how to be.

"I guess I didn't look at it like that. I wasn't trying to infringe on your . . . business. Pushing drugs isn't really my thing. I came across a few Molly pills on my travels here to Miami."

"Where did you come to Miami from?" he asked.

"Georgia," Bianca said. She hadn't lied. Georgia was actually where she'd left her car and where she'd taken the Greyhound into Miami.

"Let me guess: Atlanta. The place where everyone goes these days if they can't make it in their town." He laughed.

Bianca let him laugh, deciding not to confirm or deny his assumption. "I figured since I had them, I might as well make a little extra money unloading them until I got my real business all set up. A girl's gotta eat."

"Real business, huh?"

"Yeah, a real business. Something that I have and you're missing."

He laughed again. "Let me guess. Since you don't ordinarily push pills, what is it you usually push?" He turned and looked at Bianca then said, "Girl Scout cookies?" He laughed again as he got up. He then abruptly stopped laughing and turned around. "I'll take all the Thin Mints

you have in stock, and then after that, I don't want to see
your ass around The Den ever again. You hear me?" He
was right in Bianca's face, nose-to-nose. His threatening
voice and facial expression didn't even make her flinch.
He smiled while pulling back. "Rocco was right. You are a
wannabe bad-ass. He was wrong about you being the law.
Too young and dumb to be five-oh."

Bianca had figured out that that was why Rocco had
ripped off her dress—to check for wires. She'd proven
that she wasn't wearing one, so she at least thought they'd
show her a little bit more leniency for that. Either way,
Bianca wasn't going to just sit there and allow this man to
continue to belittle her.

"Look, I don't want any problems. I'm new to town and
just trying to find my way."

"What do you do? Dance? Sell pussy?"

"No. Neither." She turned up her nose at the thought
of him assuming that about her. "I don't knock nobody's
hustle; it's just not my hustle."

"So you don't dance, and you don't sell pussy, and you
not going to sell no drugs. What are you here for? Who
sent you?"

"Nobody sent me here. Actually, I was invited here
and just thought that since I had a few pills, I would sell.
Honestly, it was no disrespect."

"No disrespect, huh?'

By the look in his eyes, Bianca could tell there was an
underlying message behind his words.

"Look, the people who brought you here are going to
be dealt with. That's it; that's all. Yogi's little boyfriend,
Tree, for letting your ass in, and that fucking Yogi, are
going to pay.

"She ain't know nothing or have nothing to do with
what was in my purse."

"I don't believe you," he shot back with no emotion.

140   Nikki Turner

"Look, she was just being nice. She knew I was new to town and invited me out to have a drink."

"So she didn't even know you?" he said. "That's even worse."

"Look, it was innocent. Don't blame her for what I did."

He shook his head then took one last puff before putting the blunt out in the palm of his hand. "And I really liked Tree, too. We were first cousins."

"Were?" Bianca asked.

"Of course." With the unlit blunt, he pointed at the shirt Bianca was wearing. "You didn't think that was your own blood on that shirt now, did you?"

Bianca looked down. Her own blood curdled at the thought that she was wearing the shirt Tree had more than likely been killed in. Vomit came up her throat. She had a knee-jerk reaction, but did not open her mouth and let it rip. Instead, she swallowed the vomit and tried not to throw up again on the thought that she'd just swallowed a mouthful of vomit.

The entire time, the gentleman stood there watching Bianca. She figured he was trying to get a reaction out of her, so she gave him nothing.

His eyes on her were like laser beams. At that very moment, she knew that she wasn't playing for marbles; she was playing for her life. These people's "Den" she had fallen into was a real web of dangerous stuff that was way over her head and out of her pay grade. His long, silent, empty look shook her inner core, but with everything in her, she couldn't let on that he intimidated her. With everything she had been through in her life, she wasn't going to start begging for a break now. If she was going out, she was going down like a warrior, not like a coward begging for mercy.

"You like me, don't you?"

"That's what you did, came here so I could fuck you?"

"What?" She shrugged. "That's really not my style," she said with great confidence, not letting him know that she was indeed, without a doubt, scared shitless.

"Exactly what is your style?" he asked. "Tell me who you are. Where do you hail from, little girl?"

Bianca gave him the side-eye. "For one," she spoke boldly, "I'm not a little girl. I'm all woman." She gave herself a once-over with her fingers. "As you can see." She laughed then continued. "And for two, I'm sure that Rocco fellow told you all about me already. No need in me wasting my breath to repeat myself." Bianca placed her bottom back on the bed. "So now that we have all that out of the way, I know Rocco, I know Yogi, I know Tree, pardon me—" She drew an invisible cross across her chest—"I *knew* Tree, so who the fuck are you?"

All of a sudden, Bianca could hear him breathing heavily out of his nose. She imagined fire coming out like a dragon. He stalked back over to her, and then it was déjà vu. He had her by the neck.

"I'm your worst fucking nightmare if you ever come back here trying to take a shit in my house, you fucking hear me?"

Although he had her by the throat, at least, unlike Rocco, he wasn't trying to squeeze the life out of her. He had a nice grip, but it wasn't even as tight as the grip Caesar used to have around her neck when he was having sex with her.

Bianca reached up and touched his hands. He was probably expecting her, just as Rocco had, to try to pry his hands from around her throat, but she didn't.

"You and your friend Rocco got a thing for domestic violence against women, huh?" Bianca managed to get the words out.

With that, he did tighten his grip around her, jerking her slightly.

"You don't want to hurt me, Mr. . . . whatever your name is," Bianca said. "If you wanted to hurt me, you would have done it by now. You could have even had your pit bull Rocco do it. The fact that neither has occurred means only one thing."

"And what is that?" he asked. "Do tell."

"Come closer," Bianca whispered, secretly wishing he'd release his hands from around her throat.

With fire in his eyes, he leaned in.

Bianca put her mouth to his ear and said, "You don't want to hurt me. You want to fuck me." She then pulled back and looked at him, licking her lips. She had no idea how crazy she must have looked right at that moment. Lord knows her hair was all over her head. She was sure her lipstick was probably gone, or smudged all over her face. But she had an aura about her, and she had sex in her eyes. That would have to be enough.

He released her with a push down on the bed. "You wanna fuck, huh? You came here to fuck, or did you just come here to fuck with me? I really believe someone sent your ass."

"Nobody sent me," she insisted.

"So, you want to fuck, huh?"

Bianca noticed that every time he got angry and started cussing, she could hear his Latino accent come out.

"Well, guess what, *puta*? You are the one who is about to get fucked!" He angrily walked over to the door and banged on it. The fact that he couldn't get out on his own let Bianca know that the door locked from the other side.

"Yeah, boss," a man said as he opened the door, gun drawn. "You okay in here?"

"I'm okay," the boss replied. He then looked to Bianca. "But that one over there isn't." He looked at Bianca with a wicked grin on his face. "She came here to get fucked, so before she goes home tonight, make sure she gets exactly what she came for." His evil grin spread further before he exited the door, leaving Bianca alone in the room with the stranger. With one last remark, he maniacally teased, "By the way, my name is Fitz."

CHAPTER 18

"Are you okay?" Sammy asked after he pulled up in front of The Den, practically on two wheels, and jumped out of the taxi. He'd even left his door open. He rushed over to Bianca, who looked like she was recovering from the worst hangover in the world. He grabbed her by the elbow to walk her over to the taxi.

Bianca jerked away from Sammy. "I'm fine," she snapped.

Sammy held his hands up in surrender. When she realized her words had come out a lot harsher than she'd meant them to, she said it again, much softer. "I'm fine."

Sammy walked over and opened the door for Bianca. He didn't try to touch her again to help her inside the vehicle. Once she was all the way inside, he closed the door and got back into the driver's seat.

"Back to the Marriott?" Sammy asked, putting the car in drive. He looked in the rearview mirror at Bianca.

Bianca had her ripped dressed wrapped around her, clutched in her hand along with her purse. With her heels still on, she sat with her feet up under her, staring out of the window. She looked like her mind was in a faraway place.

Sammy exhaled. He'd seen things like this before. Not this Bianca literally, but in other young girls like her, girls who thought they were big and bad and grown enough to handle cities like Miami and places like The Den, only to be in for a rude awakening. He didn't even bother repeating himself. He just drove slowly through the five a.m. early morning streets with barely any traffic, trying hard not to hit any bumps. His mission was to perhaps give her time to gather her thoughts. Maybe even to possibly forget anything that could never be forgiven.

A half hour later, Sammy pulled up to the Marriott. He looked in the rearview mirror at his passenger. She was still in the same position. She hadn't budged. Probably hadn't blinked an eye either. "We're here," he announced as sympathetically as he could. Still, Bianca didn't respond. He got out of the car and went and opened the door for her.

Even after doing so, it took a minute for it to register in Bianca's head that the cab was sitting in front of the hotel. She looked around the cab, not that there was really anything for her to gather, with the exception of her clutch. She then pulled her feet from up under her, flinching at the pain of forcing her legs to move after having been in the same position for so long.

Again, Sammy didn't try to help her out of the cab. He just let her manage on her own in getting out, which was pretty difficult for Bianca to do while trying to hold her dress together. Once Bianca got out of the car, she stood and adjusted her dress as best she could. It didn't necessarily look torn. It did make it look like she had gone overboard on the slit up the side, which really wasn't a slit at all.

She looked right past Sammy. He was staring into her blank, empty, lifeless eyes. In just the blink of an eye, she was no longer that same young woman full of zest that he'd dropped off at the club just a few hours ago. She'd been violated. He'd seen that same look before in other women's eyes that had hopped into the backseat of his car after a wild night that got out of control, having drunk too much, been slipped a Mickey, or just outright violated. Their souls were gone.

Bianca took a step toward the hotel doors. "Oh," she said, stopping in her tracks. "The fare." She opened her purse. Just when it seemed her facial expression couldn't have gotten any gloomier, it did. She stared down into her near empty purse. There was nothing there.

Her money was entirely gone. Eight one-hundred dollar bills and loose bills were gone. There were no pills, either, or her phone. Everything was gone; there was just a tube of opened red MAC lip-gloss that had spilled everywhere, and Sammy's business card. She'd placed it back in her clutch after being allowed to call him for a ride to come pick her up from the club. She was too relieved to be getting out of that spot to even notice her missing items.

"Don't even worry about it." Sammy waved his hand. "This one's on the house." It wasn't really on the house considering that Bianca had overpaid him each time he'd driven her somewhere.

"No, just let me go upstairs to my room and get you some money." Bianca had only carried a thousand dollars on her that night in the form of ten one-hundred dollar bills. She was glad, seeing as though someone had taken the liberty of sticking her for her paper and pills, that she hadn't carried more than that on her. In regard to the pills, she had actually taken the majority of her supply, and now she only had a few left up in her hotel room. She had plenty more cash, though.

"Bianca, honey, get you some rest and you can get me next time."

Another thing Caesar had always taught Bianca was to never be indebted to someone. He said it didn't matter if the little old lady in line gave her sixteen cents because she was short on her grocery bill. She should go out to her car and dig and scrape until she found sixteen cents. Otherwise, take down the old lady's name and address and mail it to her.

Bianca had laughed about it, but Caesar had kept a straight face.

"When your goal is to become a boss," Caesar had said, "on your way up, never make it so that someone can say, 'Remember that one time I did this or did that for you?' Before you know it, depending on how successful you are, that lousy sixteen cents can turn into sixteen hundred dollars or more."

Even though Caesar's words echoed through Bianca's head, this would be the first time she didn't take heed. She was too tired, too hurt, too dazed, and too confused about where her life was. Maybe she'd gotten herself into something much bigger than she thought it would be. Perhaps she was in over her head. Considering all she'd been through in just her first night in Miami, jail might be like a picnic compared to this jungle.

"Okay," she told Sammy then walked off slowly. "Next time," she said over her shoulder. "I'll take care of you next time."

"Yeah, next time," Sammy said with a trumped-up smile and a chipper voice. He waved cheerfully. He knew Bianca wasn't going to turn around and eagerly wave back at him. Miami had already gotten the best of her in a matter of hours. "You got my number. Call me." He gave out one last shout as Bianca walked through those doors, knowing that if she did call him, it would more than likely be to take her back to that same Greyhound bus station where he'd picked her up.

Bianca didn't receive the same type of attention going back through the hotel lobby that she'd received when she'd first come through it. It was the wee hours of the morning, and not many guests were milling about the hotel lobby. She walked over to the elevator, hit the button, and the doors opened right up. She climbed in the elevator and took it to her floor. When she got out and walked to her room, she reached into her purse for her room key.

"Nooooooo, please no," she said softly then began to vigorously rummage through her purse that still held the same items it had held just five minutes ago down at the cab. "No, no, no." She pulled the lining up out of her purse as much as it would go. She checked to see if it had a hole in it or something that her room card might have slipped through. She came up with nothing. She thought for a moment, figuring she must have dropped it in the cab or something. Maybe it had fallen out of her purse in the club or gotten mixed in with the all her money that someone had stolen from her. She couldn't imagine anyone wanting a random key to the Marriott.

All Bianca could do was shake her head. This was just too much. She was exhausted physically and mentally. She did not have the energy to go back down that elevator, into that lobby, and get another key. She didn't have an ID anyway to even present. She leaned her back against the door and just slid down to the floor. She stared at the room across from her for a moment before her shoulders began heaving up and down and tears began to fall.

"You okay, ma'am?" a woman said, exiting the room next to Bianca's with a cart in front of her.

Bianca briskly rubbed her eyes. Any tears that even thought about falling had now been stopped in their tracks. Bianca looked up at the thick, older Caucasian woman wearing a housekeeping uniform and pushing a cart. It wasn't hard to figure out that she was one of the housekeepers she had tipped the other day. "I'm fine," Bianca said, pulling herself off the ground. "It's just been a long night, and I lost my room key. I'm just tired." Bianca's voice broke as she tried to keep it together.

The woman stared at her for a moment then pulled a key ring out of her pocket that had several key cards on it. Without saying a word, asking Bianca her name or for her ID or anything, she walked over to Bianca's door and opened it with her master key. She held it open and then looked at Bianca.

Bianca stared back at her for a couple seconds. "Thank you," she finally said. She then held the door open with her own hand as the woman walked back over to her cart and kept it moving.

Closing the door behind her, Bianca just stood against her door for a moment in her dark hotel room. She hadn't closed her drapes, but the lighting outside and the teasing sunrays that hadn't fully sprouted for the day didn't create much lighting. She allowed her dress to drop to the floor, as well as her purse. It had all become the weight of a cannon, too much to hold onto. She stepped out of her shoes and walked butt naked to the bathroom. Like her hotel room key, her panties had gotten lost somewhere during tonight's journey as well.

Bianca walked over to the shower and turned on the water. She didn't even play around with the temperature. She just stepped in and allowed her body to adjust to whatever temperature the water ended up being.

After allowing the water to beat against the front of her body, she turned around and allowed it to wash down her back. She took two steps backward until the water was pouring over her head and down her face. Within seconds, her shoulders began to heave up and down again, and just a few seconds after that, Bianca began crying. Her crying turned into a wail, until she found herself in a fetal position on the bathroom floor.

How long she stayed there, crying, she had no idea. The cold temperature of the water wasn't a dead giveaway either, as whether or not the water was hot, warm, or cold hadn't mattered to Bianca when she got into the shower. All she cared about was the water washing away any remnants of tonight off of her body. She felt sore all over her body, from where she'd been kicked and stomped by Rocco. She had bruises around her neck and under her ribs. It really hurt to cough. She wondered if her rib was broken.

Finally, she tried to wash some of the filth, the hurt, and the pain away from her body. Unfortunately, now that she'd rid her body of that horrific night, how would she do the same for her mind?

Bianca pulled herself up off the shower floor and turned off the water. She grabbed one of the thick, white cotton towels hanging on the towel bar. She wiped her face dry and then tied it around her hair. She then grabbed a second towel and began drying her body.

She laid across the bed and took a deep breath, and before she could exhale, she jumped up and ran over to the closet where she had her suitcase. As soon as she touched it, she knew something was wrong. The clasp was broken. When she opened it, her worst fears were realized.

"Noooooooooooo!" She screamed at the top of her lungs, racing around the room helplessly and hopelessly. "Fuuuuuuuck!" Suddenly, a knock sounded at the door, but she was paralyzed. She couldn't budge from the space in the closet.

Another knock, if she even heard it, was ignored, but was followed by the opening of the door. "Miss, are you okay?" It was the same housekeeper who had let her in.

"Yes," she managed to say in between sobs, but inside she wasn't. The dirty bastards had beaten her to her hotel, used her room key, and taken her fucking money. Those motherfuckers! Now what the fuck was she going to do?

CHAPTER 19

When Bianca finally opened her eyes, she found herself on the floor. She glanced around the strange room and tried to acclimate herself. Where was she? For a moment, she thought she was back in Virginia with Caesar, but then, without warning, the previous night of beatings came hurling back at her in a rush. She cried out in anguish, just remembering what she had gone through.

As soon as she tried to budge, her body ached and throbbed like a toothache. She was sore from her head to her toes. She slowly eased into a sitting position.

"Ouch!" She stretched her arms outward, then inward, and tried to rub her ribs and stomach. As she raised herself up off the floor, she was still unsure if she had had a nervous breakdown or just had a flat-out nightmare. She climbed up on her feet and stumbled into the bathroom. She looked into the mirror and saw that her eyes were scarlet red. Evidently, she had cried herself to sleep last night. As she splashed cold water on her face, she remembered the worst thing that had happened to her last night. Her money had been stolen right from under her nose, and that alone hurt like hell.

"Fuck!" She knew this wasn't a nightmare; this was the real deal, and she had been got. But did Yogi have something to do with it? How had this happened? And most importantly, why did it have to happen at this point in time, when she was just trying to get up on her feet?

She rationalized the situation. *It happened because you didn't have you.* Something inside of her told her, *You rushed too soon to make your moves. You are new. You know nothing or no one. You must study everything— people, places and things.*

Although she didn't want to believe it, one thing for sure was that this was real—her house of cards had come crashing down on her. What astounded her was that it had happened like this, and so soon after her arrival in Miami. What had she done to deserve this? How could she be taken away from her home and relationship that she had fought to establish and maintain? To have her life, as she once knew it, just pulled from under her, and now to be on the run for a crime she didn't commit? And to have been robbed of all of her money and product in a city where she had no juice card or allies? The answer couldn't be karma. Or was it? Maybe it was the Universe's way of making her pay for taking all of those stores' stuff. Maybe not. Those stores were insured, and they got well more than the worth of it from their policy.

And even so, why? She had never in her life stolen anything from anyone (since she didn't count boosting from the overpriced stores)—well, besides the pills from Caesar, but that didn't really count. That was the cost he paid for not having her back like she'd had his.

Well, she knew that the piper had to be paid, but she hoped the Universe wasn't coming to collect any more from her any time soon. There had to be a way that she could pull herself up by the bootstraps and make some understanding out of this situation.

Suddenly, she felt afraid. What if someone came back to her room to finish her off? Bianca started by coming out of the bathroom, getting down on her knees on the side of the bed, and saying a prayer. Though she believed in God, she had never really been a religious person.

Never the one to point fingers or make up excuses as to why she didn't go to church on a regular basis, she'd always been one to pray. Most of her ill feelings toward going to church were due to the fact that Grandmother Williams, who went to church every single Sunday, was so heavenly bound but no Earthly good.

What she did know was that there was a reason for everything. Maybe that was why she'd found herself on the floor when she woke up, so she could get down on her knees to talk to God.

God, I don't know why this is the life that I was given, but through everything, I trust you, Lord. Though I'm alone, I know you will never leave me or forsake me. I trust you to love me and to surround me with good people who love me as well. I trust you to keep me in your care and to give me peace and protection as I go on this journey. I'm grateful I still have clothes in the suitcase. In your name I pray. Amen.

She got up off her knees. Suddenly, she felt grateful that she was still alive. "Thank you, Lord," she said. She headed to the bed, turned on the television, and then she plopped down on the bed.

For a split second, she thought about calling Caesar, but then she decided against it. Her pride wouldn't allow her to call him and admit that she couldn't hold her own after not being gone even a week. Plus, she knew if she heard his voice, she'd begin to miss him and their life together. That alone could change the game for her. She couldn't see herself going back to Virginia and winding up in prison. No, she had to keep moving forward. She couldn't look back.

In the midst of her thoughts, she noticed the napkin on the night table. A light bulb went off in her head. What did she have to lose?

She picked up the phone and dialed the number that was scribbled on the napkin.

"Hi, Black?" she said, her voice lilting upward, since she wasn't sure if he had given her a bogus number.

"Yeah, and this is?"

"It's Bianca—the girl you met yesterday."

"Oh, okay."

There was a brief silence between the two of them, like he had muted the phone. When he did come back on the line, she could hear the noise in the background, as if he had a lot going on around him. "Did I get you at a bad time?" she asked.

"Ummmm . . ." He paused. "Listen, baby, I really want to talk to you. I can't lie. I been waiting on your call from the second I gave you the number."

She smiled through the phone, listening to the game he was kicking. It had been a while since she had dated, and she really wasn't looking forward to the back and forth ping pong of dating.

"And you might think it's game—" He read her mind— "but it's real." Then he said to someone else, "Hold on. I got you, but I'm on an important call." Then he came back to her. "Bee, baby," he called out to her in the sweetest demeanor, "is it at all possible that I can call you back at this number right here?"

"Um, no problem," she said, "but it's my hotel number."

"What's the room number, and how long you going to be there?"

"It's Room 2308, and I will be in here until about two or three. I'm going to move rooms, 'cause I got robbed." She knew that changing rooms should be no problem, because they still had her thousand-dollar security deposit downstairs.

"Wait—you got robbed? Baby, how that happen?" he asked with what sounded like sincere concern.

"It's a long story. I will tell you later, but I just don't feel like rehashing now."

"Damn, baby, I'm sorry. And I told you don't be trusting nobody."

"You did. You did." She had no other choice but to agree with him. She now wished she had listened.

"Baby, since you didn't get around to get your phone yet, I got my old iPhone. I just upgraded it. You can have it. I'll bring it to you."

"No, it's okay." She declined the offer. "I appreciate that."

"Didn't you say you just got robbed?"

"Yeah, I did."

"Oh, okay. Then look, I gotta go. I'ma drop this phone to you, and a few bucks so you can get it cut on. You can go get it cut on near where I saw you. And whatever I gotta do to help you, I will."

"That's sweet, but I can't."

"Look, you don't have no family out here. Shit is hard and fucked up, so I will help you. You seem like a nice chick, and everybody needs some help. Shit, just blessed I had an a'ight night last night that I could help."

She took a deep breath. "I appreciate that. Like, real talk."

"It ain't nothing. Look, I gotta go holla at somebody real quick. Meet me in the lobby of your hotel in twenty minutes and I got you."

"Thank you," she said. She really didn't want to accept the help. For her, it was almost impossible to accept help from someone.

"It's going to be okay, ya hear?"

"Okay. Thanks again," Bianca said.

Once she hung up the phone, the cord got stuck in the drawer of the night table, and when she tried to get it out, the drawer opened, revealing the Holy Bible, which allowed her mind to drift off. Had God sent Duck Boots to her? Was he her guardian angel?

As Bianca drifted off in deep thought, she was quickly snapped out of it when her room phone rang and startled her. She sat paranoid for a minute, then realized it had to be the front desk or Black.

She picked it up and just held the phone and listened. "Hellooooo?" She heard Black on the other end.

"Hey," she said.

"I'm about to be there in three minutes. Come down. I gotta drop this to you and keep going. Got a lot of shit going on, but I ain't want you to be without."

"Okay," she said. "I'm coming."

As she exited the room, she began to wonder what Black's ulterior motive was. What was it that he wanted? But then again, she reminded herself that maybe there are some good people in the world, and maybe he was the one good person in Miami.

The second she came outside the hotel revolving door, there he was, sitting on the bench. Black handed her the cell phone, along with a hundred and fifty dollars. For the first time, she got a good look at Black. He was about six feet tall, ebony-skinned, and he resembled a younger Barry White. He really wasn't bad looking in a rugged kind of way.

"You can go down the block and set the phone up. This should be enough to take care of that and put something on your stomach. Call me once you get it on."

"Thank you," she said. "I—I really appreciate it."

"Ain't nothing!" He flagged his hand in a dismissive manner, "Talk to you soon, a'ight? Be safe." He turned to walk away. Then he turned back. "Ayo."

She looked up at him.

"I almost forgot." With his hand turned in a downward manner, he handed her a switchblade. "Keep this with you at all times, and don't be afraid to shank a mofo."

She smiled. "Thanks, honey. And I ain't scared to hurt somebody trying to hurt me. Never again."

He nodded. "Cool. A'ight, later," he said and walked off.

Since she was just at the store the day before, she managed to get her same number connected to the new phone. It didn't matter, because no one really had the number anyway. It just was easier that way.

When she put all her apps on it, she went back to her room to change. She logged onto her Instagram account and was bombarded with countless direct messages from Bella. Though she wanted to hear what her sister had to say for herself, she didn't even open them. She didn't want it to show that they had been read.

Then, somewhere in between Bella's countless messages, she noticed another one from a guy named Viper. Though he was her follower on Instagram, she had never met him in person. They had communicated through his responses to her posts of clothes she was selling. She also had her picture on Instagram, and she'd modeled an outfit or two.

She clicked on it. It read: HEY GORGEOUS! ARE YOU IN MIAMI BY ANY CHANCE? I THOUGHT I SAW YOU ON LINCOLN ROAD.

Damn, this damn social media is a real bitch!

For a split second she thought about it and wasn't going to respond to him at all. But then she had to come to terms with the fact that she couldn't exist in this city alone. Her back was against a wall. She had nothing to lose. Shit, she needed all the friends she could get.

She answered back: YES, GOT ROBBED AND BEAT UP. EVERYTHING WAS STOLEN.

He responded back right away: THAT'S FUCKED UP! WHERE ARE YOU? DO YOU NEED A PLACE TO STAY? ARE YOU OK? CALL ME 305-777-9311.

She took too long to respond, so he hit her up again: WORRIED ABOUT YOU- CAN YOU PLEASE CALL ME? THIS PLACE NOT SAFE FOR A LADY OUT HERE BY HERSELF.

I never said I was alone, did I? she wondered.

Before she could hit Viper back, her cell phone rang.

"Hey, you!" she said through the receiver.

"Throw on some sneakers. I'ma pick you up in five minutes," Black told her. "Take you down to South Beach and get you something good to eat."

"A'ight, sounds good to me." She hung up and put her sneakers on and headed to the lobby. While she waited on the valet bench outside of the hotel, she pulled out her phone and responded back to Viper: I'M DOING OK AND WILL CALL YOU A LITTLE LATER.

V: YOU PROMISE?
B: YES.
V: PROMISES AREN'T MEANT TO BE BROKEN.

Before she could respond back to Viper, Black pulled up on a scooter. She smiled. "Now you know good and well you too damn big for this scooter," she quipped.

"Huh? What you say?" he asked. "You rollin' with me, or what?"

Bianca sighed. She was hungry, and so far, Black had shown himself to be a friend. She'd never ridden on the back of a motorcycle or on a scooter before, but then again, she'd never been in Miami, broke, or with no one to call on. Her whole life had changed overnight. She was trying not to dwell on it. Having a life was way better than being six feet under. With that being said, there was nothing else to do but make the best of the life she still had.

"Just don't drive all fast. My life is literally in your hands," she said as she hopped on the back, and off they went down the block to the Ocean Drive strip on South Beach. She ached with each bump he hit, but she enjoyed the wind blowing through her hair. It felt soothing. The hot shower she took earlier had loosened up her muscles and taken away some of the pain.

The two ended up at the same spot where Black borrowed the ink pen from the hostess to write his number down. They took their seats at the Oasis Restaurant with a perfect view of the crystal blue ocean. She gazed off, letting her mind run wild with thoughts of living the life of luxury, but she kept being brought back to reality with the ringing of Black's phone.

"Them chicks blowing you up, huh?"

"Not even."

"Negro," she joked, though she was so serious, "you know you got a bunch of chicks calling your phone."

"I do, but trust me, I ain't on that. I'm on money, in the worst way."

"Don't I know it? We got that in common."

"And chicks, all they want to do is take from you, and if you ain't got none, they ain't got nothing for you."

She turned her head from side to side, taking in what he said, and she had to agree. "I can't front. You right."

"I know, so all I can do is focus on that, be a good person, and God will bless me with a good woman and money too."

"God will provide, that's for sure."

"What about you?"

"What about me?"

"The guys chasing you?"

"Not really, but the only thing that I care about that has anything to do with a chase is Chase bank."

He laughed then his phone interrupted them again.

"Everything okay?" she asked.

"Just business."

"By all means, don't let me stand in your way." She didn't have to wonder what kind of business he was in. It didn't take a rocket scientist to figure that he was into selling some kind of drugs.

"Naw, I'm going to go handle it later after I drop you back off, but I just wanted you to eat."

"Thank you. That's sweet." She really did appreciate Black. He wasn't her type of guy per se, but was definitely her knight in shining gold teeth. His entire persona was the total opposite of Caesar. He was as dark chocolate as they come, and was kind of chubby, whereas Caesar was in the best physical condition. He wore baggy clothes, whereas Caesar dressed very conservative preppy. There wasn't much physical attraction to him, and she almost felt bad. She was sure she didn't want to lead him on, though, but was so grateful to have him.

As she sat finishing up the lobster dinner—the special that the host was trying to get them to try the other day—she was taking in how beautiful everything was.

Black asked, "So what's up with the room? How much is it for another week?"

She shrugged her shoulders. "I don't even know. I gotta find out." Sad to say that she hadn't even wrapped her head around that issue. What was she going to do?

"Well, I'ma try to take care of it for another week for you."

"No, I can't do that. I really can't accept that from you."

"Look," Black said, "I'm not the richest man or anything like that, but whatever I got, you can get. And that's real."

"Nah," she said. "I'm going to get some money. Don't worry."

"Look, real talk, you can't be going into these people's stores down here and boosting they shit. The tech is a li'l different, and I don't want you late," he said, being that he came to her rescue the other day when she was trying to boost from a store.

"Yeah, I know." She listened. What he was saying was sinking in. The truth of the matter was that she did need a crew to make things happen the way she used to, and she was playing in an entirely different arena. "But trust me, I'm going to figure out something."

"I believe that," he said to her, "but until you do, I'ma do what I can."

She took a deep breath. "Why?"

"I mean, you got anybody else out here?"

"Nope," she admitted.

"Look, it's like this. Everybody need somebody to hold them down in tough times, to have their back at all times."

"True." She couldn't deny that.

"To catch them when they slipping, celebrate their successes," he said, looking at his phone. "You know, we all need somebody."

"You are right," she replied, still skeptical. "But why me? Why you?"

"Well, why not you? And if I don't have you, who else is going to?"

She sat silent for a minute as she thought. That was some real live shit he was kicking to her. It made good sense, and the reality was that the answer to the question was what it always was: Nobody!

Before she could say thank you and graciously accept his help, she could hear Caesar in the back of her head. *Never accept anything from people, because you have to look a gift horse in the mouth.*

Suddenly, Black's s phone rang. "I gotta take this." She nodded and began to people watch as he politicked over the phone.

"You want anything else?" he asked when the waiter came with the check, as he still talked on the phone. She shook her head and then continued to watch the characters from all walks of life that strolled the strip.

As he paid the bill, she caught sight of someone and got up from the table quickly. "I'll be right back."

Her Air Maxes felt like roller skates as she made her way down the crowded sidewalk. Her eyes never lost sight of their target. In her mind, it seemed like she was moving in slow motion, but Bianca was swift on her feet. In a matter of minutes, she was on the woman's heels. She grabbed her from the back. "You snitch-ass bitch!" Bianca said as she yanked the hell out of the stripper who had been wearing the zebra-print outfit and told Rocco that she had the Mollies. She was with a masculine-looking female. Bianca hauled off and punched her.

"What the fuck?" she screamed, and the crowd began to swarm to see the cat fight going on.

Zebra was in shock and didn't know what to do, so the butch-looking girl who was with her began hitting Bianca.

"Fuck off of her, bitch!" That's when Black body-slammed the butch one onto the pavement.

Bianca wouldn't let go of the hold she had on Zebra. She had her on the ground and was on top of her, punching her and choking her. "Bitch, you almost had me killed."

"Come on, we gotta go! We gotta go!" Black was trying to tell Bianca, but Bianca had snapped out, and the only thing that ran through her head were snippets of how Rocco had beat her ass in that bathroom in The Den, and that her bag of money was gone. She couldn't see or hear anything else.

Not even Black's voice screaming, "Run! Run, B!" Out of the corner of her eye, she saw that he was being detained by five police and was rumbling with them. He was throwing blow after blow, trying to keep them away from Bianca, but it took two police to pry her hands from around Zebra's neck.

When she snapped out of her trance, police were using their stun guns and Mace to try to calm Black down so they could get him in handcuffs. Meanwhile, they already had the silver bracelets on her.

CHAPTER 20

"Bianca Alexis Williams," the old, crusty-looking Confederate judge said in a tone that sounded like he had a mouth full of chewing tobacco. "The Commonwealth of Virginia sentences you to twenty years in a state penitentiary. The Department of Corrections will take custody of you. May God have mercy on your soul."

Bianca imagined her future sentencing. These were the only words that kept playing over and over in her head as she sat inside the paddy wagon, so disappointed in herself, waiting to be transported to jail.

Damn! She knew better! She had so much at risk. Why would she let this stupid, hating-ass stripper girl get to her like that?

"Bee, you over there?"

"Yeah, I'm over here," she said through the walls of the paddy wagon. She was relieved that they were in the wagon together.

"You okay?"

"Hell, naw," she said.

"I know, man. Look, I got some cash in my pockets. I'ma get us out."

She had a lump in her throat. She was so angry with herself for acting on such impulse. She didn't even want to say it aloud and give her words life, but the truth of the matter was that she was going to have to go up the road. There wasn't going to be any bail, not today or any day. Her stupid, emotional ass was going to be shipped back to Virginia to face trial.

"I hear you. I appreciate you. What's your name?" she asked Black.

"Mark Black."

"No talking," a deep-voiced police officer said. "Be quiet." Then the door came open and the guard looked in. "Come on, ma'am."

"Where am I going?"

"Booking." He took her out of the wagon and into the police station. As soon as she walked into the compact police station, she heard a loud voice, "Ayo, Bee? Bee? Bee?"

She ignored it because she knew good and well nobody knew her there, but as much as she tried to block it out, the voice kept calling out, "Bee! Ayo! Bee—is that you?"

She turned, thinking, *Fuck! Ain't this a bitch? The fucking world is small after all.*

"Dana, got-damn!" Bianca said with a smile, though she was cringing inside at the fact that she had run into someone she knew. This wasn't good at all. She was surely going to be outed now.

"Girrrl, I thought that was you. I would know that walk from anywhere, even in handcuffs," she said, getting closer and closer to Bianca.

Dana's grandmother lived around the street from Grandmother Williams. Dana would come down to Virginia from New York City every single summer when they were little girls. The two would play together and have the best time. Dana would always promise to keep in touch when she'd go back to New York City, but she never did. Bianca had not seen Dana since she was thirteen years old, and a lot had happened since then.

The officer had her in the hall. "Stand right here until I get us an office."

"No problem." Bianca felt much obliged so that she could talk to Dana.

When Dana approached, Bianca leaned in and said what she wanted to say, but didn't want to say in earshot of anybody else. "Um, girl, no disrespect at all, but I thought you were dead."

Dana's smirk was wiped away real quick. "Girrrrl . . . " She paused. "You know I burned my daddy's house down, and when they thought I was dead, I ran with it. I had so much bullshit in the streets, and, girl, I needed a clean slate. So I fled to South Florida and mixed in."

"How long you been here?" Bianca asked, meaning Florida.

"Seven years."

"Seven years, huh?" she thought out loud. She was interested, thinking if Dana could survive these mean South Florida streets for seven years, so could she.

"Yeah, and I got a got a bench warrant on some traffic bullshit."

"Come on now," the officer said to Bianca and took her into the small office.

The police officer placed Bianca in a chair, still in handcuffs, and then came back with her purse and placed it on the desk.

"Please, sir, can you take these off?" she said in a nice, calm voice, hoping the policeman would feel her pain.

"Wait a minute," he said then left the room. He didn't return for another twenty minutes. "Look, let me do this and then I will take them off, okay?"

"Alı right, I guess."

He asked her a series of questions, starting with, "What's your name?"

"Bella Alexis Williams." She spoke up without pausing. She knew her sister's record was squeaky clean.

He stared at her to search her face to see if she was lying. "You don't have an ID in your bag, so how can you prove to me that you are who you say you are?"

"I don't know. I guess trust me, Officer Kane." She read his nametag, and immediately he reminded her of the old school rapper Big Daddy Kane. Ella had always loved him when Bianca was a little girl. The officer was tall, built, with sleepy eyes, just like the hip-hop star.

"Trust you?" He let out a slight chuckle. "How do I know you are not a mass murderer?"

She smiled as she batted her eyelashes. "With a name like Kane, how do I know you are not a big cocaine dealer?"

He burst into laughter to cover up the fact that he was speechless and that she had a good point. He nodded. "Okay, Bella. What's your social?"

Bianca took a deep breath and rambled the nine numbers that belonged to her sister. So far so good, but at any second, this could all go to hell. She smiled on the outside, but on the inside, her heart was indeed in her Victoria's Secret panties.

Officer Kane typed the numbers in the computer and she heard a beep. "Okay, and your birthdate?"

With no hesitation, she recited Bella's birthdate as well.

He asked a series of other questions, and she answered those too. He looked at her and smiled. "A'ight now, Bella. I'ma take these cuffs off of you, but no funny mess, you hear me?"

"You have my word. No funny mess."

He took off the cuffs then left the room, leaving her purse right on the desk.

In a matter of seconds, she had gotten her phone and earpiece out of it, hiding them before he came back to tag her property. When he left the room again, she quickly pulled out her phone, went to her Instagram, and got Viper's number.

Bianca calmly checked to see if the coast was clear, and then she put her Bluetooth in her ear and stashed the phone so no one would see it. The phone seemed like it took forever to connect, and each ring was dreadfully long. The anticipation was driving her insane, but finally Viper picked up.

"Yeah," he said.

"Viper," she whispered.

"Who?"

"Look, it's Bianca," she said under her breath. "I'm locked up, and I need you to please come bail me out if you could."

"Huh? Well, damn, baby."

"Promised you that I would call, just sorry that it's under these circumstances."

"A'ight, a'ight. No pressure. Now, what's up?"

"Nigga, this damn bail—and getting out of here."

"I feel that. Are you in Dade or Broward?"

"Dade County, under Bella Williams."

"A'ight, I'm on it. I'm going to get you soon as you get a bail."

"Promise?" she asked.

"Yeah."

Then she reminded him, "Promises aren't meant to be broken."

He chuckled. "I got ya, li'l momma. Don't worry. I'll be there."

After Bianca was moved to another jail then placed into a holding cell, while praying and holding her breath every single second of her stint in the jail, fourteen hours later, God had definitely shined on her. Viper had indeed made good on his word! She was outta there.

CHAPTER 21

"Free at last, free at last! Thank God Almighty, I'm free at last," she said when she jumped in the front seat of Viper's Camaro. "Oh my goodness. Thank you so much," she said to him. "I honestly can't thank you enough."

"Just carry your crazy ass to court. Don't make me have to come looking for yo' ass," said the brown-skinned, full-bearded guy who had to be at least ten years her senior.

Bianca frowned her face up. "Man, I wouldn't do that to you," she assured him.

"Better not," Viper said firmly, in a tone that she'd always imagined that the older brother she'd never had would use with her.

"Can you find me a lawyer to help me get it dismissed, please?" she asked in her sweetest voice.

"Ain't nothing," he admitted dryly. "Know a few good guys fit for the job. I'll get you some numbers."

Her mind wandered off as to how she was going to pull off going to court under her sister's name, but she was thankful that she was even able to not only think to use her sister's name, but to actually finesse it like she had with such ease.

"You are pretty as hell, girl. Too pretty to be fighting and carrying on like that." He put his asthma pump up to his face and inhaled.

"Thank you," she said.

"And what you must know is, you can't be fighting or committing no crimes, not even fucking jaywalking on

South Beach." He whistled and shook his head. "These motherfuckers do not play about South Beach. They don't allow nothing or no one to fuck up that tourist money."

"I hear you, and I don't bother nobody, but when someone deliberately tries to hurt me—"

He cut her off, wanting to make his point. "Look, baby, no more fighting, especially on South Beach. Not for nothing, but you are a lady, and too pretty to be getting into fights," he added, taking another puff of his inhaler.

"But I've been a victim so long that I'm tired. I'm not letting nobody else get away with controlling my destiny. I mean that."

He nodded. "So what are you trying to tell me?"

"I'm saying I appreciate you so much, and I'm going to get your money back to you. Give me a week." She didn't want to hear his lecture.

"Ain't nothing. Whenever you can."

"No, I'm going to pay you back." She winked. "Just in case I need you to come and get me again."

"Look, li'l momma, don't cut me off or blow me off. Honestly, I ain't tripping off that money. For real, I ain't. You give it back, it's appreciated. If not, I'm not crying."

Bianca just listened to him as he went on.

"And that chip on your shoulder needs to go." He looked up from the road and into her eyes. "This ain't the place for you to be Bianca or Bella Bad-Ass Bullshit. This place is dangerous. Don't let the palm trees, blue water, and white sand fool ya."

"I understand."

It seemed kind of crazy that she was riding shotgun in a car, getting a lecture that she was actually going to take heed to, from a complete stranger, someone who she had never even met face-to-face before now. For some strange reason, she didn't feel the least bit uncomfortable.

"Social media a real motherfucker, huh?" he said.

"When I tell you I'm so grateful to it right now, though, I can't even front. Direct Message is a wonderful thing."

Viper smiled. "Isn't it?" he concurred.

"So, enough about me. What do you do?"

"Is it really important?"

"Ummmm . . ." She thought, unsure how to respond to his bluntness.

Viper noticed that he had her speechless for the first time, and he didn't want her to be uncomfortable. "I do some of this this and some of that, but for the most part, I'm retired. Was really successful when I was younger, and retired and been chilling ever since."

"Damn, life good, huh?"

"I'm not wealthy or rich, but I'm living, and the most important thing is that I ain't starving. I got a little pension."

"Well, that's nice. I see you travel a lot on your page. What else do you do in your free time?"

"Nothing heavy. Just chill out, watch sports, the normal shit."

"So, are you married?"

"Nah," he quickly said. "Not at all."

"No old lady?" she questioned.

"Nah."

"Why not?"

He was quiet for a while. "Just got too many demons and shit."

"Meaning?"

"Just demons that I don't discuss, that's it," he said firmly, with an expression that let her know not to even think of asking or trying to pry to get it out of him.

She took heed. "I think we all have demons riding our backs in one way or another."

He was quiet for a few minutes, and when she finally gave up on him responding, he said, "You right about that, li'l sis. You right about that."

So that made it clear that he wasn't interested in trying to date her, and that was fine with her. He was an old head, in his mid-thirties, and it would probably be a blessing if she could ever get him to drop his guard so she could pick his brains. If all else failed, she was just blessed that, for whatever his reason was, he was in her life and that she had him to bail her out of jail. She was grateful to him that she wasn't still sitting in jail, being expedited back to Virginia to face the music for the one thing that sent her to Miami in the first place.

As he pulled in front of her hotel, he said, "Look, I know I'm a weird kinda guy."

You don't say, she thought.

"And it's a lot of things about me that you don't know and probably won't ever know, but know that I'm a good guy. I will never steer you wrong. Anything that you need to know, call me, and if I don't know somebody, I will ask around for you. No more hasty moves, okay?" He smiled at her but seriously meant every word he said.

Bianca smiled back, said thank you, and hopped out of the car. She looked up at the sky and prayed. *I don't know why you sent this guy to my Instagram, but thank you, Lord. You sure do know how to put the right people in my life at the right time.*

Soon after Viper dropped her off, Black called her to let her know that everything was okay. Bianca started to feel so blessed to have two good friends in her life.

Black couldn't resist. He asked her the same exact question that she had asked herself. "No judging, but how in the hell you let a trick-ass stripper ho get you out of your character like that?"

"Look, I'm not playing with these people out here. Off the break, I'm not cutting corners, because the bitch deserved it! Bottom line, the bitch is a snitch bitch, and—"

Black cut her off. "Say no more, baby."

"It's a long story, and I will tell you about it when I see you."

"Look, if you do, cool. If not, that's cool too. Whatever it is, from what I can tell, you had good reason."

"Look, I came here for a new beginning, and I know I'm going to get something big going here. I don't know what, but what I do know is that this whole new chapter, new life, is about living on my terms and not taking no shots or bullshit from nobody. I'm coming to understand that when you are the new girl, whether it's at a school, in a city, or whatever, you gotta teach these people the lesson that you ain't to be fucked with."

"Well, I bet she won't do it again," he said.

"I bet she won't either."

The two fell into laughter.

"And you, I can't believe you jumped in the fight."

"Told you I had you."

"But, nigga, you ain't have to get locked up for me," Bianca said to Black, but in a sick way, she loved that he had. No one had ever really gone out of their way and risked anything for her. Her relationship with Caesar was so uneventful. Their love was pure and exactly what she needed to feed her need to be loved; however, seeing that someone really had her back gave her another feeling. She felt like part of a family—something she hadn't felt since she was gang raped then blamed for the pregnancy by her mother. Now she knew what unconditional support felt like. Her own mother hadn't even given her that. Her mother had given her love and support with conditions. As long as Bianca made good grades and made her mother look good, Ella gave her love. Once Bianca got pregnant, her mother withdrew her love and approval.

"Shiiiiit, I wasn't going to let you get locked up by yourself. I couldn't leave you alone. Come on, now. You already know that wasn't gon' happen."

"I didn't know, but I appreciate it. I appreciate you more than you could ever know!" She really did, because no one had ever done what he did for her.

"So, what you up to?" she asked.

"Going to be out hugging the block all night."

"Why?" Bianca worried.

"'Cause I gotta get this money so you can pay dude back, plus the money for your room."

"No, I'm going to do that."

"Naw, I told you I was, and I am," Black insisted.

"No, I'm going to go out tomorrow and try to make things happen."

"Not a good idea. You can't risk getting arrested."

"Well, let me worry about that."

"Don't argue with me," Black said. "Look, I got work. Just gotta dump it. That's all."

"No cash in the stash?" Bianca boldly asked.

"Naw, I told you I ain't rich. I'm just a small-time dealer trying to make it from day to day, but I'm going to make sure you don't have to do nothing crazy. I'm going to get this bread and we going to eat. Watch me."

"I hear you. Well, I got your back too," she said, wanting Black to know how much she truly did appreciate him. "Who got your back?" Bianca asked.

"Nobody got mine," he said with great pride, "but I got mine." She could hear him poking out his chest through the phone.

"That's not true. All that you do, somebody got you. Got to."

"No! Nobody don't. My momma some shit, my sisters be on they own shit until they need me, my li'l brother it's another story, and homeboys, you know how that shit go. So, I try to stay on the good foot with all around me, just in case I do need something, but all in all, I know I got me, and that's all I need."

"Deep!" she said.

"Yup," he had to agree.

"I get it now." She understood more about Black in this conversation. "That's why you always let me know you got me and go all out for me, because you know what it feels like not to have anybody."

Black's mother was some shit. She had always used him and had taken cold advantage of him for as long as he could remember. The only thing she had ever given him was her ass to kiss, and then pointed him in the right direction to get a job as a lookout when he was still in elementary school. From that time on, he'd been hustling, getting his own, taking care of his mother, sisters, and pretty much anybody else. Whatever he made, he blessed everybody else.

"Yup!" he agreed. "But I don't do what I do because I want you to return the favor, 'cause I know expecting people to do for you as you do for them ain't realistic. Just 'cause I do, don't mean you gon' do. Shit don't work like that. This the real world."

"I know and understand firsthand, and if you don't know anything, know that I got you like you got me," Bianca promised. "And that ain't no bullshit."

Though she hated making deals with money, merchandise, or resources she didn't have, at the end of the day, her heart was pure. If she didn't have anybody else, she had Black, and she would roll with him until the wheels fell off—best believe that.

CHAPTER 22

After Bianca spent at least ten hours in the holding cell with Dana, who now insisted on being calling Diamond Diddy, the two girls had made the time they were locked up speed by, reminiscing about the old days. They brought one another up to speed on pretty much all their war stories and get-money sagas—and the things in between—that the two old friends had missed in each other's lives.

After being out on bail for almost three weeks now, things were moving not as fast as Bianca needed them to; but with the help of Black and his nickel and diming, and her online sales trickling in, she was somehow making ends meet. But Bianca had still not made good on her word. She'd promised Diamond Diddy that they'd hang out.

"Girrrrl, this shit just ain't right. You been blowing me off for a couple of weeks now," Diamond Diddy complained on the phone.

"I know. I'm just still trying to get settled out here."

"Girl, you can be out here for five years and you still not going to be settled. This is just one of those cities where, no matter what you do, the transition is just hard, so you thinking you can't go nowhere until you feeling one hundred is not going to work."

"I hear you," Bianca said in a dry tone.

"Now, look. I already know you done hit the stores up, so you got some cute shit you can throw on." Diamond insisted that they go out and have a great time. "Not to mention, after the time you've had since you've been here, you need a night of lots of drinking, giggles, and real Miami fun!"

Bianca couldn't deny it. "You ain't lying. Now that I think of it, I could really use a night of excitement." She leaned down and polished her toenails a topaz color.

"All right, so are you up for it?"

She hesitated, her mind flashing back to her first night out on the town and how disastrous it had turned out. "I guess . . ." Before she could shut it down and change her mind, Diamond cut her off.

"Okay, then it's all set. I got something in mind."

"Nothing heavy, but I do wanna get out of the house."

It was settled, and tonight was the night.

Bianca was running unusually late as she rushed inside of Gypsy's Lounge, only to realize that it was definitely the place to be. The huge warehouse-style building was so unassuming from the outside. No one would have ever known what was behind the walls. There was no denying that on this night, it was definitely the place to be. It seemed like everybody and their grandfather was hanging out.

There was a huge boxing match going on, and for those who hadn't made it out to Vegas for the big fight, Gyspy's seemed like it was the only place to be. There had to be about twenty-five hundred people in there, crowded around the mega screen televisions in the sports bar part of the strip club. The actual sporting event drowned out the fact that the establishment was an upscale gentlemen's club that catered mostly to white men, and the girls that worked there were Caucasian and wore evening gowns.

But tonight, the sports bar aspect definitely catered to all kinds of men—black, white, Chinese, Cuban, and anything in between.

With a jam-packed house, the chances of her finding Diamond through the tight, standing-room-only crowd was slim to none, so she grabbed her cell phone from her purse and called her.

"Girl, where you at?"

"In the parking lot waiting for you."

"I'm inside."

"Is it thick?"

"Thicker than a Snickers," she joked, but Bianca was looking around, wondering where they were going to sit. There was literally not an empty chair or table in sight.

"Okay, well, I will be in there in a minute."

"A'ight," Bianca said. "Just come to the back near the small bar in the corner. I will be standing over there."

"Okay."

Bianca stood in her tight stretch jeans that showed off her curves and her fitted T-shirt, with her Giuseppi studded heels and purse to match, trying to figure out where in the hell they could sit.

"Hi, how are you?"

"Hey, honey," Bianca said in a friendly manner to the guy standing in front of her with small, shoulder-length, neatly done dreads pulled back in a bun. He had another big, Godzilla-looking guy with him. She didn't know him from a can of paint, but Ella had always told her and Bella that it didn't cost a thing to speak.

"You by yourself?" he questioned.

"No, just waiting on my girlfriend to come in."

"Where are y'all sitting?"

She breathed in, let it out, and calmly shook her head. Her hands clutched her purse, and she kept her trembling on the inside. "The jury is still out on that one," she said with a flirty smile, not letting on that she was worried.

"Well, you seem like a cool chick. We got a few tables over there. You welcome to come sit with us. All the food and drinks you want are on me."

"Really?" she said, thinking how that was right on time.

"Yeah." He nodded. "We right over there."

"Where?" She looked at him to clarify exactly where they were, because with the big crowd, she could easily lose him in it.

"You see the big dude standing over there in that orange shirt?" he questioned as he pointed through the crowd of folks.

"Do I?" she said. There was no way she could miss the guy, who stuck out like a sore thumb. He had to have stood at least seven feet and weighed over four hundred pounds. "Good God almighty!"

"Exactly," he said, laughing to himself.

"Okay, cool. So I'm going to go to the bathroom, and hopefully by the time I get out, she will be in."

"Well, I got you. Just come over when you get wit' your friend," he said as he walked off.

By the time she came back from the restroom, there was Diamond. "Perfect timing," she said.

"But where in the hell we going to sit, girl? This shit is bananas," she said.

"You ain't never lied, but listen." Bianca leaned closer to her friend to tell her the game plan. "I just met this guy. There's a group of them, and they invited us to sit with them. Now, I can't front. They look a little big and crazy, but they said it's definitely somewhere to sit, free food and drinks. We gone make it work."

"Did you say free food?" Diamond smiled. "And drinks?"

"Yeah, he said he had us," Bianca confirmed.

"Then why in the hell we still standing here?"

When Bianca started making her strides in their direction, with Diamond in tow, she saw her new friend waving her over to them, while one of his homeboys was passing chairs, placing them down beside where he was sitting. She smiled, thankful for him, because the shoes she had on were not meant for standing.

He directed her to the chair, and Diamond to the one beside her, so that Bianca would be in the middle. Then he said, "Um, hey, friend, this my brother, D. D, this is . . ."

"Diamond," Bianca spoke up. The brother was happy to get to know Diamond better, offering her a drink right away. Then Bianca turned to her new friend, "And I'm Bianca. You never gave me your name, honey."

"Rap."

"Nice to meet you, Rap, and thank you again for inviting us."

"Pleasure's all mine. I think you are so pretty." He looked into her eyes.

"Thank you," she said, taking her seat.

"Are those your real eyes?" he asked of her gray contacts that she'd been wearing for the past couple of days.

She thought for a second and said, "Not today."

"Oh, well, they still pretty, but you prettier."

"Thank you."

"What are you drinking?"

"Water is fine." She smiled, still taking everything in.

"Water?" He turned his face up. "Baby, you can have anything your heart desires." He motioned to all of the buckets of bottles of various brands of liquors that were on the table. Some were still full to the brim and untouched.

"I know," she said, "but I would like to have water, please."

He didn't understand her choice, but nodded. "As you wish, beautiful."

Their section and tables were definitely the place to be, and the fellas she was with were definitely the right people to know, judging by all the people coming over to the table to show respect, give dap, or just stop to drop jewels or jawbone. These guys were definitely in the know, and Rap was definitely a very important man. He was in the middle of everything and calling all the shots. Everybody wanted his attention, but Bianca was the one he was interested in giving his attention to.

"Where you from?" he asked.

"I just moved here like a month ago."

"You like it?"

"Honestly, it's not what I really expected."

"That's 'cause you hadn't met the right people." He lifted his drink to his lips, trying to conceal his smirk. "But you have now."

"Really?" She smiled, taking a sip of her bottled water.

"Yup." Rap tried to assure her then took another shot of his Rémy Martin 1738, which he wasn't slowing down with. He was taking them to the head, shot after shot.

"So you have family down here?" he inquired.

"No family."

"Where you work?"

"I'm a consultant," she said.

"A consultant?" Rap questioned with another shot to the head.

"Yes, a sales consultant."

"That's what's up," he said, knowing good and well he was still unclear about what exactly she did for a living. "So, can I take you out sometimes?"

Before she could answer, his brother D turned around and said to the waitress, who was bringing more bottles, "Ayo, let's do shots."

Rap took another shot of his 1738, hit his glass on the table hard, and then said, "Double shots for everyone."

Everyone was happy, following his lead. The three waitresses filled the glasses with the double shots of 1738, but Rap had a triple shot.

"You not doing no shot?"

"Naw, baby, I'm good. You g'on and do mines for me." Bianca slid it over to the side.

"What, you don't drink at all? You gotta live a little," Rap said.

"Yeah, I drink, but just not feeling it tonight for some reason."

Diamond heard him. "That's why I brought her out, so she could loosen up."

"Well, we ain't doing no good job," he said in slurs.

Bianca was glad she wasn't drinking. She could really see how people who seemed witty when she was drinking, now seemed inebriated and silly. This was her first turning point. She said she would not drink around people she was watching and getting to know.

"Don't worry. I'm going to do hers for her," Diamond said.

"Thanks, boo."

"You know I got you." As Diamond went to reach for Bianca's shot, Rap took it and drank it.

He smiled at her and imitated the people from an "oldies but goodies" commercial. "Naw, playgirl, you gotta get your own."

Diamond, who was also kind of juiced up along with the fellas, burst out into laughter.

"You are so funny," Bianca said.

When the fight was well into the eleventh round, Rap handed Bianca his cell phone. "Put your number in my phone so I can take you out tomorrow."

"Okay," she obliged, "but you gotta take your pass code off the phone so I can put my number in it."

He took one more shot, and as he took the phone out of her hand, she moved the bottle of 1738 out of his reach. "No more for you. You've had enough. We're done with this." She put her foot down as he struggled to put the passcode in. It took him twice as long to log the right numbers in it, because his equilibrium was totally off. He finally handed it back to her.

Bianca logged her number in the phone and saved it for Rap, while he snuck and took another shot when he thought she wasn't watching. "Come on, Rap. I said no more. You've had enough," she said firmly, giving him a look, letting him know she wasn't at all happy with him.

"All right, party pooper," he said, trying to make light of the situation. "No more for me, because you can be the boss of me. But only you can boss me around, though."

"A'ight, I won't abuse the privilege," she said with a smile.

"Did you put your number in the phone?" He stuttered a bit. "I mean the right number?"

"Of course I did," she assured him. "I'm actually looking forward to our date."

"Let me see it." He dug into his pocket to get his cell, which seemed like such a chore for him to retrieve it out of his jeans pocket. "Show me."

"You don't believe me."

"Not that. Just wanna make sure," he said then, by mistake, to keep from knocking the bottle over, he knocked her purse off the table, causing things to fall out.

"Take the lock off it," she said as she proceeded to gather her contents that had fell out of her pocketbook.

Diamond got up and went to the bathroom. "Girl, too much drinking. I'll be right back."

He struggled to punch in the passcode and kept putting the wrong numbers in. It was official, he was drunk! After trying three times, the phone locked him out and shut off completely. He shot her a look of daggers.

"Why you do that? Why you do that to my phone?"

"What?" Bianca said to him. "I didn't do anything to your phone." Realizing that there was one more thing she had left by mistake on the floor, she bent down and picked it up.

"I know who you are, and it ain't shit you can do to me anyway," he said.

"What?" She was dumbfounded. "I don't wanna do nothing to you."

"I'm so glad I ain't in the streets no more." He shook his head. "I swear, if I was still in the streets, do you know what I would do to your kind?"

"Boy . . . " she said, looking at him as if he were crazy.

"Ayo, D, man, dey the po-po."

D laughed. By now, he and Diamond were friendly.

"Look, nigga!" Bianca said in her boldest tone. "You are officially fucked up, and you really drunk as shit." She stood up. "I'm 'bout to get the hell out of here."

He grabbed her hand and pushed her down. "You ain't going nowhere."

"Nigga, let my motherfucking hand go." She tried to jerk away from him.

He leaned in and got right in her face, and she could smell the 1738 reeking on his breath.

"Nigga, you are crazy, I'm not nobody's fucking police," she said, staring him back in the eyes. "And let me the fuck go!"

He squeezed tighter. "You think I'm stupid? Nobody knows you, you not drinking, no family, no friends, then you do something to my phone so you can tap it."

She tried to push him off with her other arm, but it wasn't working. She looked around at all the guys who were sitting with them and searched their faces to see who could help her, but she knew none of them could or would. "So you niggas call yo'selves men, and you gon' let him hold me against my fucking will?"

"Bitch," Rap said, his hand still squeezing her. The guys around stood up and surrounded her.

Before anyone knew it, with her free hand, she had a knife at Rap's throat.

"Ohhhhhhh, shit!" the guys echoed, unable to believe their eyes.

"Muthafucka, now I asked you nicely to let me fucking go, but you wouldn't. You want to torment me because I don't wanna get drunk tonight? This is why, 'cause I don't trust you Miami muthafuckas."

The guys surrounding them were in shock.

"Don't try me, nigga. I will kill this motherfucker! See, you right, you motherfucking right. You don't know me. I'm out on bond for quadruple homicide charges, and killing a motherfucker ain't shit to a heartless bitch like me."

She saw a little fear seep out of Rap's eyes as she bullshitted them all. He slowly let her hand go, but she still had the switchblade that Black had given her at his throat.

Rap was speechless. He really believed that she was crazy. She wasn't shaking, and she had not flinched or stuttered at all. She was as serious as world peace, and at this point, she didn't give a shit if she was disturbing the peace.

D tried to talk her down. "Baby, it's all good and love. You know niggas be paranoid and shit. That's why I told my nigga not to drink."

"Shut the fuck up, D." She looked into Rap's eyes. "So you were just going to bully a lady around, huh?"

At that moment, she heard a voice she'd never forget say to her, "Come on, baby." He charmed her and then said in a firm tone to the fellas, "Clear the way so the lady can leave."

It was what she needed, because who knows what would've happened if she had taken the knife away from his neck with all of those guys surrounding her. She stared in Rap's face for another thirty seconds then removed the knife, grabbed her purse, and said, "And nigga, you guessed it. The date is fucking off."

CHAPTER 23

The man who had come to her rescue was the same one who had caused her such trauma at The Den: Fitz Pierre-Louis. Dressed in all white, he grabbed Bianca's hand, whisked her away from Rap, and out the front doors of Gypsy's Lounge. Once they were outside, the valet guy went directly to Fitz's car and opened the door. It was a beautiful black Bugatti, parked dead smack in front on display so everyone could see it. There were a few people trying to sneak and pose for pictures in front of it, until the valet shooed them off.

Bianca stopped in her tracks, "Ummmm, I'm not getting in the car and going anywhere with you. Not today, not tonight, or any night."

"Come on. You can't stay here. I'm afraid you've worn out your welcome here, sweetie," he said to her, not wanting to make a scene.

"Excuse me, sir," she said to the valet, who was now reaching for the door, "Can you please get me a cab?"

He totally ignored Bianca's request and looked to Fitz, who smiled and said, "She's fine," and firmly said to Bianca, with this sexiness mixed with cockiness and confidence, "Get in the car, honey."

She stood there and didn't budge for a few seconds. The valet guy strolled a few feet away so they could have a little privacy.

Fitz waited until the valet was out of earshot and then walked around the car to come face-to-face with her. He

softly placed his hand under her chin, lifted it up a little so
she could look at him as he spoke to her in a firm tone just
above a whisper. "Look, I spared your disrespectful ass at
my club. Yes, I'm sure I shook you up with the Jedi mind
tricks, making you think that they were going to rape you
that night when I left the room, which I'm sure scared you
shitless," he admitted. "No doubt, it was a sinister plan to
teach you a lesson, but I just saved your ass from a group of
animals who were going to do God knows what to you for
putting a knife to their boss's neck." He didn't blink as he
searched her face for some sort of understanding, but she
didn't blink either. Then he added, "That guy was a really
big-time dope dealer. I only want to help. That's all."

"Yeah, but you sent someone to steal my money out of
my room."

"What?" He looked as surprised as she had been when
she went back to her room and found out that her money
was missing. "Now, I don't know a thing about that."

"Listen, I was robbed of my key and basically all the
contents of my purse at your spot, and when I got back to
my hotel, my room had been ransacked. All of my money
that I came down here with to start a new life was stolen.
So why would you think I would go anywhere with you? I
mean, really? Plus, my friend is still in there."

"I had my guy take care of her. She's okay."

"Just like you took care of me?"

"Listen, get in the car, honey. I know a lovely little place
with delicious food and great wine that we can go off to.
If you don't like it, I will drop you home." He grabbed the
passenger's door so she could get in.

For a few seconds, she just stood there with her lips
poked out, but through her peripheral vision, she saw
Rap and his homeboys coming out of the front door.

"No strings attached. Just want to make it right, that's
all," he said with his hand extended to help her get inside
the car.

Bianca took his hand and stepped inside one of the most expensive cars that money could buy, placing her Zanottis on the floor of the car and her round bottom in the bucket seat, which hugged her like she was the love of its life. She took a deep breath. Inhaling the car's scent gave her a contact high. There was no other way to describe it; it smelled like new money, and it was intoxicating.

Fitz made his way around to the driver's seat. Once he was in, he made eye contact with Rap, who was by now hassling the valet to hurry and get his car. The look said: *Nigga, stay in your lane.*

Fitz put his Bugatti in gear and calmly eased off the gas, allowing the admirers of the spaceship to get one last glimpse before he'd disappear into thin air. He turned up the music, Jaheim's "I Choose You," which blared through the speakers like it was live in a studio. She'd never been a Jaheim fan, but there was something about the way it sounded through the vehicle's surround sound that was mesmerizing.

It seemed the car's engine gave Fitz superpowers, putting him in his own little world. She studied him, but he paid her no mind as he mimicked Jaheim. He acted as if she wasn't there. He was too busy into his own world, catching his own vibe. She just stared at him, fueling his performance.

He sang aloud to the words for a while. "All the places I can be and the people I can see . . . the decision was easy to make. I choose you over everything," Jaheim sang, before Fitz turned the volume down.

"Let's get off to a fresh start," Fitz said, like he wanted peace.

Bianca gazed at him, but he was still smoothly moving to the beat of the song while in full control of the 1500 horsepower at his disposal, as he waited for her to respond.

Bianca couldn't deny that Fitz was definitely fine—in fact, he had to be the finest thing she had seen since her feet had touched Florida's soil. There was something about his tanned, caramel complexion in that white Robin jeans outfit he was wearing, paired with his watch, whose diamonds were so bright they lit up the Miami skyline as he maneuvered the $2.4 million car.

"Really?"

"Serious," he said to her, sincerity written all over his clean-cut face.

Before she could respond, he turned up the volume. "Hold on, baby. I like this part right here." He played the song to its ending then played it again, pumping it up almost as loud as it could go, while putting the pedal to the metal, handling the car with precision.

All she could do was lay her head back on the headrest, close her eyes, and allow the Miami wind to blow through her hair from the convertible top. For the first time since she arrived in Miami, she was relaxed and was able to allow her mind to run wild like the roaring engine of the best luxury-car engineering.

Deep in her euphoric bliss, she was brought back to reality when her phone vibrated and she looked at her text message:

BISH, WTF HAPPENED? HOW I GO TO THE BATHROOM AND ALL HELL BREAKS LOOSE? YOU BOUT TO MURDER A BIG TIME MIAMI DRUG BOY BUT THE KICKER IS THE LEADER OF THE DAMN PERUVIAN CARTEL SWEPT YOU AWAY. WHAT THE FUCKKKKKK???? MAKE NO MISTAKE YOU ARE MY BISH THO!

Bianca read her text message from Diamond two more times to make sure she was reading it right. Then she looked up over at Fitz, who was still in his own world, rocking out to the music.

B: HUH GIRL? WHAT YOU MEAN

D: RE-READ MY SHIT. AIN'T NO TYPOS IN THERE

B: DAMN GIRL, MY LIFE! BUT ARE YOU OK?

D: YEAH PABLO ESCOBAR MADE SURE HIS PEOPLE CAME AND GOT ME AND WALKED ME TO MY CAR AND MADE SURE I MADE IT HOME SAFE. BUT I AIN'T EVEN GET DEE NUMBER!

B: YOU FUNNY. LOOK CALL YOU ONCE I GET TO MY ROOM.

Bianca tried not to hide the slight smile that had taken over her face as she put her head back and closed her eyes again, trying to get back into her rhapsody as her mind took over again. Hell, Diamond couldn't believe it? Bianca couldn't even believe what had transpired herself, and she was living it. How in the hell had she cabbed it to Gyspy's but was now riding shotgun with a damn drug lord? What did all this mean? Better yet, what did he want with her? He had to be at least fifteen years older than her, and that swagger was on five billion.

After the song ended for the second time, he tried his hand again at her.

"So, listen. There is no denying we are both tough as nails. Neither one of us is going for the other's bullshit."

Bianca looked at him with the same poker face that she wore at all times, never letting on that she was a little taken aback with him as she listened to him and studied his whole being.

"So, this is the deal," he said, using one hand to drive and the other to talk. "You are going to be as absolutely nice to me as you can possibly be. I know you have it in you. And I'm going to be nice and as thoughtful as I can be to you as well. We're going to be friends—no bullshit, no beef. Everything from the past is water under the bridge."

"But—" She started to say something, but he wouldn't let her.

"No buts, ifs, or ands," he said then immediately changed the subject. "The place I wanna go is right up ahead. You are going to love it."

Before she could fix her lips to object, he said it again. "Trust me, you are going to love it. The food is delicious, the view is simply breathtaking, and the service is superb."

"Okay, looking forward to it." The truth of the matter was, she was now hungry, and after everything that had happened, she needed a drink bad. She decided that she'd be on her best behavior. He seemed like he could definitely be an asset to her.

When they rolled up to the fancy restaurant, she saw ladies in cocktail dresses making their way through the entrance. "I don't think I'm dressed properly."

"Don't worry. You look beautiful." He was trying to make her feel secure in her jeans, fitted tee, and heels as he pulled up to the valet.

He opened the door, she stepped out, and he grabbed her hand and walked toward the entrance of the five-star restaurant.

It wasn't until she was out of the car and they were walking hand in hand that she noticed Fitz's security a few feet behind them. He realized that she had noticed them.

"They usually stay out of the way. They will allow us our privacy," he said, clutching onto her hand.

The second they hit the door, the hostess immediately focused all her attention on him. "How are you, Mr. Pierre-Louis?" She gave him a smile bigger than the one on the Kool-Aid commercial. "Oh, what a beautiful lady who will be dining with you."

"Absolutely," he agreed. "She is gorgeous, isn't she?"

"She is." She nodded. "Right this way." She whisked them off to the private room as quickly as Fitz had whisked Bianca out of Gypsy's Lounge.

Real VIP treatment, she thought as she sashayed in front of him, after the host. Bianca made it her business to be sure her butt was shaking more than normal as he followed behind her to their table. As they were led off, up a few stairs and into the private room in the back of the restaurant, she noticed that they had passed a few rappers and reality television stars sitting in the dining room.

The ambiance of the back room was quiet, quaint. It could hold about twenty-five people comfortably on any given night. A man was there, playing a white baby grand piano. When they approached the table where they would be seated, he pulled out her chair for her and then took his seat.

"Thank you, Michelle." He nodded, accepting the menu from her.

"No problem, Mr. Pierre-Louis. Jan will be your server for the evening." She never let that smile leave her face as she exited the room.

"Snazzy," was all Bianca would find to say as she looked over the menu and smiled at the man who played a few more songs for the next thirty minutes, until the music began to come over the speakers. The songs were perfect R & B picks. Song after song made her smile. "The music here is everything."

"Yes, it's my playlist."

"Really? Now, how did you pull that off?"

"My father owns the place, that's how."

She tilted her head to the side and twisted her mouth in approval. "Very nice and exquisite place. I can't even front."

There was something about Fitz's aura that inspired her. He was like her inspiration or something. She found herself wanting to be more polished when she was with him, and less aggressive and vulgar. She desired to act more like a lady—the lady that she always knew she could be.

"Have you ever eaten conch?" he asked.

"No." Bianca furrowed her brow in distaste. "What is that? I've never even heard of it."

"It's comes from the ocean."

"Should I order it?"

"No, not from here. Besides, they don't even serve it. I know where we can get the best conch. Don't worry. I will take you for some soon. In the meantime, have the filet or the halibut."

They had a wonderful six-course dinner. The private chef had pulled out all of his stops for Bianca and Fitz. Once the dessert came out, she asked, "So, do you wanna get down to business?"

He raised an eyebrow. "Business?" He put his fork back down before he cut into his cheesecake.

"Yes, that's why we are here, right?"

"Is that why?" he asked.

"I would guess so. We both know it's not a date. You told me back at the club that you were not interested in 'little girls' and that I wasn't your style, remember?"

"Is that what I said?"

"Pretty much."

"Well, why can't this be a social call?" he asked, drinking his tea.

"Because I'm sure you have a wife, a number one hooker, a few side chicks, and several jump-offs in your stable, just waiting for you to come home to them."

He threw his head back and belted out a hearty laugh. "You get right down to the point, don't you?"

"Well?"

"Honestly, I don't. I live alone. Yes, I have a staff and security detail, but I'm really a loner. No wife, and definitely no hookers, because they want nothing but money.

I watch them at my club all day, all night. No loyalty to nothing or nobody. Side chicks are just everybody chicks, and if everybody can have it, baby girl . . ." He never let his eyes leave hers as he made clear, "I don't want it."

"Okay, good observation." She nodded her head in agreement.

He gave her a direct look. "I've been around a long time. Seen everything, so not at all moved by a big butt and smile. Never have and never will be."

"Well, everybody got somebody."

"You are right in most cases. So who is your somebody?"

"Well, I have a boyfriend back home. We are separated, for the obvious reason." She took a deep breath and was on her third glass of wine. She had decided a few minutes ago that this would be her final glass. She liked how she was not too high but had a nice mellow buzz. Her thinking wasn't impaired. It was just highlighted. "I'm here, and he's there."

"Why, may I ask, did he not come with you?"

"Honestly, he didn't want to, and besides, let's just say it's very complicated and I'd rather not get into it." She thought about Caesar and their love for each other. She wished so badly that she'd be able to get back what they had one day, but she knew deep in her heart that things would never be the same between them. Although their relationship meant everything to her, the truth of the matter was that it was a casualty in her bullshit-ass past of a life that she once had.

However, there was no denying her sense of loss. "But I do love him very much. In fact, he was, and is, my first real love, and we experienced so much together." She shifted the conversation back to him. "And you? What about you?"

"Well, I've never had a shortage of women chasing me, but none that I can say I was passionately in love with, or who honestly captured my heart."

"As old as you are?" She shot from the hip, knowing good and well it had to be the vintage red wine talking for her. "Do you even have a heart for someone to get into? Because honestly, you seem like the iceman, if you ask me."

He chuckled. "Well, I see I must bring you for wine more often. You are such pleasant company, and the bad-ass seems to leave the building when the wine comes. You let down your guard and seem to be a little more . . ." He searched for the word. "Ahhhh, soft."

"No, not at all. The wine doesn't do anything. I'm well aware of everything going on around me. I'm trying to keep my word with you to be nice." She smiled. "We did make a deal, right? And the bottom line, if I don't have my word, I ain't got shit. That's it, that's all." She looked into his hazel eyes that blended perfectly with his tanned caramel complexion, giving it an almost reddish tone. "Now, sir, don't try to put the spotlight back on me. There is still a question on the table for you to answer."

"Hmm, I do have a heart."

She drank her wine and used her eyes to say, "I'm not sure that's true, but okay."

He took a sip of his and then spoke to her. "Well, I was always taught to make money. For the longest time, that's always been my focus. For decades now, I've always been married to my family business. Was groomed for it from my childhood, and when I got old enough, I eased into the CEO position, still under my father's command at times. So that's always been my priority."

"Well, I can understand that. That's my only focus now—money. I just want to get me some money, to create endless options for myself and those who have my back. And once I get my money, I will marry it! If I can't spend it, I can't use it."

"What do you need so much money for, may I ask?"

She gazed at him as if he were crazy. "The same thing you need it for. Options! Just life, whatever my heart desires. And I have no problem working hard getting it. Now, if you don't have a wife or kids, how are you going to pass the family business along?"

He nodded and gave her a conspiratorial grin, as if she had a great point. "It's so funny you should ask. My father asked me the same thing, just the other day." He chuckled as if he had something on his mind.

She didn't really care about the answer to this man's personal life. She was more into his business life, which she knew was going to be hard to pry into, because a man of his stature would never have loose lips or share his business details with her or anybody else. All she wanted was an opportunity, just like she was sure most of the other folks he came in contact with wanted.

"So, is there room for opportunities for me in your business?" she asked.

"Not really." Although he sounded pleasant, there was a note of finality in his voice.

"So you're not an equal opportunity company?"

He chuckled. "We are, but listen. This isn't the time or place to have this conversation. Besides, on my level, I deal with people who have a lot of cash and resources. A pretty face and nice shape just don't move me."

"Then why bring me out to insult me?"

"I wouldn't insult you. Just was trying to be nice. I heard you were out for a lovely night on the town, and instead of dining alone, I thought maybe I could use a little company for dinner. Show you a nice time. That's all this is about."

"Whatever," she said as she drank the last little bit of wine, not knowing that so much more was about to be poured on her.

CHAPTER 24

After dinner, Fitz took her to a nice little salsa spot, and she had to admit, she had a wonderful time. They danced the night away, and the sun was coming up when he dropped her at the hotel. The sunrise cast an amber glow on the world, and that's exactly how Bianca felt—glowing. She couldn't understand how this man had gone from being her arch-nemesis to becoming somewhat of a friend when she was in need. Contented, she had slept pretty much the entire day away when she was awakened by a call from Black.

"Hey, you!" she answered.

"Hey, I was worried about you."

Bianca filled him in on everything that had happened the night before. "You really do be my lifesaver. Man, if I hadn't had that knife that you gave me, I don't know what would've happened to me."

"Why you go over there by yourself?"

"Well, I told you I was going to meet my homegirl, Diamond, from back home."

"Man, I don't trust her either. None of these hoes you be with. Come on, she mysteriously disappears and goes to the bathroom when shit 'bout to get real?" Black made a great point.

"She was drinking . . . and peeing. You know that goes hand in hand."

"Listen, I told you from day one, you can't trust none of these hoes. Didn't I tell you? Now look, every time you with one of them, shit get crazy!"

Bianca sat on the side of the bed, listening to Black
lecture her. She didn't argue because he had a valid point.
Knock! Knock! Knock!

"Oh, shit, someone's at the door." She was sure it was
the maid, since she'd moved to another room. She was
relieved, because she had had enough of his protective
speech anyway. "I'll call you right back," she said and
then disconnected the call from Black.

Bianca dashed over to the door, still in her boy shorts
and camisole tank top to match, her hair in a doobie,
wrapped under a Louis Vuitton scarf. She looked through
the peephole. "Who is it?"

"Me."

"Me, who?" she asked, grabbing a short satin robe to
put on, then opening the door. She was surprised by who
she saw standing on the other side of the door.

"Yes, sir, to what do I owe this visit—and don't you
know how to call?" she asked as she moved to the side
so that Fitz could come in. "Just so you know, normally
I don't answer the door for people who don't call. I know
you know it's super rude to just show up at people's door
all unannounced."

"For the record, I did call, but your room phone was
off the hook," he said. "Plus, I wanted to make a special
delivery to you." He handed her a bag.

"What's this?" she asked, gladly taking the Louis duffle
bag off of his hands.

"Your money, your ID, and a few more items that I
think are yours as well."

Before even saying thank you, she let off. "I knew you
sent your peoples to rob me." As she unzipped the bag
and saw all the cash inside, along with a plastic bag with
her ID, gum, and iPhone, a huge smile took over her face.

"Honestly, I didn't. I really didn't," he admitted with a
sincere face. "I don't operate like that."

"Then how do you explain this?" She pointed to the bag and pulled out the money.

"When you mentioned it, I investigated, and I am embarrassed to say one of my employees did it. And I'm not happy about it."

"So your employees running around here, taking ladies' purses and bags and shit, and you don't want to give me a job?" She shook her head. "You got some nerve," she said, but was then brought back to reality and shifted gears. "Let me say, I can't tell you how much I appreciate you for putting it in your heart to bring my money back," she admitted. "I can't front. I've been scrambling without it." She gave him a huge hug. He put his arms around her and embraced her back.

"So, now you have your money. You can definitely open you a little boutique or something like that. You don't need to sell no pills or do nothing illegal."

"Yeah, right," she said, rolling her eyes in the top of her head, shutting him down. "Thank you for the little ideas, but no boutique is going to satisfy my hunger or ambition. I want big bucks—no whammies!"

"Oh, yeah? Well, you have to start from somewhere. It's called building."

"Okay. You right." She shrugged him off, knowing good and well that this was a conversation they were not going to see eye to eye on, so she shifted it back to the matter at hand. "Look, thank you so much for bringing my money back. I totally, totally can't tell you how much of a blessing it is and is going to be. I appreciate last night and this." She lifted the bag that possessed the cash, shaking her head in appreciation. "This just really puts the icing on the cake."

"Happy I could make you smile," he said dryly.

"You really did. You know, it really is about being blessed to be a blessing to someone else."

"Good way to look at it. So, this is where you call home now?" He stood in the middle of the floor and looked around. "Nice for a Marriott, I guess."

"A'ight now, you about to get an invitation to the other side of the door with your wisecracks." She pointed to the door.

"No, listen. This isn't really a place a nice lady such as yourself should be."

"Well, since I have cash, don't worry. I'm going to get me a place."

"You're going to put all that money back under the bed, this time for the maid to take it?"

"No, for now, in the safe," she said to him as if it was no-brainer.

"Listen," he said on a serious note, "I have a place you can stay in until you find yourself the right place. It's a lovely beach condo, overlooks the ocean. Nice, clean, marble floors, gym in the building, pool, valet, security. Just a real nice look for a nice lady such as yourself."

"Thank you, but—"

He cut her off. "Listen, there's no need in giving an answer now. You can just think about it for now. It's definitely an option. Now get dressed. We need to be outta this hotel by about—" He looked at his watch. He was wearing a different timepiece today—"I can give you forty-five minutes. I will be waiting, so, baby, please don't have me waiting forever."

"Who said I was going anywhere with you?"

"Listen, come on now. Time is ticking. It's for your own good."

"My own good?" she questioned.

"Yes. I'm taking you to the gun range because you most certainly need it. Honey, you can't be taking a knife to a gunfight."

She let out a laugh. "Real funny. Ha ha ha!"

"Last night that bullshit-ass blade worked for you, and Lady Luck been on your side in a bigger way than most, but, baby, better to prepare and not need than need and not have."

Bianca couldn't say anything but "Okay," because Fitz was right.

He knew he had her where he wanted her. "I'll be in the lobby waiting."

When Bianca got out of the shower, she had three orders of business she had to take care of. First and foremost, she prayed and thanked God for bringing her money back to her, because that was the only way to explain a half a million dollars being returned back to her.

Secondly, she counted and secured the money into the safe in the closet. Thirdly, she called Black to tell him that she had ten grand that she was going to invest into helping him get some product, and she would meet up with him a little later to give him the money. He wanted to know the particulars, but she told him, "Look, Black, no questions asked. Just know, how you be having me, I got you."

As she got dressed, she thought, *Hell, the cartel business must be going really well, because Fitz had to be real bored to be hanging out with a little sassy-ass girl from Virginia.*

Whatever it was, inside, she was happy, because this was the part of Miami that she had always envisioned: living the glamorous life, eating the best food, drinking the finest wine, rolling in the hottest automobiles with the most powerful men in Miami—hell, maybe in the whole country. The roller coaster ride of Miami, with its twists and turns, was getting more intense by the second.

They two walked into a huge gun store, where everybody greeted Fitz and was happy to see him. He was led to his locker, which, when he opened it up, looked like the artillery from *Terminator* or some gangsta movie. Hell, what did she expect? After all, she was with a real life gangsta.

He purchased her a pair of ear coverings. "Here, honey. You are going to need these, and I will have someone bring you some eyewear as well. Have you ever shot a gun before?"

"No, I haven't," she admitted, secretly wishing she had.

"Fitz, how are things?" a guy greeted him.

"Going great. We have to get a nice piece for Ms. Bianca here."

"Well, we have some new stuff over here." He pointed to a case.

Bianca looked into the case.

"Baby, pick whichever you want."

"I can get the one that I really like?"

"Yes, baby. You can get any gun in here," Fitz said. He was a little preoccupied with talking to his one of his gun buddy friends.

"We have 22s, 25s and 380s here, some really nice ones," the salesman told her. "These are very popular with the ladies."

Bianca didn't respond to him.

"We even have them in pearl handles, and pink ones as well."

Bianca kept looking at the guns, until she decided on one that clicked with her spirit. "Okay, so that's it." She tapped on the glass of a gun that was in the case by itself.

"Are you sure?"

When the guy hesitated, she called out to Fitz. "Baby, I want this one," she confidently said.

Giving his homeboy dap and assuring him, Fitz said, "She can have whatever she wants." He walked up to see what she picked.

"She picked the TrackingPoint rifle."

When Fitz heard what she had chosen, a proud smile covered his face. He was definitely impressed that, having no knowledge at all of guns, she picked a powerful one.

"Are you trying to stop a person or a truck?" the guy asked.

"No, sweetie, it's fine. It packs a lot of power," Fitz informed her.

"I like power."

"Well, I got power for you." He grabbed the gun and boxes of ammo, then they headed toward the door and into the back of the store.

Before going down the stairs, he looked at her and placed the earmuffs over her ears. Once at the bottom of the stairs, she could smell the strong scent of gunpowder. Inside the range, there were a bunch of folks already shooting. Bianca and Fitz were greeted by the range master, who was in charge.

"Give me five minutes," he said to Fitz and then went to all of the patrons and whispered something in each one's ear. They all cleared out within minutes, so that Fitz and Bianca could have it to themselves.

Afterward, Fitz placed a target up, sending it on the string about one hundred feet away, and sending hers about fifty feet away.

"You ready, li'l mami?"

"Let me see what you got, big papi," she joked with her hand on her hip.

He placed his glasses over his eyes and proved he had the aim of a sharpshooter as he let it rip, bulls-eyeing every single shot.

"Oh, wow! Impressive!" She gave him a high five. "Yes, baby, yes!" Bianca looked at him, wearing black from head to toe, holding his black 40-caliber H&K P2000 handgun, noticing how sexy his physique was. She tried not to stare, but her body betrayed her. She hated that she could feel her thirstiness for his hotness. The way he gripped the pistol made her feel so protected and secure.

"Good job, honey!"

Though neither would admit it, Fitz felt the electricity between the two of them as well. He leaned in close to her, moved her earplugs to the side, and whispered in her ear in a sexy tone, "Baby, always know that I hit the target and the spot every single time."

"I'm not mad at that. I'm going to definitely give your props. I *always* give them when they are due."

He helped her getting aligned, holding her waist while being seductive in a flirty kind of way. "Now, assume the position like I showed you, and let her rip."

She did as she was told, studied the target, and then let off, hitting every one, just as he had.

"What?" He sat in shock. "Hell, naw!"

"Hell, yeah!" she said as a smile took over her beautiful face. Holding that gun in her hand made her feel invincible.

Fitz waited for the proof to come in, because he still couldn't believe it. Then, after grabbing the target and studying it with his own eyes, there was only one way to describe it: "Beginner's luck!" Fitz said it, but he was secretly more excited than she was. "My little fucking marksman!" He gave her high five. "Well, excuse me. I've created a marks-lady. My shooter! My shoota! This could go real good . . . or a *lot* of motherfuckers could be in a bunch of trouble." He was happy, boasting on Bianca's target practice. "You're a natural."

And just when he least expected it, she had to rub it in and go in for the kill. She leaned into him and seductively said back to him, "You hit the spot every time? Know this: I always hit the mark every single time."

"Well, we might be able to do something." He smacked her hard on her plump behind, wondering what the hell he had done, putting a pistol in the hands of a crazy chick with heart and hunger. He couldn't help but worry about who would fall victim to her aim.

He shook his head and said, "Lord, have mercy on Miami and the mayhem ahead."

CHAPTER 25

An urgent phone call caused Fitz to grab Bianca and bounce, with Bianca riding shotgun as Fitz bent corners like someone's life depended on it. He listened to old school Scarface the entire ride and turned down the music when they entered into the city morgue's parking lot.

"Why are we here?" she asked.

"I have to identify a body, that's all." The car fell silent. Like always, Bianca kept on her game face, but her heart began palpitating.

Fitz turned to her. "You can sit here in the car if you'd like, or sit in the waiting area if you want," he suggested. "This shit might be kind of too gruesome for you."

If he would've bet cash money on her, he knew what her answer was going to be. She said what he thought she would. "No, I will come with you. Even an iceman like yourself needs some kind of support," she said as compassionately as she knew how.

"Why, thank you," he said as he opened his door and quickly made his way around to hers.

They walked into the Dade County morgue, two of his security guys in tow. The building was air conditioned and extra cold. Their footsteps echoed on the marble floor.

"Hi," the cavalier medical examiner who met with them said. He shook both of their hands. He didn't look like someone who she thought would be working at the morgue. He looked to be fairly young, in his late twenties, with a dark, short crew cut. He wore a white lab coat and some black motorcycle boots.

"Wow. It was kind of funky gruesome," the flighty examiner said then looked to Fitz.

Bianca could tell that the examiner recognized exactly who Fitz was, and she immediately started to talk. "Is it at all possible to just please get this over with? You know, it's a hard time for everybody." She redirected his attention. "I'm sure you could imagine."

"I'm sure this is going to be hard on you," he said to Bianca in a friendly way, as if he knew her, and she just played along.

She took a deep breath as she got into character. "Do you know what happened to him?"

"Well, from my observation, he just bled out."

She sighed and dropped her head. "Lord, have mercy on his soul," Bianca said, with much empathy.

"Yeah, no substantial blows or beating." He looked to Bianca with sincerity as he continued to deliver the news. "Just the amputation of his hands, that's all, and he just bled himself to death."

She allowed tears to form in her eyes as the examiner searched her face. She knew that he was a little intimidated by Fitz, but Bianca's performance was so airtight that it made the examiner more comfortable with Fitz.

When they got to the huge room with white walls and bright fluorescent lights, he stopped by the desk and handed Bianca some tissues before heading over to a long wall with several doors in it. For an awkward moment, he stood there as if he were preparing to make a presentation. He opened the door and pulled out the stretcher with the lifeless body on it.

The moment of truth came.

The examiner slowly pulled back the sheet, and Bianca saw that it was Rocco. "Oh my God. It's him," Bianca said. She could sense the man wanted some kind of emotions, and she didn't cheat him of any as she fell into Fitz's arms. "Oh, why? Lord Jesus! Why? Nooooo . . . not him!"

An emotionless Fitz put his arms around her to try to console her. "It's going to be okay."

"The really sad part about it is, he would've lived had he not been tied down. It looks like he was tightly tied to a chair and could not run or get loose. I'm so sorry. I'm sure it was painful to him, because his life had to flash in front of him," said the examiner.

Her sobs grew louder and she uttered, "I'm just so glad I was able to get a babysitter for the kids." She sniffed, and a waterworks of tears started to pour out as she buried her head deeper into Fitz's chest.

"I'm sorry," the examiner said as he pushed Rocco back into his new resting place. Then he was quiet for a few minutes, feeling bad about adding the last bit of information and drama. "Now, I know I told you on the phone that I wasn't going to be able to get the property released until the other lady comes in, but I can get it for you if you like. It hasn't been officially logged in, and I know you said that there were some very important papers in it. Would you like to take it?"

"No," Fitz said, shooing it off.

"Yes, I will take it," Bianca spoke over Fitz, wiping her tears away, sneakily pinching Fitz in the arm to play along. "I would very much appreciate that," she managed to get out in between tears and sniffles.

"Yes, no problem." He left and returned with a big MCM backpack with studs on in it, and handed it to Bianca.

"Thank you so much," she said again, blowing her nose into the tissues then taking one of the straps and putting it on her shoulder. "Thank you so much for all your help."

He dropped his head. "My deepest, sincere condolences to you." He patted her on the back.

Fitz looked at the guy and said, "Thank you, too." He put his arm around Bianca's shoulder and escorted her out of the morgue and into the car.

Once inside the car, he said, "Damn, girl! I never knew you were an actress. I think I'm going to make some calls for you to get you some roles. My sister, who's deceased, had a lot of friends who were actresses."

She burst into laughter. "No, thanks. I'm not interested in being no struggling actress, and with black Hollywood not really working, please, that will definitely send me back to the store boosting," she said.

"With that performance you pulled back there, you'd definitely be able to be Hollywood's leading lady. I can't lie. I was impressed."

"Thank you." She paused. "But maybe I should be really saying thank you for . . ." She struggled with the words.

"Yes, what are you trying to say?"

"Umm, like, I can't believe you had Rocco, your right hand man, killed. His hands were cut off." She felt like this whole thing had been staged. This couldn't possibly be real, right?

With no remorse, he said, "That's what happens to thieves."

"But he was your man, your right hand."

"But he stole, and he was skimming money. He stole that money from you and never breathed a word about it—using my club as a backdrop to that larceny. And I found out he'd done it to some others, too, and I didn't really appreciate it."

"Why not fire him or make him pay it back?" she questioned. She recognized the irony, as she was a booster, which some may call a thief, but she never stole from anybody on a personal level.

"Because his behavior is unacceptable, and it's a little deeper than that."

"Look, I boost, but I never stole from a person—ever. I can't even front. I've gotten damn near every major store, but a person . . . naw, I don't do that."

He laughed. "That's way different. His sins have nothing to do with your hustle."

She nodded then reached for the backpack.

"Besides, you know he couldn't be around anymore anyway, especially since you are becoming a friend of mine. In fact, a special friend of mine."

"Really?"

"Yup! And why is that?

Bianca heard him loud and clear, but she was more into checking the backpack. "Who do you think called?" she asked.

"I'm not sure, but maybe one of his women."

She pulled out a T-shirt, some Polo boxers, a brush, some checks and gift cards, about $5,600 in cash, a do-rag, and a few more items. Once everything was out, the backpack still had something else inside. She just had to get to it. There was a hidden button that slid to the side when pressed, exposing the inside of the lining of the tricked-out backpack.

"Oh, shit!" It was dope inside. She pulled it out. "Oh la la, would you look at that." She smiled as she looked at the contents of the bag. She started dancing The Snake, in her seat. "Look what I recovered. Who's bad?" she said in her Michael Jackson voice.

Fitz looked over.

"You see how the other day you were saying that there was no room for a lady in your organization? See how a pretty face got you your work back, and look at this cash!"

"You did do that." He had to agree with her. "You can keep the cash and gift cards if there's anything on them. Buy yourself something nice. I'll take the work."

"No, I will take it."

"No, you have money that was returned to you, and cash here, and plus I will get you whatever you want. You are not starving for anything."

"Look, I'm independent. Always had my own hustle." She gazed into his eyes with a serious look. "Always got my own. I'ma need you to respect that. This here—" She pointed to the heroin—"You wasn't going to miss it or claim it. Ten minutes ago, it was about to be left in the hands of the medical examiner."

Fitz tried to cut Bianca off, but she wasn't having it. She kept talking. "Look, a'ight? We been going back and forth on this matter, and me getting some money from the very first day we met has always been the issue. So, let me see what I can do with this. If I mess up, I will never say anything to you again about my business. Okay?" She flashed her big, beautiful eyes at him.

Fitz smiled at how Bianca was always on her own money chase. Though he hated allowing women in the game, he had to respect her grind. At least she wasn't chasing some man's pocket or sucking dick and pushing pussy. She was out to get her own, and though he didn't like it, he really did respect it.

He took a deep breath. "Girl, you know you are a pistol, don't you? Not typically how I do business, though."

"I'm sure." She agreed with a smile. "But this right here, what we got, what we are building, isn't the typical kind of friendship you normally have, right?"

"Not at all." He had to agree, thinking about how from the day Bianca met him, she had never walked on eggshells around him, like most everybody else whose path he had crossed. She had to know that he was the most powerful and treacherous man north of the Equator and that his father was "the" Señor Manuella of Peru, and that neither one played popcorn games. They'd have a bitch killed at the flip of a dime. Maybe she didn't know. Or maybe she did, and she just didn't care.

"Well, we should be able to do something then, right?"

He nodded. "Go ahead."

Bianca was shocked. "You for real?" she questioned.

"Yeah, but always know that fair exchange is never robbery."

"I know."

"I'd like the opportunity to take you on a real date. I haven't had a real date in a long time. If I suck at it or fuck up, I won't press you again."

"Normally, I don't really mix business with pleasure. I've always felt like either we are going to get money together or we're going to fuck. You do your thing and I do mines. But since you seem to be a special kind of character, I guess I can make you the exception to my rule," she said.

"Well, this one time, I can make you the exception to my rule too." He nodded. "Go ahead and take it."

She leaned in to the driver's side of the car, letting her cleavage be exposed to him, and kissed him on the cheek. "Thank you, babe! I promise I won't disappoint you."

CHAPTER 26

Fitz dropped her off, and now she had so much work to do. Immediately, she gave Black the work and, as she promised him, the shop was opened. Black dumped the work in the streets quick and had the money together. In the meantime, she got a small beachfront apartment and moved in.

She had finally caught up with Viper and was now about to head to his house and pay him back the money that she owed him from bailing her out. When she wasn't too far away, Fitz called her. He'd already informed her that their date would be this afternoon.

"Can be ready at two p.m. sharp?" he questioned.

"Just have one errand I need to run, so if you could pick me up in about an hour, that's cool. I just have to go pay my friend back for doing me a favor. As soon as I swing by there, I can meet up with you. I have money for you too."

"Really? Just wait until you have all of it, and then I will get it from you."

"No, I do."

"Really?" he asked.

"Yes. Told you I be about my business," she said as she parked in front of Viper's building.

"Okay, but I wasn't calling for that. I was calling to make good on our date."

"Looking forward to it. See you in an hour?"

"One hour. I will call you," he said before disconnecting the call.

***

The building was a swank high rise that looked over Biscayne Bay. The doorman had been expecting her and said she could go right up. She took the elevator to the tenth floor. Apartment 1007 was the fourth door on the left. No one answered when she knocked, which was odd, because Viper knew that she was coming. She tried the knob to see if the door was locked. It wasn't, so she let herself in, hoping that he didn't have company.

The apartment opened up to a wide foyer, which led to an expensively furnished living room and an open kitchen with all new stainless steel appliances set straight off to the left. She heard music coming from the den, apparently his man cave, further down the hallway.

"Viperrrrr."

He didn't answer when she called his name. Bianca rolled her eyes. She had told him over the phone just twenty minutes ago that she would be in a hurry and needed to be in and out.

"Hellooooo! Big brotherrrr!" she called, because she didn't want no problems for him or herself, being that Viper was probably getting better acquainted with one of his hoes that he claimed he didn't have.

She and Viper had grown to be friends, like brother and sister, so Viper's sex life didn't bother her, unless one of those chicks was trying to get over on him. That was a different story, but Viper was a big boy and was more than capable of taking care of himself. Until he wasn't.

When Bianca stepped into the man cave, she found Viper alone. "Shit!" She ran to his side.

He was sprawled on the floor, butterball naked and unconscious—or was he dead?

"Fuuuuuuck!" she screamed as her heart dropped. "Nooooo!"

Bianca went into her purse to get her phone to call the ambulance, but then she spotted a needle on the floor.

"Got-damn! Don't tell me this nigga shooting up!" She took a deep breath, trying to figure out what to do.

Let me see if this nigga dead or alive first.

She grabbed her mirrored compact and put it under his nose to see if he was breathing. She wasn't sure, but she thought she saw his nostrils moving. She reached for his wrist and he had a weak pulse.

Thank God. Okay, so he's alive!

"God, please, help me! Viper, please, baby, don't die on me."

She didn't want to call the police for Viper to get a drug charge, so she grabbed her phone and Googled "drug overdose." The service was moving super slow, maybe because of the building.

"Shit! Shit!" she screamed in a panicked voice and ran to the kitchen to his freezer. She opened it up and grabbed the ice bucket out of it. She went and poured it on his balls. She didn't know where she had heard it from, or what movie she had seen it in, but she did it. She kept putting the ice on him and calling his name. "Viper! Viper! Please! Please! Come back! Come back! God, help me! Help Viper!" she cried out.

By now, her Google search had come up and she skimmed through it. One site instructed her to keep hitting his chest, and she kept desperately pumping his chest and putting the ice on his testicles like there was no tomorrow. She really didn't know what else to do.

Breathing hard, feeling beads of perspiration from anxiety on working so hard at trying to bring him back, Bianca knew that she didn't have much time to play with. Her heart was pounding with each pump she did on Viper's chest. He had foam running out of his mouth, and she didn't want to do mouth-to-mouth resuscitation if she didn't have to. She really had never taken CPR classes, so she didn't want to make things worse. Her last resort was to call 911 to get the help, but she knew he might get a drug charge and the police might search his place. The shit she was doing clearly wasn't working, and the last thing she wanted to do was see him in jail, but at the same time, she'd never forgive herself if he died on her watch.

It went without saying that she'd rather see him in jail than dead any day. She took a deep breath and decided to try one more time, and if it didn't work, she was left no choice but to call for help.

More ice, more rubbing his chest, and more praying and begging to God.

His eyes sprang open and he popped up. "Fuck my inhaler at?" he asked.

"Oh my God! Thank you, Jesus!" Bianca said with a sigh of relief and immediately looked around until her eyes caught sight of his inhaler. She grabbed it and handed it to him.

He took it from her hand and was sluggish for a few seconds as he used his inhaler. She sat down on the floor beside him then closed her eyes, counting his blessing for him.

"Where the hell my money at?" he abruptly asked.

"Nigga . . . " She turned her nose up at him. "I just saved your fucking life, and not to mention your punk ass gave me the scare of *my* fucking life, and all you can ask me about is your money?" She shook her head and then bopped him upside the head "And cover that shit up." She pointed to his long, medium-sized penis. It wasn't too big, but it wasn't nothing to play with either.

He laughed at her. "Man, go grab my robe for me. I'm still the patient." She got up and went to his bathroom to get his robe. He called out to her, "And grab yourself a cooler or a beer out of the fridge. Shit, yo ass need it."

Bianca threw him the robe as she dropped some towels on the floor to get the melted ice up. She handed him the Corona so he could open it up for her. "I don't even drink this shit, but you got me drinking it though." She rolled her eyes at him.

Viper passed the opened bottle back to her and scooted closer. He put his arm around her, looked her in the eyes, and said to her, "You are truly my li'l sister, you know that?" Then he kissed her on the cheek.

She was quiet for a second. "Sweet, but I decline."

"How do you decline?" he asked.

"Because I never had a brother before, and all my life I wished I had one to protect me."

"Well, you got one now."

"See, my expectations of my big brother are tall, and if you high and using all the time, then how you going to protect me? And if you die, then what?" She shook her head. "I honestly can't take no more heartaches and pains. You would think after everything I've been through in my life that I would be immune to it, but not quite." She zoned off and looked into space, trying not to think of the things that had hurt her. She almost didn't want to risk her heart and suffer any more losses. She'd already lost too much.

"Look, I'm not going anywhere. I'm going to be here for you."

"Man, why you gotta do that shit?" She pointed to the needle on the floor, shaking her head in distaste. As much as she'd been through, she was not an addict.

"Just my demons, that's all," he said.

"What demons could you possibly have that would drive you to this? I mean, you have a really nice place, which symbolizes you do okay for yourself, and you had thirty-five hundred dollars at your disposal to come and get me out on bail. Doesn't seem like you hurting for it, because you didn't call me one time to pay you."

"Yeah, I do have a good life. I can't complain. But it's not this life; it's my past life that's so filled with demons."

"Okay, so if I'm going to be your sister, it's a no-judgment zone. After all, I do some real crazy shit, and I don't want you judging me either. So, with that being said, you gotta confide in me," she said.

"These demons are heavy."

"Trust me, I'm sure they're not as heavy as mine. Why you think I came here? To run away from mine."

The truth of the matter was that now, reflecting on everything that had happened with Peanut, she knew that if she had stayed and faced the music and had gotten a good lawyer, she could probably beat the murder charges on her baby. The real thing that she didn't want to face was finally having to face her abuse. It was just too painful to try to tackle such a traumatic experience that she had held in and had harbored deep in the pit of her stomach and in the back of her mind for so long. It was so much easier to avoid and act as if it didn't happen than to face it. It was just easier for her to leave. Bianca knew in her heart of hearts that she would eventually prevail, but the pain . . . well, that was another story.

She wasn't ready to deal with her hurt now, still, but she knew one day in the near future, she would be.

"What demons could drive you to this? We are siblings now. We must learn to trust each other," she said.

Viper thought deep and hard. "Yo, this shit is so fucked up. I never told nobody this shit. Nobody!" he said as he stared off.

Bianca just sat and waited patiently.

"Look, it's like this. . . . A'ight . . . " He tried to fix his words and search for the right ones to convey. "I'm just going to keep it real with you. No judging."

"No judging." She reached for his hand to give him comfort.

"Look, it's like this. I used to get a whole lot of money. I mean *money*, money—like kingpin-status money. No bullshit."

"I believe that."

"So when a nigga getting stupid, ridiculous money, it gives him all kinds of options in every which a way—like countless options, countless bitches, just whatever a nigga want. Just options! Whatever a nigga want, think he want, or don't want."

"Right," she agreed.

"So, I had this amazingly beautiful woman, who I loved with all of my heart. I swear I got up every day and hustled for her so she could do whatever she wanted. She came from money out the gate, but I took care of her so she could have independence from her family. And it was her family which I was in business with. I loved her, and I know people say there is no perfect person, but she . . ." He nodded. "She was perfect." Viper took a puff of his inhaler.

Bianca wanted to ask questions about her, but her gut told her to just listen, because at that moment, Viper needed a sympathetic ear.

"She was just beautiful and gorgeous in every which way. Did you go into my room?"

"No." She shook her head.

"I still to this day have a beautiful picture of her hanging on my wall. I don't care who I'm with. I will never take it down."

"Come on, now," she said. "We going to work on that, but go ahead."

"She made all of my wrongdoings in the street right. She took my dirty money and made it clean by doing right by the children and doing work in the community. Just an all-out good soul."

"So what happened to her?" Bianca asked.

Viper was silent for a few beats, and then he shook his head. Bianca looked at him with much compassion, and then he spoke. "With having so many options, I don't know. . . . One night, my girl was out of the country, one of those fashion weeks—I think Paris." He stared off into space.

Bianca just waited for him to continue.

"So, I was out drinking, drunk as a skunk, horny as fuck, and I met this girl. We got a room, and she gave the most amazing head. Best head I ever had in my life. The sex was out of this world."

"Okay," Bianca said. "All men cheat. What's new?"

"Didn't have any indications it was a guy until the next morning, when I walked in and he was in the shower."

"Get the fuck outta here!" She was stunned.

"I said the same shit too."

"What did you do?"

"I dragged that nigga out of the shower and beat the living shit outta his ass."

"God damn, brother. But how you didn't know?" she questioned.

"'Cause he put my dick in, and I was drunk, and he just got away with that shit. Long story short, I liked it."

"So you're bi now?" she questioned.

"That's another story."

"Well, that's different, but a lot of people are."

"But you haven't heard the worst," he said.

"I'm listening."

"So, shit got crazy. I started working with her brothers, and I was getting so much money. Way more than I was getting before, which allowed her to travel around the world with no limits. Me and her brother worked hand in hand, and one night we used X, and then we started fucking around."

"What? You mean . . . ?"

"Yup! You heard me! Shit got cold-blooded!"

Bianca sat in disbelief as Viper told her the rest of the story about how the girl ended up dead. It was like something from a movie or a book.

She gave him a hug. "Brother, well, it's a lot, but you must face your demons, as you call them. You can't keep using drugs to escape everything. You need counseling, like some real intensive therapy, as well as rehab, because you, too, are running from your demons."

"You're right." He nodded.

"I know you a hardcore kind of guy and think help and therapy is a joke, but it really works."

"You speaking from experience?"

"Shiiiiit! Hell, naw! I need it too." She laughed. "I do need therapy to work through my family issues. I really do," she admitted.

"So you going to share your demons after I done gave you my deepest, darkest secrets?"

"Next time. I promise, next time!" She got up and looked at her phone. "I hate to break this up, but I got a date. Remember how I told you I had to be in and out? We've been here for two hours now."

"A date with who, sis? You know I gotta approve."

"Well, I will tell you everything next time. I'm massively late now! I enjoyed the bonding time, but I gotta go, big brother." She kissed him on the cheek and headed out.

"You know I owe you."

"One word—five letters!" she said as she left out of the door. "Rehab!"

CHAPTER 27

As soon as Bianca left Viper's house, Fitz called.

"Hi, honey." She was extra nice because she knew that she was extra late.

"I been calling you. Is everything all right?"

"Yes, just had the scare of my life. Went to my friend's house and he had OD'ed and all this craziness. Had to put ice on his balls, and then we had a heart-to-heart. You know, just another day in my world."

"Really?"

"Yup, so, baby, please forgive me. I had to save a life. You know that's the only reason why I would be late when it's concerning you," she joked.

"Stroking my ego will get you everywhere," he joked back.

"I'm gon' keep that in mind."

"So, where are we off to? What should I wear? What do you have planned?"

"Nice sundress and bathing suit."

"I can handle that."

"How long before you'll be to the hotel? I'm here waiting," he said.

"No, honey, I moved. Let me give you the new address."

"Oh, you moved, huh?"

"Yes, nothing big, just a little place so I don't have to live in the Marriott anymore. Can you pick me up from there in like thirty minutes?"

"Yes."

***

Fitz was impressed at how in a week's time, Bianca had pulled herself and everything together. She had gotten a place, a cute BMW, and had his money straight. "You are a real go-getter. I can't lie. I did underestimate you."

"Most people do."

"Well, I won't." He kissed her on the cheek as he drove to Key Biscayne, where he parked his car and they boarded a seaplane. "I wanted you to see how beautiful the coast and the water is, so I thought I'd take you to have some conch in that little place I told you about in the Bahamas."

She put the headphones on and enjoyed the ride to a little private island down in the Bahamas. They circled the island to get a better view of the huge house that, from the air, looked to be shaped as a letter *M*. There was an infinity pool, crisp white sand on the beaches that bordered the island, and a man-made dock that led out into the water with several boats, including a huge yacht. The smaller guest houses that surrounded the main house were beautiful too.

"Oh my goodness, look at the beautiful lighthouse," she said.

"You mean the watchtower," he corrected her. "But lighthouse, watchtower, whatever you wanna call it, baby. We can go up there if you want to get you some beautiful pictures."

"Wow! Is this where we are going?"

"Yes!"

"OMG!" It was definitely hard for her to keep her composure.

"This is where I go for the best conch in all of the Bahamas."

Once the plane landed on the island, they were greeted by a warm Spanish man wearing a soft pink polo shirt, some khaki shorts, and brown leather flip-flops. He gave

Fitz a hug. "Looking good, son! I see what this glow over you is all about." He smiled.

"Papi, this is Bianca. Bianca, this is my pops."

She smiled as he kissed Bianca on both cheeks.

"Welcome to my home, beautiful Bianca."

"Why, thank you for having me, and what a beautiful home you have."

"Thank you. So, you are the reason my son is smiling." Before she could answer, he continued, "I met this gorgeous lady named Bianca about thirty odd years ago, when I was young and handsome."

"As you still are," she added.

"Son, you gotta keep this girl around. She's special, you know."

"I know, Papi."

"Aw, thank you."

"You do know you are special, don't you?" he said and she blushed. "Anytime he brings you here to meet me, you are a special lady. You know the last time my boy brought a little lady home to me?"

Bianca raised an eyebrow, knowing that his father was going to tell it.

"He was about . . ." He looked up as if he was thinking. "He was about fourteen years old, and he told me he was in love with this girl and was going to marry her." Señor Manuella started to laugh.

"What happened?" Bianca asked as an older lady wearing a traditional maid outfit came and presented Fitz with a drink in a coconut. He took one and passed it to Bianca.

"Thank you, Magda," he said to the housekeeper then looked to Bianca. "Try these. These are legendary. They are so delicious."

Bianca took a sip. "Mmmm. Yes, it *is* good!" she complimented, then focused her attention back on Papi. "So, what happened?"

"She broke his heart."

"Oh, no!"

"Yes, she started liking his best friend, and that, my dear, was the last time he brought a lady home to meet me."

"Are you kidding?" Bianca was surprised.

"Sad but true." Papi nodded. "But now you are here, with me, and I had to promise that I would not talk too much and that I would not pull out his pictures from when he was a little boy."

"Okay." She smiled.

"So, the best conch comes out of my ocean out here, and out of my kitchen. We eat dinner at around eight p.m. In the meantime, please make yourself at home. Mi casa es su casa." He turned to Fitz and said, "Give her a tour of the place."

"Yes, sir, I will," he assured his father as Papi raised up from the table and kissed her on the cheek. "If he isn't good to you, you call me."

"I will. Thank you so much," she said, and butterflies fluttered around her stomach. This couldn't be real. She had entered into another world, another dimension, and the one thing she was sure about was that she didn't want to leave.

"Come on, babe," he said as he grabbed her hand.

Magda was walking toward them. "Everything is prepared in your quarters, just the way you like it, as well as how I think for you," she said in broken English with a thick Spanish accent.

"Gracias," he said to her.

"You speak Spanish?" Bianca questioned.

"Yes, but I requested that while you were here, everyone speak English, because I didn't want you to feel out of place."

"Thank you, baby. How sweet."

"Told you I was going to be nice to you."

"You did."

Someone rolled up in a tricked-out golf cart and hopped out. "Mr. Fitz, here you are."

"Thanks," he said to the groundsman. "It's so much easier to do the tour of the island by golf cart," he said as they hopped on.

The island looked like a resort, and the staff was deep. Once he got to his quarters, she saw that it was a huge house too, which had to be about 10,000 square feet.

"This is my house, where we will be staying," he said. "My dad insisted that he build me this house when I turned sixteen. He says every man needs his own house. I think he just got tired of me throwing wild parties at his house," he joked.

As he opened the door, she was greeted by a huge bouquet of six feet tall long-stem roses. "Oh, how beautiful." She smelled them. "For moi?"

He nodded. "Of course."

"You are so thoughtful."

"You make me want to make you happy," he told her. "Change into your swimsuit so we can get some sun, snorkeling, jet skiing, whatever you want before we prepare for dinner."

"I want it all," she said and spun around.

"You can have whatever your heart desires, if you continue to be everything you've been."

After they both were in their swimsuits, Papi approached. "I have to take picture of you two. This is a moment to remember. My boy smiling, happy, courting a beautiful lady." He smiled and kept talking, a little under his breath. "Who knows? I may have a grandbaby soon."

"Papi, stop. Cut it out. It's only our first real, official date."

"It only takes one date to fall in love if chemistry and feelings are there. It's okay, son," Papi said as he took a few pictures and looked at them. "One more, and smile. Your madre needs to see this big smile on your face."

"Papi, come on. Don't send that to Mami. She's going to jump to conclusions and start to ask me questions every day."

"I have to. She worries about you. She does. She calls me every week. 'When will Fitz find love? There has to be something more to this life than business.'" He mocked Fitz's mother. "I have to send this picture to get her off of my back, son."

"Okay, so to get her off your back, you going to put her on my back?"

"Yes," he admitted.

"Okay, Papi, take this." Fitz grabbed Bianca, leaned her over his arms, and blessed her with a long tongue kiss.

Bianca's face turned red from the embarrassment, but she secretly loved every moment of it.

"You happy now?" Fitz said.

"Yes, and I'm sure your madre will be, too."

"So your father and your mother are not together still?" Bianca asked.

"No, they're not, but they are very close friends. The situation is very complicated. I will share it with you one day." He didn't bother giving Bianca the story of how Señor Manuella had adopted him and raised him as his own. In fact, he didn't talk about it to anybody. But most likely, one day, he'd share it with her.

"Okay, sounds good, but it does seem like they love you so much. Especially your father."

"Yes, I'm his only child. I did have a brother and a sister. They were twins. Both are no longer with us. We had the same mother, but I had a different father than they did."

"So sorry to hear that," she said.

"Yeah, me and my brother were never close. But my sister . . . I loved her with all my heart. She was my baby. There was nothing I wouldn't do for her," he said, letting his mind drift to thoughts of Annalise.

"Your father's not what I thought he'd be."

"What do you mean?"

"When we were at dinner the other night, you spoke about him as if he was a tough businessman who only wanted you to work."

"Well, he is, and he is indeed a shrewd businessman who doesn't fuck around by any means. But now he's older, and through everything, he has always wanted nothing but the best for me," Fitz said.

"Well, I adore your father. He's so kind and cool, and he seems like he likes me."

"He does."

They spent the rest of the day just lying on the beach, chatting and enjoying getting to know each other. Every second around Fitz made her fall deeper and harder for him.

Dinner went off without a hitch. It was the best dinner she had ever had, and the company and conversation were even better. A mixture of too much red wine and the sheer thrill of excitement caused Bianca to doze off to sleep.

CHAPTER 28

Waking up in the middle of the night, in Fitz's, strong, muscular arms, had to be the most amazing feeling. So she thought, anyway. She would've liked to get up and jump in the shower, but she didn't want to move out of her comfort zone.

The second he realized she was up, he asked in a whisper, "Are you okay?"

"Yes, in your arms, it makes everything okay."

"Is that you or the wine talking?" he asked, running his fingers through her hair.

"All me, baby," she said. Then she moved in closer to him to inadvertently back her butt on his manhood, and as she did, she felt it was hard as wood. *Good God*, she thought to herself.

"Why are you teasing me?" he asked, beginning to massage her shoulder.

"No tease here." She grinded a little bit against him.

"I don't think you are ready."

"Maybe it's you that's not ready."

"You know you are going to be mine," he said in her ear as he began to rub her legs.

A flame of fire began to light under her. There was passion and anxiousness that she couldn't control. As bad as she wanted to turn the heat down, there was no way that she could. Before he could even touch her again, she was on fire.

Fitz's touch was like butter, melting her as he ran his
fingers over her body and gently licked on her nipples,
making his may his way down toward her secret place.
When he touched it, it was like Niagara Falls, so wet and
juicy.

He gently caressed her clit with his lips as his tongue
circulated around it. He kindly pushed her legs toward
her stomach and inserted his tongue into her waterfall,
before softly going in and out of the coochie with his
tongue, prompting her to climb the walls.

"Don't run," he quietly said, bringing her back to him.
He continued licking her with such pride and passion,
every which way, driving her crazy, immediately sending
her into an orgasm. The way he used his tongue, it felt so
good that it brought tears to her eyes. All she could think
about was pleasing him, and she did.

Bianca had never had this kind of passion and arousal
before. All she wanted to do was jump on top of him and
ride him. The sex was perfect and incredible, and the best
thing about it was that she had not taken a pill or a drug,
yet this man had her in ecstasy.

They went on for the next hour, until the sheets were
wet and they both were worn out, spent. They fell off to
sleep in each other's arms.

CHAPTER 29

The next morning, they were both awakened by his phone vibrating. He rolled over and looked at his phone. He sat up in the bed. "Oh, shit!" he said.

She turned over. "What is it, baby?"

"Nothing to worry your pretty face about. I just need to go take this call in the other room."

"Okay. Will you pass me my phone too?"

He handed Bianca her phone so she could check her messages. Of course, one was from Black, checking on her, and then another from Viper, telling her he was going to go to rehab. She smiled when she saw his message.

Meanwhile, in the bathroom, Fitz was on the phone with his mother. "Where did you get that from, Mommy?" Fitz grilled his mother as he whispered into the phone, pacing back and forth.

Fitz sat on the edge of the tub in the huge marble bathroom. His mother had just sent him a picture of a sleeping Bianca, informing him that Caesar had sent that to her some weeks ago. He'd always suspected that his mother was sneaking behind his back, talking to Caesar, even though she said she had not.

"I told you that he had a woman that he was in love with."

Fitz was messed up for a minute, but now what could he do? He had fallen hard for Bianca himself, and, on another note, he could really understand how Caesar could love this girl so much. She was an amazing lady.

What he did know was that he no longer had a brother. In his eyes, Caesar was dead to him and had been buried back at that cemetery with his sister. The fact of the matter was that Caesar may have cared deeply for Bianca, but he was willing to bet his life that Caesar would never, or could never, love Bianca like he could.

He pulled himself together and exited the bathroom. It didn't bother him that this may have been his brother's woman. She had told him she had been in love with someone, but they were separated for complicated reasons now that she was in Florida. He just hadn't known it was his brother.

"Is everything okay?" she asked, noticing that something just didn't seem right.

"Yes! It is! In fact, better than okay. What are you smiling about?" Fitz asked Bianca as he got back under the covers with her and took her into his arms.

"Just happy that my homeboy, the one I told you about yesterday—"

"Yeah, the one you brought back from the OD?"

"Yes. He's checking himself into rehab. I'm so glad. He really almost let the dope addiction kill him."

"Well, why you didn't just call the ambulance?" he asked.

"Babe, that was going to be my last resort. I know if I would've called the ambulance, they would've filed a report, or the hospital would have, and he would've gone to jail."

"Good point."

"But literally, like, five seconds before I was about to give up, he came around. But I was thinking, I'm sure he would have rather be convicted by twelve than carried by six, that's for sure."

Fitz chuckled, looking at Bianca, thinking how beautiful she was and how things could go so well for the two of them in the future. He liked everything about her, and he wanted her to be his. He asked, "What's that nigga story? I don't want you around them people."

"He just got demons, and they are cold-blooded, too."

"Man, what kind of demons make you put that shit in your arm?" Fitz said, not having any sympathy at all.

"Well, his was big time," she said.

"They usually are."

"I'm going to make a long story short."

"Please do," he said.

"Well, V, he got a lot of money, was madly in love with his woman," she started.

"Typical shit."

"Then he started messing with her brother, who he was getting a bunch of money with. One day, they fucking—"

"Chicks?"

"No, each other!"

"Mm-hmm. It happens," he said.

"And the sister comes in and catches them in the act, goes plum crazy, threatens to expose the brother. And the brother just kills her."

Fitz was speechless. She was waiting for a response, but there was silence. He said nothing. Nada. Not a word.

"Babe, did you hear me?"

"Yeah, you said what?"

"I said the brother killed the sister, and my boy been carrying around the guilt for all these years, trying to conceal his pain and guilt with the drugs. But anyway, he's going to rehab. He said that he found a program that will have a bed available in the next forty-eight hours, and I'm welcome to stay at his place if I want. It's a whole lot nicer than the apartment I rented."

Fitz shook his head. "You not staying at his place. You moving in with me when we get back."

"Umm, I hear you, but I don't know. I have my own spot now, and I'm trying to stand on my own two feet," she told him.

"Listen, before you say anything, I want this to be serious. I'm going to get you a nice-ass promise ring, and I'm promising you that I'm going to be different than the rest. I'm going to be committed to you, and we going to work to make this whole relationship official. Baby steps, I know, right? But I just want to be with you. To be around you, to spoil you, to build with you, to live with you, to grow with you and love you."

It warmed her heart to hear that someone like Fitz could really love her and want all these things with her. "Look, I want these things too, but I must get closure first from my past relationship," she said.

"What relationship?" he asked abruptly. She noticed he had a weird look on his face.

"The one I had in Virginia. Remember, I told you about it?"

"Yeah, I know all about it. You call that a relationship?" he said.

"Yes, we were very much in love before I moved here."

He sucked his teeth. "Are you serious? I mean fucking *serious*?" he snapped.

"Yes!" Now she was getting pissed.

"You can't be fucking serious," he said with a chuckle.

Bianca was in shock. She was dumbfounded, and she had no type of understanding as to why Fitz's entire demeanor had changed. "What are you talking about?" she finally had to ask.

"You really don't know?" He answered her question with a question.

"No, I don't." She glared at Fitz.

"I just don't understand. How can you possibly consider a relationship with a man who is fucking gay?"

"Huh? What are you talking about?"

"Your man, Caesar, he's a fucking punk-ass nigga. He's gay. Been undercover in the closet his whole entire life."

"What?" Bianca said, her mouth gaping open. "Why do you wanna lie about him? You don't even know him!"

At that point, Fitz broke it all down to her, about how Papi had sent the picture of the two of them from yesterday to his mother, and then she had sent back a picture of Caesar with Bianca.

"Babe," he said, "Caesar is my brother. And you . . . you were the only woman that nigga ever been with in his life," Fitz let out. "There, if you didn't know, now you do, and furthermore," he went in, "that nigga is a fucking pussy. He's soft in every aspect. I'm not hating, just giving you the real deal shit. He's never going to protect you from harm, hurt, or danger. Get in trouble, watch how that nigga flee." He said it with such fiery malice.

Bianca burst into tears. His words were like sharp daggers that went through her heart. She sobbed, and when Fitz saw her tears, it tore him up to see her falling apart. Fitz felt awful and helpless that he had spilled the beans. He immediately took her in his arms, realizing he had really hurt her feelings. "Baby, my apologies, but I had to be real with you, always. I just gotta be!" He wiped her tears away as they flowed endlessly down her face. "I know the truth hurt. I know it do." He did his best to console her from the blow he had just delivered.

Bianca was trying to figure out if it was the words, or the truth of the matter that hurt most. In her heart, she knew that Fitz was right. It all added up. The anal sex all the time, him needing the Mollies and Ecstasy just to perform and have sex with her, and rarely ever having any vaginal sex. How had she not put it all together? Indeed, love was blind. Why would Caesar do her like that?

She shook her head, angry, mad, and disappointed, knowing it was true that everybody played the fool sometimes, but it hurt like hell that she wasn't the exception to the rule.

CHAPTER 30

The news that Fitz had delivered knocked the wind out of her. The hardest part was pretending to be okay around Papi and the rest of the staff. Fitz and Bianca laid out at the pool for the reminder of the day. Though he held her hand, there was silence for the most part between the two. Both were in deep thought.

Bianca thought about the way Fitz made love to her. It was indeed mind blowing, and the intimacy and passion that they had shared was nothing she had ever felt from Caesar. She was confused. How could this have gotten past her? Was something wrong with her? Was she falling off of her game? Could she even trust her judgment now?

Fitz didn't want to leave the island, because at least he was there with her, and he knew she couldn't run away from him there. Once back in Miami, it wasn't a real lock. He felt she could disappear and he'd never hear from her again. But, at the same time, he had some unfinished business to take care of, and he needed to get back.

Fitz noticed her deep in thought, and he went and put his arms around her. "I know you are doing so much soul searching, and you are questioning your judgment and you're unsure of everything, but rest assured. The one thing you can be sure of is this . . . with me, with us. It's real! I give you my word." He looked her dead in the eye and gave her a tongue kiss that almost took the breath out of her.

And that's all it took to convince her. Intense passion like that didn't come along every day, that's for sure!

Once the two set their feet back on Miami soil, they kissed and went their separate ways. Fitz said he had something to do, but he promised to be back home to her by dinner.

Meanwhile, she was just arriving to Viper's house to see him off to rehab when Fitz called to check on her. She entered Viper's apartment and sat on the couch to talk to him while Viper was in his room, packing.

"So, tomorrow, we're going to get promise rings," he said.

"You sound kind of excited."

"I am," he said. "I never did anything like this before, and though I was taught to never wear my heart on my sleeve, I do trust you with my heart."

She heard a voice in the background. "Flight 643 to Richmond, Virginia." And then the phone went dead.

What the fuck? She tried to call Fitz back at least ten times. Each time, it went straight to voice mail. She sat, trying to put things together, then Viper called out to her.

"Hey, sis."

"Yes," she said, making her way to his bedroom.

"Look, come get this key and this shit for me."

She entered his room, and what was staring at her stopped her dead in her tracks. "What the *fuck*?" she uttered in disbelief. She was astonished. Frozen in space, she couldn't move. Her feet felt like concrete blocks as she stared up at the big, Mona Lisa–style picture looking back at her.

"Oh my God!"

"Isn't Annalise beautiful?"

She was in shock, because though it was Annalise in the picture, she was the spitting image of Caesar, just with hair and makeup. She looked just like him.

"Um, I have to go," she said in a strangled tone as she backed out of the bedroom. She ran out of the building, into her car, then drove straight home. As she raced across the Causeway, everything was coming together.

The second she got home, she threw a few things in a duffle bag, along with some cash, and booked herself on the next thing smoking to Richmond. She was about to get to the bottom of this.

CHAPTER 31

Glen Allen, Virginia

A black-on-black Maserati, running 25 miles per hour above the speed limit, hooked a hard right off West Broad onto Pump Road. It had been raining, so the roads were slick, but the low-profile tires on the sports car hugged the pavement as if the two were reunited lovers, refusing to release its hold.

Caesar had a relentless need for speed, and he appreciated the way the Maserati performed under his skillful touch, obeying his every command. Few things in life made him feel more alive than going fast. Whether in a car or on a bike, it didn't matter, as long as it moved fast and he was the one in control. Along with a being a speed freak, Caesar was also a control freak.

Everything had to be his way or no way—his sexual relations, the food he ate, in business, and at play. Everything. The only thing in Caesar's life that he didn't have a snowball's chance in hell of controlling was his brother, Fitz.

That needs to change, he thought as he turned onto Snow Peak Lane. A touch of an app on his phone screen raised the garage door. The Maserati settled in between a cocaine-white Rolls and a crimson-pearl Bentley coupe. Adjacent to the garage was a $1.1 million hideaway pad, which he shared with Tracey, one of his many lovers. Since being exiled from Miami by Fitz, and since Bianca moved away to his old stomping grounds, a lot of things had changed for the better. This was now his home away from home.

Yet, today, something felt off. He'd used the kitchen entrance, and although nothing seemed out of place, he felt a pain in his stomach the second he walked in. Was it paranoia or a gut feeling? Either way, whatever it was, he felt uneasy. And where the fuck was Tracey?

He shouted, "Traceyyyy!" A few beats went by.

No answer.

"Trae, baby?" He called out again.

A couple of beats later, he heard a familiar voice say, "Tracey is no longer with us." The voice came from the living room.

But how the hell did he find me? Caesar thought. *And better yet, why is he looking?*

Fitz waltzed into the kitchen with an arrogant half-grin on his face. "I bet you're wondering how I found your bitch ass."

It wasn't like he was hiding from his brother. Caesar had just chosen not to let him, or anyone in the family, know where he was staying.

Fitz looked at Caesar in disgust. Caesar grabbed a vase and threw it at him.

Fitz stepped to the left and laughed. "You still a pussy-ass nigga. When are you going to ever get some balls?" Fitz asked Caesar.

Caesar just glared at his brother. "What the fuck do you want? Why are you here?"

Fitz ignored the question. "Oh, but you did finally get the gumption about yourself. You out of the closet, living with a flaming-ass gay man." He shook his head.

"You would never let me do it in Miami."

"Me?" Fitz pointed to his own chest. "I wouldn't let you? Now, how does that measure out? I wouldn't let you be gay in Miami? One of the places where damn near anything goes?"

Caesar's nose started to sweat. He was so angry. "I stayed in the closet out of respect for you, for the business, for the family."

"For me? Hardly. You stayed in the closet because you didn't have the balls to come out and face the music. Because you are soft and you are a pussy, probably more pussy than that thing in there."

A light went off in Caesar's head. "Where's Tracey?" Caesar asked.

"Your gump fuck partner? Oh, he's dead," Fitz said. "Two to the head, nice and neat."

Caesar charged full speed toward his brother, screaming, "You fucking bastard!" The reckless move sort of caught Fitz off guard. Caesar's shoulder slammed into Fitz's midsection, blasting some of the wind from his lungs. But Fitz recuperated quickly and kneed Caesar in the face. The blow knocked Caesar straight on his ass.

Fitz, sucking air, said, "Your bitch ass killed our sister to keep the filthy little secret that you and Viper were fucking! You murdered our sister! Our fucking sister!" The way the word "fucking" came out, it could have killed Caesar. "You didn't think that I'd never put it together, did you? You didn't think that Viper would ever tell a soul, did you? Well, guess what? He did!"

Caesar stammered. "Y–you don't understand. I h–had t–to do it."

"You had to do it, huh?"

Fitz pulled out a pistol. *Probably the same one he used to kill Tracey*, thought Caesar.

"No, I don't understand," Fitz said as he squeezed the trigger.

Somehow, Caesar had managed to get his hands on his own Glock. He didn't want to shoot his brother, but Fitz hadn't left him much of a choice.

BOOM! BOOM!

Both brothers unloaded on each other at the same time.

CHAPTER 32

While waiting to board her flight, Bianca had finally called Bella, who had been sending her Instagram messages, apologizing and practically begging for her forgiveness. When she left, Caesar had met up with Bella and shared everything with her about Peanut. So now, going back to Virginia with God only what waiting for her, Bianca decided to call her sister.

"Sister," she said.

"Oh my God! Thank you for calling."

Bianca cut her sister off before she started on an emotional roller coaster. "Girl, it's okay. Listen. I don't have time for the apologies and the whole reunion right now. Just know some heavy shit is going on, and if I never needed you, I need you now!"

"Say no more. I got you. I'm sorry about the situation. I will never do anything to hurt you, and I will do whatever you want to do about Peanut."

"Fuck Peanut. He's going to have his day. Don't worry. He gon' get his! But this is what I need: I'ma need you to pick me up from the airport in two hours. I'll be at US Air."

"Um, I don't have no car."

"Okay, so listen. Don't worry about it. It's all good. I will catch a cab."

"No, I'll figure out something. Don't worry. I will be there. Hook or crook, I will be there."

"Okay, thanks, sister."

"I got you," were the last words Bella said to Bianca before she hung up the phone.

Bianca came in on Jet Blue, but she had told her sister US Air just to make sure there was nothing funny going on. Once she landed, she called Bella. "Where are you?"

"At US Air baggage claim, like you said."

"Okay, come to Jet Blue."

"Okay, I'm going to come back around."

Bianca stood at the airport curb, looking, wondering where her sister was. She studied every car, and then all of a sudden, a black hearse slammed on its brakes.

"Bitch, where you get this from?"

"I told you I had you. You know I work at the funeral home now."

"I ain't know shit."

"Yeah, so I told them I had an emergency."

Bianca was laughing so hard that she couldn't even get into the car.

"Girl, get in and come on. You said you got urgent business."

Bianca put her bag in and climbed in.

"You know you can put your bag back there."

"Bitch still crazy. You know good and got-damn well I ain't putting my damn bag back there where the dead people be. You got me fucked up."

"Shit, it ain't never the dead people. It's the alive people that get you every time."

At that moment, Bianca remembered just how much she loved and missed her sister. On the highway, she shared with her what had happened. In retrospect, Bella told her all the tea on Caesar: how he had moved to this big house and was living with a flaming gay man.

"How you know?"

"Because one day, I met up with him, and that's where he had me to come to."

"A'ight, well, take me there then."

Bella navigated the hearse like she was a skilled driver, all the way to Caesar's front door. They knocked, but there was no answer. Bella went around the back and managed to pick the lock without the alarm going off.

Bianca turned her face up. "Girl, where you learn to do that?"

"Chile, please, it's so much you don't know about me."

Once the door was opened, she went in and got the shock of her life. Caesar was laying on the floor, bleeding. "Oh my God!"

He smiled when he saw her. In spite of him playing her as his beard, she still loved him, and he still had a place for him in her heart.

"Hang in there. Everything is going to be okay." She held his hand. "Please just hang in there."

"I'm sorry," Caesar managed to get out. "I'm glad you are back. I love you."

She ignored him. "Look, everything is going to be okay. You are going to be okay." She tried to be as encouraging to Caesar as she could.

Bella was on the phone, calling the ambulance.

Just a few feet away from Caesar, in the dark, Bianca heard some coughing, and that's when she realized it was Fitz. "Oh my God! God, nooooo!" She quickly dropped Caesar's hand and raced to Fitz's side, leaving Caesar to fend for himself.

"Baby! Please, baby! Please! You just hang in there!" she cried out as the blood was seeping out of the side of his mouth. "Just please, baby! I love you! Please fight, fight for us!" She looked into Fitz's eyes.

Caesar managed to turn his head and see Bianca at his brother's side. Tears formed in his eyes.

Bianca had all her attention focused on Fitz as she sat between the two bleeding brothers, who were both once her lovers, trying to be strong. "Baby, please, look at me," she said to Fitz.

"Where the fuck is that ambulance?" she cried out to Bella.

"I love you." Fitz smiled. "I love you until . . . death do . . . us part."

"I love you too," she said with tears in her eyes. "You are going to make it. We got too much we gotta do. I need that promise," she told him.

Bella screamed, "They're on the way. They are three minutes away."

Bianca looked into Fitz's eyes. "I need you to hold on, baby. Please," she said with tears in her eyes, but she saw him drifting away. "Help is coming."

"All the places I can be and people I can see . . . the decision was easy to make. I choose you over everything," she reminded him with the Jaheim tune. "I love you so much."

Fitz opened his eyes. "Manuella," he croaked.

"Baby, don't talk, please. You are making it worse."

"Manuella. Call him." Fitz struggled with the words but managed to get it out.

Sirens rang out, getting closer and closer.

"I know, baby, I'm going to call your father. You know I'm going to let him know what happened. Don't worry." She kissed him on the forehead. "They are almost here. Just please hang in here with me! Baby, just a little longer. Please, baby." She begged him.

"No," he said, gasping for air. "No!" He kept insisting.

"Baby, please. Baby, don't talk. Hang in here for me, for us—for our life, for our promise," she said, looking into Fitz's eyes, begging him to fight.

"They here! They here!" Bella screamed.

"They here, baby. Fight. You'll be okay. I love you!" Bianca said, for the first time realizing that Caesar's eyes were on her as the blood was still pouring out.

"Over there! Over there!" Bella anxiously demanded.

"Manuella, baby." Fitz was gasping for air. "My pops is . . . connect!" He pushed the words out and struggled to take another breath, and then the EMTs came in and took over, prying her hands from his.

Bianca was pushed off to the side, watching and praying, not knowing the fate of the only two men that she had ever really loved or cared for. She was also not fully understanding or realizing exactly what her new destiny would be. In time, she would understand Fitz's plan for her. She would call Manuella for the connect. She was destined to become Miami's next kingpin!

ORDER FORM
URBAN BOOKS, LLC
97 N18th Street
Wyandanch, NY 11798

Name (please print):_____

Address: _____

City/State: _____

Zip: _____

QTY	TITLES	PRICE
	16 On The Block	$14.95
	A Girl From Flint	$14.95
	A Pimp's Life	$14.95
	Baby Momma	$14.95
	Baby Momma 2	$14.95
	Baby Momma 3	$14.95
	Bi-Curious	$14.95
	Bi-Curious 2: Life After Sadie	$14.95
	Bi-Curious 3: Trapped	$14.95
	Both Sides Of The Fence	$14.95
	Both Sides Of The Fence 2	$14.95
	California Connection	$14.95

Shipping and handling: add $3.50 for 1st book, then $1.75 for each additional book.
Please send a check payable to:
Urban Books, LLC
Please allow 4-6 weeks for delivery

ORDER FORM
URBAN BOOKS, LLC
97 N18th Street
Wyandanch, NY 11798

Name (please print):_____

Address: _____

City/State: _____

Zip: _____

QTY	TITLES	PRICE
	California Connection 2	$14.95
	Cheesecake And Teardrops	$14.95
	Congratulations	$14.95
	Crazy In Love	$14.95
	Cyber Case	$14.95
	Denim Diaries	$14.95
	Diary Of A Mad First Lady	$14.95
	Diary Of A Stalker	$14.95
	Diary Of A Street Diva	$14.95
	Diary Of A Young Girl	$14.95
	Dirty Money	$14.95
	Dirty To The Grave	$14.95

Shipping and handling: add $3.50 for 1st book, then $1.75 for each additional book.
Please send a check payable to:
Urban Books, LLC
Please allow 4-6 weeks for delivery

ORDER FORM
URBAN BOOKS, LLC
97 N18th Street
Wyandanch, NY 11798

Name (please print):_____

Address: _____

City/State: _____

Zip: _____

QTY	TITLES	PRICE
	Gunz And Roses	$14.95
	Happily Ever Now	$14.95
	Hell Has No Fury	$14.95
	Hush	$14.95
	If It Isn't love	$14.95
	Kiss Kiss Bang Bang	$14.95
	Last Breath	$14.95
	Little Black Girl Lost	$14.95
	Little Black Girl Lost 2	$14.95
	Little Black Girl Lost 3	$14.95
	Little Black Girl Lost 4	$14.95
	Little Black Girl Lost 5	$14.95

Shipping and handling: add $3.50 for 1st book, then $1.75 for each additional book.
Please send a check payable to:
Urban Books, LLC
Please allow 4-6 weeks for delivery

ORDER FORM
URBAN BOOKS, LLC
97 N18th Street
Wyandanch, NY 11798

Name (please print):_____

Address: _____

City/State: _____

Zip: _____

QTY	TITLES	PRICE
	Loving Dasia	$14.95
	Material Girl	$14.95
	Moth To A Flame	$14.95
	Mr. High Maintenance	$14.95
	My Little Secret	$14.95
	Naughty	$14.95
	Naughty 2	$14.95
	Naughty 3	$14.95
	Queen Bee	$14.95
	Say It Ain't So	$14.95
	Snapped	$14.95
	Snow White	$14.95

Shipping and handling: add $3.50 for 1st book, then $1.75 for each additional book.

Please send a check payable to:

Urban Books, LLC

Please allow 4-6 weeks for delivery

ORDER FORM
URBAN BOOKS, LLC
97 N18th Street
Wyandanch, NY 11798

Name (please print):_____

Address: _____

City/State: _____

Zip: _____

QTY	TITLES	PRICE
	Spoil Rotten	$14.95
	Supreme Clientele	$14.95
	The Cartel	$14.95
	The Cartel 2	$14.95
	The Cartel 3	$14.95
	The Dopefiend	$14.95
	The Dopeman Wife	$14.95
	The Prada Plan	$14.95
	The Prada Plan 2	$14.95
	Where There Is Smoke	$14.95
	Where There Is Smoke 2	$14.95

Shipping and handling: add $3.50 for 1st book, then $1.75 for each additional book.
Please send a check payable to:
Urban Books, LLC
Please allow 4-6 weeks for delivery